The Joyous Season

PATRICK DENNIS

AN AVON BOOK

AVON BOOKS
A division of
The Hearst Corporation
959 Eighth Avenue
New York, New York 10019

First Avon Printing, December, 1965
Printed in the U.S.A.

For Betsy and Mike

One

Well, we never thought it could happen, but here we are living with Gran at East Haddock (Mass.).

It all started day before yesterday. That was Friday because this is Sunday. Gadzeeks, *every* day is Sunday in East Haddock! I mean it's Boresville, U.S.A. Anyhow, up till Friday everything was great. School was out and Missy and I just futzed around the apartment all day and sent paper gliders down into Gracie Square and dragged Maxl out to wet in Carl Schurz Park and watched television until eleven o'clock every night and like that. Lulu took us to the movies practically every day and up to the Bronx Zoo and to the Children's Wing of the Metropolitan Museum (which is a drag) and up to her place in Harlem, where practically everybody is colored, and to a pizza place and to the East End Lanes (for bowling) because Lulu said we were poor abandoned children all alone in the world and deserved a little fun. It was cool, but we're paying for it now.

Nine o'clock sharp on Friday the men from the Scott Service came to the apartment and started rolling up rugs and taking down curtains and putting sheets over the furniture like it wasn't home any more but some kind of morgue. Lulu had all of our stuff packed—except for important things that we actually need out here in the wilderness—and by ten o'clock the doorman was hollering up the house phone to say that H. A. was waiting down front in his station wagon to take Missy and I—Missy and *me*—away. Since Missy and

I are both under twenty-one there wasn't anything we could do but go along.

Maybe I should have told you before. Missy is my sister. Her real name is Melissa, for cripes sake, and she's only six years old. She's also kind of a pain in the ass. She looks like a little angel (her picture was even in *Vogue* once; and don't think *that* made her any easier to live with) and she bats her eyelashes and curtsies to grownups the way they teach them to do at Miss Farthingale's School for Idiots when all the time she'd just as soon jump you from behind as look at you. On the other hand, she gets off some pretty funny cracks once in a while and, as baby sisters go, she's not too bad. Like Lulu says, she's all I've got and we'd better appreciate each other.

Lulu's our nurse. We need a nurse like we need a case of mumps. I mean, hell, I'm ten and eleven twelfths years old and I've already smoked over two packs of Tareytons. (They've got that extra charcoal filter, you know, for cancer.) Even old Missy can take a bath and get dressed and wipe herself without any help, which is pretty good for six, I guess. But like Mom always said, we can't go around New York alone because of kidnapers and Dirty Old Men (especially on East Eighty-sixth Street) and types like that. So Lulu drags us across town every day, me to St. Barnaby's—although she turns me loose at the stationery store so the kids won't think I'm being hauled around by a nurse at *my* age—and Missy two blocks further (or farther, whichever it is) to Miss Farthingale's. Except for that, Lulu hasn't got much to do except see that we go to bed and get up and eat and don't fight.

Lulu's quite a character. She's colored and elderly and has been with us ever since I was born. She's kind of old fashioned and hates the N.A.A.C.P. and says she doesn't want to integrate with any white people except Missy and me and that's only because she gets paid to. Lulu says that after us she needs a rest, if we don't kill her first, and she wants to retire and move back down South. Gadzeeks, *South!* I mean I don't even like Palm Beach, which is supposed to be the next thing to heaven and I'm not colored or any-

8

thing like that. Give me New York City and keep the rest. Crazy! Anyhow, Lulu tells real interesting stories and knows every kind of poker there is—except strip —and always lets us have some of her beer and hates Gran's place in East Haddock almost worse than we do. I mean Lulu is great, even if we don't need a nurse.

My name is Kerry, which is short for Kerrington, for cripes sake, spelled with a K and an E and not with a C and an A and is a very big name somewhere back in Gran's family. Like I told you, I'm ten years old—practically eleven. I go to St. Barnaby's School because I have to be kept off the streets until I'm sixteen. I am not now and never have been and do not intend to be a member of the Scouting Movement— and that goes for the Knickerbocker Greys, too.

Where was I? Oh, yes. The doorman (his name is John Peter Francis Xavier Riley) was yelling up the house phone on Friday. So Lulu and I loaded all of our luggage into the elevator and Missy pulled Maxl out from under the boule chest and down we went to the tumble (if that's what you call those things in the French Revolution) out in Gracie Square.

But it wasn't all as easy as that. Missy, the big ham, had to make a production out of leaving. She threw her arms around the elevator man, who smells like a combination of the Ruppert Brewery and the gym at St. Barnaby's, and went into her act. "Ah, Mickey, *mon cher,*" she piped, *"je t'adore. Je t'embrasse,* Mickey *chéri."* (They start French in the first grade at Miss Farthingale's and Missy takes it seriously. She also wants to be on the stage when she grows up and the combination is deadly.) "Parting is such sweet sorrow, *mon brave,*" she added. Then she gave him a big wet kiss. Mickey belched. He always feels terrible in the morning. *"Adieu mon coeur,"* Missy said, with a big, phony sob. Then Lulu gave her a crack on the tail and said, "Talk with your mouth, child, like you was born to." Well, it broke me up. Then, just as a parting shot, Maxl wet on the rug in the lobby. Maxl is a dachshund and smarter than some people, but he can't help it if he has a weak bladder.

Well, there was a big to-do about getting all of our stuff into the back of the station wagon and up onto

9

the luggage rack on the roof (it's very spiffy as station wagons go) and by that time Mlle. Missy was all wound up to camp her way through another big French farewell scene with John Peter Francis Xavier Riley, the doorman. "Ah, Jean-Pierre-François-Xavier, *mon image!*" she cried, throwing her arms around his sweaty old summer uniform and covering his face with kisses. And a good thing, because that's about all the French she knows except for useless things like table, chair, pen, umbrella and "Frère Jacques."

"Ahem, Melissa," H. A. said. "That's enough. We don't kiss people who work for us."

"Who don't?" Lulu said dangerously.

I mean you can see we were getting off to a great start.

"Now where would you like to sit?" H. A. asked, with a big, fake smile that made me think of that Spartan spaz who was having his guts eaten out by a fox or whatever.

"On my bottom," Missy said. It wasn't one of her best, but I gave it a big yak just out of loyalty.

On the other hand, Lulu wasn't having any. As far as Lulu's concerned there's our Upstairs Manners and our Downstairs Manners and we were way downstairs on Friday—and have been ever since.

"I'll smack your bottom good, child," she said. Then she got all Uncle Tom with H. A., which is a sure sign that she hates someone, and said, "Miss Melissa and the little dawg and me'll all ride in the back, sir, if that's all right with you, sir." When Lulu gets to talking like that I wouldn't like to have my back turned to her. For good measure Maxl lifted his leg against one of H. A.'s white-wall tires like he was christening the goddamned car and then they all piled in.

H. A. gave my shoulder a manly squeeze like he wanted to break it and said, "I guess we men have to stick together." Then he flashed a big, beautiful, white smile. They say that Missy has inherited H. A.'s teeth. She's welcome. I'd rather spend the rest of my life in Dr. Fulton's chair than inherit anything of H. A.'s.

"Why?" I asked, but, as H. A. wasn't paying any attention and as there wasn't any place else for me to sit, I got in front next to H. A.

H. A., I guess I should tell you, is Gran's son and Mom's brother. That makes him our uncle, see? Only not very much. I mean H. A. is a whole lot older than Mom, who wasn't even born until after H. A. left St. Barnaby's. (Flunked out, if the truth were known.) They were never what you'd call close, like Missy and I—I mean Missy and *me*.

H. A. actually stands for something fancy like Heathcote Applegate, also very big names in Gran's family. Daddy always said it stood for Horse's Ass and Daddy was right. H. A. is about ten feet tall and very good looking—even I'll give him that—but there it stops. He's a real re-tard and like all people who don't have any children, he claims to be nuts about them and to be a real authority on how they should be raised. If he's so big on kids, he must mean somebody else's children, because he certainly isn't fond of us and vice versa. But he puts up kind of a front for a little while, at least, until his naturally lousy disposition takes over.

"I envy you and Melissa, Kerrington." (No nicknames, you notice. Although we always have to call him just plain old H. A. and not Uncle Anything so he'll sound younger. H. A. is very elderly—in his forties—and sensitive about his age since he still gets invited to coming-out parties around New York. Everybody says he's very eligible, whatever that means.) "Just imagine the wonderful time you'll have up in dear old East Haddock."

Missy said "Echhhh!" from the back seat and Lulu said, "Hush your fuss, child."

"Anything the matter with Melissa?" H. A. asked.

"Oh, she just gets a little carsick now and then," I said. H. A. looked like he'd been stabbed. Actually Missy doesn't get carsick or seasick or airsick or any other kind of sick unless she wants to. Neither do I, but I thought it would give old H. A. a jolt. It did. "Well, if you want to stop, be sure to tell me," H. A. said.

I wanted to stop right then and there and we weren't even as far north as Ninety-sixth Street, but I know when I'm licked. Like I said, Missy and I had no choice.

"Yes, quite a place, East Haddock." (Chuckle,

chuckle, chuckle. Gadzeeks, old H. A. was carrying on like Lord & Taylor's Santa Claus.) "Your mother and I used to spend all of our summers out there when we were children." I noticed that Mom was never in any tearing hurry to get back to dear old East Haddock after she was grown up and married. She used to shudder whenever the place was mentioned. "And your grandmother spent her summers there when she was a little girl. . . ." Well, to hear H. A. carry on about the place you'd think George Washington had chopped down that cherry tree right on Gran's lawn it was all so historical.

H. A. went on and on about the woods around Gran's house and the barn and the stables (the horses all died of old age years ago) and the beach club and the active sports like croquet and horseshoes and birdwatching.

Then Missy piped up, "Oh, we love birds. 'Specially Maxl. He catches them and eats them." Maxl chases pigeons around New York, all right, except he's so fat and his legs are so short that he couldn't catch so much as an egg, but that was enough for H. A. For about the next million hours he gave us a long lecture on our feathered friends and how sweet their songs were, exetera, exetera, exetera, and didn't run down until he had to pay a toll. Then he said he hadn't anything smaller than a ten-dollar bill and started cadging dimes and quarters from poor old Lulu. (Like Daddy always said, H. A. isn't the fastest one with a buck. Mom always said so, too, although she didn't like it whenever anyone *else*—especially Daddy—mentioned how tight her brother was.)

After that we rode along in silence, except for hearing the twelve o'clock stock market reports on the radio. H. A. is very hot stuff on Wall Street, or so he says. Daddy always said that if H. A. had been born something like plain John Smith and didn't have all of Gran's dough to play around with he wouldn't be hired to sweep the floor of a bucket shop—whatever that is. H. A. muttered something about the damned Democrats and snapped off the radio. Then Maxl gave the back of H. A.'s neck a swipe with his tongue, which is very long and pink and wet, and that almost sent the

12

car off the road. Since we happened to be at a Howard Johnson's, H. A. decided that it was time for lunch and we all went in and sat at the counter. (Personally I *prefer* the counter, but I knew that H. A. wouldn't want to sit at a table with Lulu because she's colored and he'd be afraid that people would think that they were married and Missy and I were their children, so I said that I'd rather sit at a table. We ended up at the counter, but H. A. was mopping his forehead like it had sprung a leak. Ooba dooba, what a boob! Everybody knows that Lulu's already married to a steward on a freighter who is hardly ever in New York, which suits Lulu just fine.)

There was some trouble about paying the check—not that it was added up wrong or anything. H. A. was still hanging onto that ten-dollar bill like it was a life preserver. But Lulu said that *she* didn't have anything smaller than a hundred. I had a little dough, but I wasn't going to give it to a tightwad like H. A., especially when I knew that he'd gouge the whole lunch check out of Gran. Gadzeeks, no wonder he's so well off. Finally H. A. broke the ten—and his heart, too, I guess—then we hit the road again.

I asked H. A. if I could tune in the game between the Yankees and the Chicago White Sox and H. A. said no, he saved the radio for important things like stock-market reports and world affairs and anyhow baseball was vulgar. That didn't sit very well with Lulu, who's a big fan, although her enthusiasm for the game kind of burned out since the Dodgers left Brooklyn.

So we rode along, nobody saying anything until we got outside of Boston, Mass., in quite a lot of traffic. Then Maxl threw up and out of sympathy Missy threw up, too. I can burp any time I feel like it, but I can't be sick. In some things Missy's a real *artist*—and only six years old! For kind of an encore, Maxl wet the seat. I thought I was almost going to do the same thing just trying to keep from laughing.

Poor old H. A. stopped the car right then and there and hopped out trying to mop up the mess with a wad of Kleenex from the glove compartment and then a greasy old rag and finally with one of his genuine Irish linen hankies while about a million truck drivers

13

honked their horns at him and called him all kinds of a rat fink. He was sweating bullets when he got back in, stalled the car and then finally got going, but he said, "Feeling better, Melissa, dear?" like he wished she were dead.

Then Missy did the eyelash bit and said, "Yes, thank you, H. A.," like she could almost hear the choir of angels. The kid's got talent!

We got to the town—town, my eye, *crossroads*—of East Haddock about four o'clock. I don't know exactly what we were expecting, but at least civilization. I mean like a Loew's or even a Trans-Lux and maybe a bowling alley and certainly a pizzeria. You know. Like the place was alive. Well, East Haddock is strictly Tombsville. One drugstore, one garage, one general store-and-post office, a town hall where they show a movie on Saturdays *only* and two churches. And that's East Haddock. Before you're in it you're out of it. Keep on driving a couple of miles through a real spooky wilderness until you see some big, ugly iron gates. Turn in. Drive another mile and you're at Gran's big, ugly house.

Before I get in too far with the story, there's something I should tell you and that is that you've got to excuse me if I keep running off at the mouth. The St. Barnaby's psychiatrist wrote in his report: "Kerrington has a marked tendency toward oververbalization with a vocabulary incompatible with one of his years." It didn't make any sense at all until Daddy said, "He means you talk too much, kid." Why couldn't the psychiatrist say that in the first place? I also suffer from something known as "total recall."

St. Barnaby's is very ancient, as schools in New York go, but when the old headmaster was put out to pasture we got this jazzy new ball of fire that wears bow ties and sports jackets and he's the one that's trying to make St. B's very modern. Like he's been hunting all over town for a colored kid to give a scholarship to. (He still hasn't been able to find one that wants to go there.) And like he's put in this psychiatrist.

Mom and Daddy got all dressed up in very serious clothes and took me around for a conference with Dr.

Epston, the psychiatrist, about my "ververbalization" and what to do about it. Daddy had what seemed to me a very good suggestion when he said, "Couldn't Kerry just shut up?" But the school psychiatrist said that would cause a lot of repressions and like that and that my "garrulity should be harnessed and channeled into verbal productivity." Cripes, even with a big vocabulary I don't know what the old kook is saying half the time and it's about *me*.

Anyway, it all boils down to that I'm supposed to talk until I run out of things to say. Isn't that a gas!

Now back to East Haddock. To begin with, Gran's house is really gross. Like H. A. said on the way out here, it's very old. But it's bad old and not good old. Not old *enough,* I guess. It's made mostly of brown shingles with a lot of fancy cutout work and stained glass and five or six kinds of brick and stone and porches and balconies and towers and like that. The roof is flat in some places and pointed in other places and round like an igloo in still other places and stabbed with a whole mess of lightning rods to keep the house from burning down in case it gets struck. They've done their job very well, which is a shame.

As the son of an architect, I try to look at every building the way Daddy would and try to decide what the man who built it was thinking about. But I can't look at this one—at least not very long. The Guggenheim Museum, for instance, always makes me imagine that somebody's cook just happened to drop a big popover on Fifth Avenue. I mean that's what it looks like to me, at least. Gran's house makes me think that a whole truckload of odd doors and windows got dumped on the lawn and some kid like Missy came along and put it all together. And, like the Guggenheim Museum, the outside isn't *half* as bad as what's on the inside.

Gran has a house back in New York which is also brown (stone, not wood) and is tall and narrow and dark and about as cheerful as a dungeon. Everything in her house on Eightieth Street that isn't brown or black is dark red or dark green. Well, the house out here at East Haddock seems to be filled with all the furniture and pictures and curtains that were too gloomy to use in New York.

15

This house has about a million rooms, all shapes and sizes. Like there's a hall and a reception room and a drawing room and a parlor and a study and a library and a morning room and a music room (not that anybody in the family could ever play so much as a kazoo) and a dining room and a breakfast room and a pantry and a servants' sitting room (where Lulu will *not* sit) and a kitchen and a linen room and a sewing room and a day nursery and a night nursery (where Missy and I will *not* stay—*nurseries*, for cripes sake, at *our* age!) and a conservatory where the sun shines in for about ten minutes a day and a flower room (which is full of empty vases, like every other room in the house) and a couple of dozen bedrooms and some miserable kind of box stalls for the help and a whole lot of attics and storerooms for anything that Gran won't throw out (which is everything).

My room is halfway up in a tower, which sounds very interesting like King Arthur or something but is just round and full of big brown old furniture and a lot of black pictures of generals (mostly related to us, it turns out) dying in each other's arms while all hell breaks loose on some battlefield. It faces north. I can tell because there's moss growing on that side of the house.

At first I was afraid Missy and I would have to share a room like we do whenever we sleep over at our *other* grandmother's. Now I almost wish we did. Instead old Missy lives in a cave across the hall. It's big and it has a lot of windows except that they're covered solid with vines. The wallpaper is all velvet roses the color of anchovies and crazy Missy has decided that if she stands too close they're going to reach out and eat her up, for cripes sake! She slays me. In Missy's room the furniture is black and the pictures are brown. There's one of a lot of horses being pulled around and one of some farmers—Dutch, I guess; they're wearing wooden shoes—bowing their heads out in the middle of a field and a great big one, all covered with spots, of a lot of religious people bawling outside of a tomb. Cheery! Missy's stuffed animals (she's got five bears, a lion, two tigers, a leopard, a giraffe, a great big panda and I forget what all else) help a little, but not much.

H. A. lives about a block down the hall in the same room he had as a boy—and it *is* the same. I mean here he is pushing fifty and the walls are still covered with pennants of the three schools, five boarding schools and four colleges he went to. (No diplomas, I notice.) There's also a splintery old oar from when H. A. rowed on the crew at Kent (he still talks about "Being the Kent Boy" like he invented the place instead of getting bounced out because he failed three subjects all at once) and about a million photos of H. A. looking like a TV star from the age of zero up till now. On your left, ladies and gentlemen, H. A. beautiful baby; H. A. in the Knickerbocker Greys; H. A. at summer camp; H. A. at Sea Island in a two-piece bathing suit; H. A. on a bike in the Alps; H. A. and the St. Barnaby's soccer team (no kidding, the ball actually has 1930 painted on it); H. A. Boy Scout; H. A. in the Browning School Glee Club; H. A. at Groton; H. A. on the Choate tennis team (and there's a silver cup on his mantel to prove it); H. A. in Harvard Yard. And on your right, H. A. dancing with Brenda Somebody; H. A. in some place called La Rue; H. A. being an usher in a dozen different weddings that all happen to look exactly alike unless you study the faces real close; Lieutenant (j.g.) H. A. in the Battle of 90 Church Street; H. A. at the Piping Rock Club; H. A. on a sailboat in Bermuda; H. A. on skis; H. A. playing golf and like that. There's also a picture of H. A. and our grandfather, who looked like a tired old seal, and one of Gran holding—you guessed it—H. A. Underneath all the pictures the walls of H. A.'s room look like Nutty Crunch Peanut Butter so maybe it's just as well that he doesn't take them down.

A mile or so down the hall from H. A.'s Cub Scout Headquarters is Gran's room—or maybe I should say rooms. First you go into a big sitting room which would be very sunny and nice if the shades weren't pulled way down to the window sills all the time. Then there's our grandfather's bedroom and dressing room and bathroom on one side. He's been dead and gone for almost twenty years and nobody seems to be

17

very anxious to have him come back, but the whole layout is set up for just that. A fire is laid in the grate. His suits are taken out once a month and aired and pressed and then put back into mothballs. His combs and brushes and bottles are left just the way he always had them and his big old inkwell is filled every week. I don't happen to believe in ghosts (Lulu does and Missy almost does) but it's enough to make you think twice. Across the sitting room from that is Gran's cozy corner—a bedroom with a big old bed, hard as a rock, with curtains and ruffles all over it. Some governor, who is somewhere back in Gran's family, is supposed to have been born in it or died in it. Died, I should think. There are a whole lot of portraits of dead people on the walls in big, gold frames and millions of photographs of people both living and dead in little silver frames on all the tables in the room. There are also a lot of doors that open so that they bang into each other. One goes to Gran's dressing room, which smells of cedar and lavender. Another goes to her bathroom, which smells like the dog-and-cat hospital where Maxl had distemper. Door Number Three goes to Gran's chapel. Gran is so religious that she'd almost be a Catholic if she didn't keep saying that Catholics are common. But she's the next thing to it, I guess. And finally there's the door that leads to the Dragon's Den—Miss Fitch's room. Miss Fitch (I'd hate to tell you what everybody calls her behind her back) is Gran's nurse. Gran needs a nurse about as much as Missy needs a brassière. But it's aristocratic to be sick all the time and if you want to know what is—and what is *not*—aristocratic, just ask Gran. Miss Fitch was our grandfather's nurse when he died (Mom always said that she nagged the poor old man to death) and she just stayed on ever afterward because Gran is a hypodermic [?] always imagining that she's sick. It's a good thing she just imagines it because Miss Fitch isn't like any of those hot-shot nurses you see on television saving lives and giving shots and like that. She's real old and mean and can't even make her own bed. But she sure can make trouble for the rest of the help and for we kids—*us* kids, I mean.

Well, this church-tomb-hospital-museum arrange-

18

ment in East Haddock is just about the same setup as Gran has on the second floor of her house on Eightieth Street in the wintertime. (For one old lady, Gran sure takes up a lot of space.) Gran is a great believer in naps—short ones in the mornings, long ones in the afternoons and then early to bed. She wonders why she can't sleep nights and she talks about it every morning until she gets worn out and has to lie down from eleven until time for lunch. She was just winding up a good three-hour snooze when H. A. dragged us up to check in.

Gran was sitting up in bed wearing what she calls "my wrapper," which sounds like something around a candy bar, and piling her white hair up on top of her head like Martha Washington or somebody. "H. A.," she said, "I thought you were never coming. You look dead." He always does—sounds dead, too.

"Hello, Mummy," H. A. said, kissing her. "Working pretty hard down in the street," by which he means Wall Street.

"Kerrington, Melissa. How nice to see you." Gran sounded like we were about as nice to see as an operation. Then she turned her cheek in our general direction to be kissed. It's like kissing a sponge, but I got through it okay. When it was Missy's turn, she made one of her big ace plays by knocking over about ten glass bottles on the portable dressing table Gran wears across her lap like a bikini. So there was a big flood of Quelques Fleurs and 4711 and Violette du Parme and all the other old-lady smells that Gran dabs on herself. (She calls it toilet water, if you'll pardon the expression.) "Oh, Melissa! You must be more careful! Miss Fitch, will you please take my dressing things away. Aren't you children going to say hello to Miss Fitch?"

"Hello, Miss Fitch," we said. Then Missy said, "Aren't you going to say hello to Lulu?" Trust old Missy not to be upstaged by *anybody*.

"How are you, Lulu?" Gran said, like she hoped the answer would be "Failing fast."

"I can't complain—*so far*," Lulu said.

Gran does not care for Lulu and vice versa. According to Gran, Lulu is "cheeky" and "lax" and "a bad influence" and doesn't have a "proper name." Lulu

19

never says anything about Gran, but it doesn't take much to get the breezes.

"Miss Fitch," Gran said, "could I please have the *boîte du bijou?*" For the benefit of anybody that doesn't understand French, such as Miss Fitch, that's Gran's jewel box. Gran hasn't got any French blood at all and says it's vulgar to use French words like our other grandmother does when there are just as good ones in English, but she had to speak French almost all the time when she was young and some of the words she uses are just a hangover from then, like *pot de chambre* for potty, *étui* for her needle case and *fauteuil* for armchair. Gran's got a lot of jewelry because none of her ancestors ever threw anything away, either, and she changes it about six times a day. She put on a couple of dirty diamond rings about as sparkly as an old milk bottle, a pin, her pearls and some earrings and that made her decent for tea. "All of these will be yours some day, Melissa," Gran said, "and so I want you to learn to appreciate beautiful things."

Missy said "Uh huh," and while Gran was saying, "Don't say 'uh huh,' Melissa, say 'Thank you Grandmother, dear,' " I could almost hear old Missy figuring out how many Almond Joys she could buy with a ruby brooch—not that she can multiply or divide or anything complicated like that.

Gran got off the bed with all of her joints going snap, crackle, pop like a bowl of cereal and said, "Well, now that we're here together, we're all going to have to get along as best we can. I'm the only one you children have."

"Oh, no," Missy said. "There's always Ga-ga." Ga-ga is our *other* grandmother—Daddy's mother—and Gran and she hate each other like poison.

"Yes," Gran said, like she was picking a dead rat out of her bed, "I suppose there *is* always Evelyn. Although I'd hate to count on her in any emergency."

"Careful, Mummy," H. A. said. "Little pitchers . . ."

"Be still, H. A., and ring for tea."

If you think one old lady can waste a lot of space, you ought to see Gran with the groceries. She eats like a bird, she says, but I think she means a vulture. At half past four every day of her life in come three

20

kinds of sandwiches, two kinds of cake, muffins, scones, toast, jam, honey, cookies and, of course, tea with milk, cream, lemon, hot water, sugar and saccharin. "I eat like a bird" Gran says and then takes a bite out of five watercress sandwiches, eats half of two cucumber sandwiches (they're round and no bigger than a fifty-cent piece), refuses a third crabmeat sandwich ("You know that shellfish disagrees with me"), eats half a scone, crumbles a slice of toast and polishes off all but a forkful of cake. That's that and I hate to think what happens to all the leftover food. ("I eat like a bird.") But just let one of us kids leave a pile of cow's guts (Gran calls them sweetbreads) or a dab of spinach on a plate and Gran goes all teary and says, "Just think of the poor little souls in India who'd give anything to have the food you refuse to touch." Just today at lunch Missy suggested that we wrap it all up and mail it to India—which struck me as a very sensible idea. Missy was sent from the table. I mean you can't win here at East Haddock.

Before tea was brought in the day we got here, Missy pulled another of her big ace plays by announcing that she and Maxl had both thrown up on the way out of New York. That took care of things just fine. Maxl was sent out to the barn to live and Missy had to settle for plain tea and dry toast, just when she'd got her big mouth all set for a lobster roll and coconut cake. It served the dope right, but even so I slipped a few cookies into my pocket while Gran was reading an interesting obituary aloud to H. A. (he *can* read) so that poor old Missy would have something to keep her going until dinner.

All this took place on Friday. Today is Sunday, but that doesn't really matter. Every day is the same in East Haddock except that there was church this morning instead of the beach club. (The only difference is clothes.) Gran is very big on religion, like I said before, and acts as though God was some kind of old personal friend who had done something *really* important like start the Colonial Dames. She's always talking up the "sweet little Episcopal church" in East Haddock like she was trying to sell it to us, organ and all.

21

But when it comes to actually putting on her hat and *going* to that sweet little Episcopal church, Gran feels hot or cold or faint or something (which gets Miss Fitch off the hook, too) and has her usual eleven o'clock lie-down instead. This morning she got all the way to the porte-cochere—hat, gloves, fur piece, prayer book and all—and then decided she was having an attack of "the vapors," whatever they are, and sent Missy and H. A. and me as a kind of substitute team, although she acted like she didn't think the three of us would carry nearly as much weight with God as she would singlehanded. Gran's parting shot was, "Be sure to pray for your poor little mother."

"Why?" Missy asked.

Luckily H. A. was talking about how Brooks Brothers didn't make seersucker suits the way they used to and how he'd seen his club's tie (in rayon) marked down to a dollar in Bloomingdale's basement, and Miss Fitch was saying, "We're not running a temperature, are we?" so nobody heard Missy and she didn't wind up with her ass in a sling as usual.

Still, it was a good question. Just what we're supposed to be saying in these prayers for our "poor little mother" is never explained to us—like a lot of things around here. If you ask *me,* Mom ought to be praying for us—and Daddy, too. Both of them are millions of miles away from this terrible place having a ball doing whatever it is that grownups do. But I guess that's the kind of thing that happens with a divorce.

Two

The divorce thing got started on Christmas Day. Daddy always said that Christmas is a joyous season when suicides and holdups and shoplifting and like that reach a new high and that the best place to spend the whole thing is a Moslem country. Mom says he's right about that, if about nothing else. After last Christmas, I guess I kind of agree.

The day began while it was still pitch dark with Missy bouncing on my stomach and pounding my chest and shouting, "Wake up! Wake up! Wake up!" in my ear. "Let's see what Santy Claus brought."

I was so doggone bushed that I almost told her there wasn't any Santa Claus and to go back to bed until morning. But like Gran says, we all try to "keep her simple faith alive." Besides, Maxl was licking my ear and by the time I got them both off me I was wide awake.

So I got up and we went into the living room, which was also dark except for the Christmas tree, flickering away in front of the middle window. Our Christmas trees are different each year—usually to match whatever color the room happens to be. Once it was white with pink ornaments and lights like roses; once it was all gold; once it was old fashioned with candy canes and strings of popcorn; another time it was blue and green; and I forget what all else. This year it had nothing but green ornaments and millions of little white lights going off and on at different times like a sign in Times Square. I mean it would drive you crazy to look at it for more than a couple of minutes at a time, but like Ga-ga said, it was very chic.

There were about a million packages under the tree that hadn't been there the night before, but they were all wrapped up—mostly in white and green, like Santa Claus was some kind of interior decorator—and in our house a wrapped-up package or a sealed envelope always meant "Hands off!"

Our stockings were hanging over the fireplace where Daddy had taped them (it's very difficult to drive a nail into a marble mantel) before he and Mom went off to their Christmas Eve bash, only now the stockings were full instead of empty. So, to keep Missy's simple faith alive, I put on a big act about how wonderful it was that Jolly Old Saint Nick had parked his sleigh up on top of the Cushings' penthouse, carefully avoiding the television antennas, and made his jolly old way through all the vents and the water tower and the elevator works with a sack full of junk and right down the chimney to dear old Sixteen East going "Ho ho ho," every inch of the way. Some kids will swallow *anything*.

Well, the stockings weren't filled with much except some candy and little things from the five-and-ten. Besides, Missy has a very small foot, so it didn't take her long to go through all that stuff and break most of it. It wasn't even 6:00 A.M. and Missy was dancing around like she had to go to the can and itching to get at the real swag under the tree.

"Maybe if I just tore the paper a little on that great big package," she said, pointing to a bundle about the size of a refrigerator off in one corner. I knew it wasn't from Mom or even from "Santa Claus" as the paper was real old fashioned and had holly and mistletoe and "Davis-Collamore" printed all over it—a store not even *I* ever heard of. One look and I could tell it was from Gran. In both of Gran's houses all boxes, ribbons, string and wrapping paper are saved like they were money.

"It's kind of torn anyway," Missy said. It sure was.

"You better leave it alone," I said. "It's not even for you. It's for Daddy." The card in Gran's shaky writing made that pretty clear.

24

"Well, what time is it *now?*" Missy said.

"Five minutes till six."

"Well, shouldn't they be getting up *now?*"

"No, they shouldn't, for cripes sake."

Missy was getting so het up that I finally took pity on her. "You can open this one and that will have to hold you till everybody else gets up."

"From Santy Claus?"

"Santa Claus, my ass! It's from me. I bought it at Rappaport's Toy Bazaar with my own money. I wrapped it myself, too."

"It looks it," Missy said.

Well, maybe it wasn't the prettiest package under the tree, but when Missy opened it, she sang a different tune. It was a genuine Martian Outer Space Squirt Gun. It holds a pint of water and, depending on which knob you turn, shoots either a hundred Instant Locomotor-Paralysis Rays or one full-pint Gamma Death Ray, which means curtains for Earth Mortals. (You may have seen them advertised on television.)

"Gee, Kerry, it's *beautiful!*" I could tell that even Missy was impressed. And she should have been. It cost three ninety-five plus sales tax. "Can I work it now?"

"Not in the apartment. Remember that time with the glass clock and the Johnny Reb Cannon?"

That shook her, but not enough.

"Well, at least show me how to fill it."

The Martian Outer Space Squirt Gun comes with a full set of instructions, but they're kind of complicated and Missy can only read beer signs and cigarette packages and "Run, Jack! Jump, Jane!" and the kind of stuff they teach in the first grade at Miss Farthingale's.

"Okay," I said, "we'll fill it, but don't shoot it at anything except Daddy's shower and *don't* make any noise."

We went to Daddy's bathroom, which is all tile and positively leak-proof (except the time Daddy let his tub run over) and has a great big shower stall with lots of water spouts that get you in terrible places if you don't watch out. I filled the squirt gun in the washbasin, aimed and fired half a dozen Instant Loco-motor-Paralysis Rays into the shower stall right at heart level. Pow, pow, pow, pow, pow, *pow!* Let me tell you, that Martian Outer Space gun was everything they claimed it was on TV. It sent out a fine spray that hit the wall so hard it splashed halfway back into the bathroom. I almost wished I'd bought it for myself.

"Now let me try, Kerry," Missy said.

"Be my guest, kid, it's your gun."

Well Missy's aim wasn't all it should have been, like with the Johnny Reb Cannon two Christmases ago, but it made five or six beautiful splashes right into the shower stall.

"Now let's fill it all the way up again and try the full-pint Gamma Death Ray," I said. Hell, I was just trying to keep Missy quiet until Mom and Daddy woke up.

Missy ran the cold water full tilt and reloaded. But when she tried to turn the faucet off she knocked over Daddy's shaving bowl. It's some kind of plastic and unbreakable but it made a terrible racket when it hit the tile floor. There was a groan from the bedroom. It was Daddy.

"Wh-who's there?" Daddy moaned.

"Shhhhhhh," I said to Missy and switched off the lights. The sun was beginning to come up over the East River and a little bit of gray dawn filtered in through the bathroom window—just about enough so that you could see your hand in front of your face.

There've been a lot of robberies in our neighborhood over the past year. (Only last week some fool dame left half a million bucks' worth of diamonds on top of her dressing table, like a cook's-night-out supper, and a burglar came in, helped himself and walked right out.) Anyhow, Daddy keeps this great big revolver left over from the Army in the drawer by his side of the bed and the next thing we knew, the door opened and there he was standing stark naked pointing the gun right over our heads at his reflection in the bathroom mirror.

"Daddy . . ." I started to say. A shot rang out and the mirror busted into a million pieces. Then Missy did *something* with her squirt gun and Daddy got it up and down his whole front with a full pint of ice-cold Gamma

Death Ray. There was a bellow like he'd grabbed a live wire and then a stream of language like even *I* have never heard. Then he made a lunge for us and *then* there was even a worse yell and worse language because he'd cut both bare feet on all that broken mirror.

By that time Mom was up struggling into her robe and saying, "Darling, what's the matter?" Missy went into hysterics and I was so confused I didn't know whether to laugh or to cry. I laughed. It was the wrong choice.

Well, what happened right after all that is still too painful even to think about. The lights went on. Daddy took one look to see that we were okay. We were. I got a good one across the side of the head and Missy got such a crack on the rear end that she forgot to have hysterics and just plain cried. Then Daddy turned all gray and went staggering back toward the bed, leaving a trail of bloody footprints on the white rug and clutching his head like he was dying. By then Mom was awake enough to start putting the whole picture together.

From what the other guys at school tell me about *their* parents, Mom and Dad got along like two peas in a pod most of the time. But this wasn't one of the times.

"My God, there's blood all over the place. What are you doing with that *gun?*"

"Only trying to protect my family."

"*Protect* them? You nearly killed the children! Kerry, Melissa! Tell Mother! Are you all right?"

"By God, if those two don't get out of here I'm just as likely to kill them as not."

"You great, drunken oaf! Look what you've done! The whole room a shambles and company coming. Just *look* at the place!"

In addition to the blood and the water and the broken glass, the bedroom looked the way it does when Daddy has a Difficult Night and is about to have a worse day. Usually he's very neat and tidy, like an architect ought to be, with his clothes all hung up and his shoes in trees and his dirty linen put in the laundry hamper. He's so neat as a rule that his keys

27

and his wallet and his cigarettes and his money are lined up like soldiers on top of his chest of drawers. He even piles his change in a stack—halves, then quarters, then nickels, then dimes—so that you wouldn't dare to swipe so much as five cents for fear that he'd know just by looking. But today was One of Those Mornings. His evening clothes were partly on the chaise longue, partly on the floor. His shirt was draped over a chair with the studs still in it. One shoe had been kicked off near the door and the other one was almost under the bed with the socks scattered in between. His tie was over a lamp shade and his underwear crumpled up on the desk. And, what with Mom's new evening dress rolled up like a sleeping bag on her dressing table instead of out of sight in her dressing room, it didn't take me long to get the general idea.

Then Mom said in that kindly cold tone of voice, "De-ar, don't you think you might try to get a little help with your drinking problem? There was a Dr. Gumbiner who did so much for Liz's first husband before he killed himself. . . ."

"Liz's *first* husband? Well, if that poor nance drank, it was because Liz drove him to it. And if your great chum Liz would serve something decent instead of her hot Swedish Glögg that nobody in his right mind would . . ."

"*I* thought it was delicious."

"So I noticed."

"And it didn't seem to me that *you* were being force fed. I mean social drinking is one thing but when it gets to the point of having hallucinations and firing point-blank at the children . . ."

"I *didn't* fire at the children. I thought it was a prowler. What were they doing in my bathroom anyway?"

"What anyone would be doing in a bathroom."

"They've got their own bathroom to use. Why don't they?"

"And look at you! You're soaking wet. Liz told me what Dr. Gumbiner said about those terrible sweats. . . ."

"Sweat, hell. I'm freezing to death."

"*And* chills. One of the first signs of acute alcoholism . . ."

"Alcoholism, my ass! One of those brats sprayed me with a God-damned hose."

"A *hose?* Now where would they get a hose? I really think you're on the verge of delirium tremens, darling, honestly I do. And would you look at what you've done to my brand-new rug!"

"*Your* rug? Who paid for it?"

"Nobody, as yet. And that reminds me, a man from the credit department at . . ."

"Oh, shut up about it!" Mom did.

Since she hadn't attracted much of an audience, Missy had stopped crying and wiped her tears on the sleeve of her robe. Now she took advantage of the silence to do things up brown. "Merry Christmas, Mommy! Merry Christmas, Daddy!" Missy yelled. "Look what Kerry gave me. It's a genuine Martian Outer Space gun." I had thought that the squirt gun had fired its full charge at Daddy in the bathroom doorway, but I was wrong. There was just enough water left in it to do a little more damage. Missy raised the gun proudly and Mom got it full in the face.

An hour or so later, with the Martian Outer Space gun under lock and key, we were all in the living room to see what Santa Claus had brought. In other years Mom and Daddy used to sit on the floor beside the tree in their robes and slippers drinking coffee while Daddy read out the names and passed the presents around. This year Daddy couldn't get his slippers on for all the Band-Aids on the soles of his feet and he was drinking a brandy-and-soda. "Do you think that's entirely wise?" Mom asked.

"You're damned right I do and if you had sense enough to come in out of the rain, you'd join me. You must feel fierce."

"Perhaps. But *someone* has to think about the children's Christmas. Besides, your mother is coming to lunch."

"Isn't yours? *And* your idiot brother?"

Mom suddenly got very interested in a stuffed gi-

29

raffe her friend Liz had sent to Missy. It was big, I'll say for it, but not all that fascinating.

The Christmas presents were much fancier than usual—especially the ones Daddy gave Mom and vice versa. I guess it must have had something to do with the big new building he designed. Daddy gave Mom a green ring and a brown fur jacket and a gallon of some kind of French perfume and quite a lot of other stuff. She gave him a whole new set of drafting instruments in a cool leather case and a kind of machine to make copies of plans right at home and some spiffy books on architecture and a couple of special golf clubs and a new squash racket. They said thank you very politely but they didn't seem to like the stuff very much, fancy as it all was.

My haul was the usual run of stuff—a few things I'd asked for and a lot of things I hadn't. Gran gave me a big old book on the blood lines in her family and she'd written, "Kerrington—This is so you'll know who your ancestors were—at least on your mother's side," on the flyleaf so I couldn't take it back to Scribner's and turn it in on something I might want to read. H. A., generous to a fault as always, did the big thing and gave me a chemistry set. It didn't look like any of the sets you see in toy departments nowadays. It was large and kind of fly-specked and dented at the corners and the boy wonder on the box top was wearing knickers, for cripes sake, but like I said, it was the *biggest* chemistry set I ever saw.

"Do you think that chemistry thing is safe?" Daddy asked.

"Do you think that my brother is in the habit of endangering the lives of children?" Mom said, driving home the point.

"Aw, come off it," Daddy said. He got up like his feet were killing him, and his head, too, and mixed another brandy-and-soda—very dark.

"Do you really think you should, *dear?*"

"Yes, I do."

Gran's present to Missy came in a box from John Wanamaker's wrapped in paper from James Mc-Creery's. Inside was a dusty velvet box from Tiffany's.

"Valuable things come in small packages," Mom said hopefully.

"Yeah?" Missy said, pulling out clouds of old tissue paper. After all the unpacking, it turned out to be a gold locket that looked like Maxl had cut his puppy teeth on it.

"Read it to me," Missy said, handing me one of Gran's cards.

"What's the magic word?"

"Please."

" 'Dear Melissa,' " I read, " 'this locket was given to me when I was just your age and I hope that you will love it as I did.' " H. A. gave Missy ten shares of stock in an oil well in Turkey which, as he said on the card, might be very valuable some day. Daddy said that the stock was selling for fifty cents a share and Mom said, "It's the thought that counts," but not with much feeling. Whatever the idea was, I could understand Missy's not appreciating it.

On the other hand, Ga-ga, Daddy's mother, is very extravagant. Sometimes I feel that she's more of a child than Missy is. That doesn't mean that she always has the best ideas in children's presents, but at least they're very expensive and come from cool places like F.A.O. Schwarz and the toy shop at Saks instead of some attic. Ga-ga's present to me was a Decline and Fall of the Roman Empire Battle of the Visigoths (410 A.D.) set. It was really keen and also educational, which was unusual for anything Ga-ga gives you. The only drawback was that it came in millions of little pieces and had to be put together. Ga-ga's gift to Missy was more typical. It was an Antoine-ette Junior Miss Beauty Salon, which contained everything needed to fix your hair and face if you happen to be a girl. I didn't think much of it, but Missy took to it right away.

I said, "Daddy, will you help me put my Fall of the Roman Empire set together?"

He didn't look very happy about it but he said, "Yes, as soon as your mother and I open the rest of our things." Then he handed Mom a very fancy box and said, "This is for you from Ga-ga." Well, even Mom brightened up a little bit because Ga-ga never thinks about anything except clothes and bridge and whenever she buys anything it's bound to be expensive and unusual. So was this, but I guess it was a little too unusual.

"Oh," Mom said, after she got the package open. Just "Oh" and no more. Then she said, "Maybe I *will* have a tiny bit of brandy in my coffee."

"What is it?" Daddy asked as a whole lot of bright beads and feathers tumbled out of the box.

"That's a good question. You name it and you can have it."

"Well, I don't know," Daddy said kind of hotly. "Mother always has pretty good taste."

"When she's buying something for herself. It looks like something that comes from one of those Men Only Christmas shops."

Daddy pulled it out of the box and held it up. It was something to wear, all right, but I don't know what you'd call it.

"I guess it's some sort of negligee," Daddy said, as though he didn't quite believe it. "It comes from that expensive place . . ."

"That's just what I mean," Mom said. "All spangles and caribou [?]. It must have cost the old id . . . I mean it must have cost your mother a perfect fortune, but a call girl would think twice before she . . ."

"What do you know about call girls?"

"What do *you* know about them?"

"I don't think it's so bad," Daddy said, but not with much feeling.

"Then why don't *you* wear it? I realize that she's blind as a bat and too vain to wear glasses, but when there are so many lovely, simple things that I'd adore to . . ."

"If you don't like it, take it back."

"Oh, of course! What better way to another woman's heart than to tell her she has the taste of a . . ."

"Tell her it was the wrong size and . . ."

"Your mother and I wear exactly the same size and she's been dining out on the fact for the past . . ."

"Well, it's your present. You decide what to do with it."

32

"I already have. Now please open whatever that great hulking thing in the corner is and then we can clear all this stuff out of the living room."

Muttering something about ingratitude, Daddy got the great big box from Gran out into the middle of the room. It took some doing, and once the old Christmas paper was stripped off there was still a long way to go. It wasn't a box, it was a crate, for cripes sake, three feet square and nearly as high as Daddy, who is very tall. It was daubed with "Manhattan Storage & Warehouse Co. Inc." and "Fragile" and "This Side Up" and built to last. Daddy broke the handle off a hammer trying to open it and said a terrible word. "No wonder the children talk like guttersnipes with this sort of influence," Mom said. Daddy said the word again and then called down to the handyman for a crowbar. Before the crowbar arrived he got a long, jagged splinter in his hand and said an even worse word. "Splendid Christmas spirit," Mom said, real sarcastic like.

Something in the air told me that we kids would do well to make ourselves scarce, so without even being told, we piled up our presents and took them to our rooms.

I put H. A.'s chemistry set down on my workbench and started to look at all the stuff inside. The set had been used. It was kind of dusty and there wasn't any instruction book. But just to be doing something, I poured three or four different chemicals into a bowl and watched the stuff bubbling away.

Just then there was a terrible uproar in the living room. It sounded like the end of the world or something and when I got there, there was Daddy standing in a pile of some kind of straw looking at the biggest, ugliest model of a building I've ever seen.

"Now what in the hell kind of practical joke is this?" Daddy said.

"My mother does *not* play practical jokes," Mom said.

"Well, im-practical joke, then."

"It happens to be a scale model of the Applegate Arcade."

The Applegate Arcade is a terrible-looking old building that Gran's grandfather put up just after the Civil War in what is now practically the Bowery. It makes the Flatiron Building look like Lever House but it was famous for something like being a skyscraper (six stories) and having the first elevators or flush toilets or like that a hundred years ago. Like everything Gran's family owns it's big and brown and grim.

"It's a perfect replica," Mom said. "One inch to the foot. Mummy thought it would be of great interest to an architect."

"So the card says," Daddy said between his teeth. "Well, as a terrible example of what a building should *not* be . . ."

"Mummy was only trying to . . ."

"Only trying to get rid of it and that's just what I'm going to do with it."

"You are going to do no such thing! It's of great sentimental value to Mummy."

"And that's why it's been in storage for the last fifty years?"

"Nonsense. I remember it from the time I was a little girl. It stood in my father's study and I always wanted to turn it into a birdhouse out in the garden."

"You could turn it into a cat house for all of me."

"Of all the ingrates! Well, if you want to break my poor mother's heart . . ."

"I'd like to break her neck. Just what are we supposed to *do* with this thing? It's bigger than *you* are and, architecturally speaking, it's a complete bastardization of . . ."

"Will you *please* watch your language in front of Kerry. No wonder he . . ."

"In that case, Kerry, you'd better leave the room, because the more I look at this eyesore, the more I feel like . . ."

"I think Daddy's got a point," I said. Most times in our family everybody gets a chance at least to give an opinion. Daddy calls it Democracy. But this wasn't one of the times.

"Kerry!" Mom shouted. "Did you hear your father? Leave the room!"

"Thanks, kid," Daddy said.

34

For such a very long morning, I don't know where it all went. Before anyone realized it, the doorbell was ringing and there was Ga-ga and her newest beau.

Ga-ga isn't really her name. It's just something I called her when I was very young and couldn't manage to say "grandma." But it fits her like a glove. Ga-ga is just as old as Gran—even a couple of months older —but she looks like Gran's daughter and acts like Gran's granddaughter. I mean next to Ga-ga, even Missy seems very mature.

Gran and Ga-ga have known each other all their lives. They were born on the same street and were in the same class as Miss Farthingale's and they like each other a little less every day. When we're not supposed to be listening, Gran tells Mom that Ga-ga is a frivolous old fool and that her family was in Trade, wherever that is. Whether anyone's listening or not, Ga-ga tells everybody that Gran is a stuffy old bore and has no *joie de vivre* (French). They both have a point.

I mean they're as opposite as day and night. For example, Gran has been wearing the same old dresses ever since I can remember, while Ga-ga hardly ever wears the same thing twice. Gran lives in great big houses both in New York and in the country with everything dark and gloomy while Ga-ga moves into a smaller apartment every couple of years with everything in it pink—even her telephone and the toilet paper! They're both widows, but while Gran acts like her husband was just about to hobble out of his coffin, Ga-ga keeps saying, "Poor, darling Charlie. He's better off where he is. He never could have stood the pace." Gran only seems to know other old widows who all sit around and talk about taxes and how they have to watch their pennies. But Ga-ga has a lot of what she calls beaux—some of them younger than Daddy —and when she isn't out dancing with them, she's got them all in her apartment playing bridge. Sometimes, when they're speaking to each other, Gran tries to tell Ga-ga how to run her life (like she does with everyone else). "Evelyn," Gran will say, "the way you're spending money you'll end up in a pauper's grave."

Then Ga-ga will blow out a big cloud of smoke and rattle her bracelets and fluff her wig and say, "But by then I'll be dead, darling, and it won't make any difference where I am. They're having the most marvelous fur sale at . . ."

"Evelyn, you're not touching your *principal,* are you?"

"You make it sound as though it were my vulva."

"*Evelyn!* Melissa can hear you!"

"Well, darling, she'll have to know about that sort of thing sooner or later, won't she? Now if you were to call Mr. Kaplan and tell him I sent you, he could give you a very good trade-in on . . ."

"Evelyn, haven't you anything more in your empty head than furs and fashions and . . ."

"Well, darling, at least *I* don't go pussyfooting around town in an old orange mink so rump-sprung that I look like someone's cook!"

"*Evelyn!*"

Then they stop speaking again.

Ga-ga is usually late, never on time. On Christmas Day she was early. She came busting into the apartment all fluffy gray furs and long gloves with her newest beau—an old Englishman named Sir Rupert Something, who looked like a basset hound. "Joyeux Noël, darlings! Here we are—hours early I know, and perishing for a drinkie. Rupert and I thought we might just be able to get up a table of bridge at the Regency Club, but not a chance. I mean people still seem to take Christmas so hard. Now, where are my babies? Really, Rupert, isn't it ridiculous—a grandmother at my age!"

I had meant to clean up my room a little and throw out the chemical experiment, which was steaming away, but Mom says our First Duty is to our guests, so I kicked my slippers under the bed, got into my shoes and jacket and went out to do my loving-grandchild act. I also had to do it for two, as Missy's door was still closed and I figured she was still trying to cram her right foot into her left Mary Jane like the dope she is.

After Ga-ga got lipstick all over me she turned her forces on Daddy. About the only times they ever see each other are days like Christmas or when Ga-ga wants some free remodeling service for "The Chicken

Coop," which is her little house in Southampton. Daddy seems just as happy to leave it that way. He looked kind of grim and Mom was white around the mouth. But, like Mom says, the First Duty exetera, exetera, so Mom and Daddy spoke to one another, whenever it was absolutely necessary, like they were total strangers and both a little hard of hearing.

Ga-ga took off her furs, set her hat at a wilder angle, squirted herself with some more perfume (she always smells very good but it's awfully strong), squinted at the mirror to mop her nose with a powder puff and dragged Sir Rupert Whoever into the living room, talking a mile a minute, as always.

She was saying what a darling little doll's house of an apartment we had (it's three times as big as hers) until she was stopped dead by the monster in the middle of the living-room floor. "My God," Ga-ga said, "what's *that?*" Ga-ga has millions of pairs of glasses, all in different colors to match whatever she's wearing, but she only puts them on in a dark theater or to play bridge or read a menu.

"I wish you'd tell me," Daddy said.

"It's a model of the Applegate Arcade," Mom said dangerously.

"My dear, don't tell me that miserable old pile is still standing. I used to go to a dentist there when I was a mere baby. Isn't it hideous, Rupert?" Then Ga-ga trained her guns on Mom. "Darling, didn't it fit?"

"Didn't what fit?" Mom asked.

"My little *cadeau*. You did get it? The negligee, I mean. Your good little wools are divine, of course, but I do feel that once in a while a woman should look utterly, utterly feminine. Now put it on this instant, *chérie.*"

"But . . ."

"Not another word, ducky. I want to feast my eyes on my *new* daughter-in-law."

So Mom went off, sore as a crab, to put on the Christmas present she already hated and Daddy went limping away to mix drinks while Sir Rupert talked (not that you could understand a word he said) about something called the Portland Club and somebody opening with a two in spades. Still no sign of Missy.

37

By the time Daddy hobbled back, fished the ice out of Sir Rupert's whisky and added lots of odds and ends to Ga-ga's drink, the doorbell rang and Gran and H. A. arrived, looking more like they were going to a funeral than a Christmas party. Gran was wearing the old fur coat down to her ankles and a hat that looked like a crow had died on her head. H. A. was got up in a morning coat and striped pants to show everyone that he'd been ushering at church. H. A. practically saluted when he heard the "Sir" in Ga-ga's beau's name and I could see Gran making a note of it to look him up in some book she has. Gran does this with all the titles Ga-ga digs up. If there's something fishy about them, Mom hears about it the very next day. If they're the real McCoy, they're never mentioned again.

Gran and Ga-ga greeted each other the way Maxl and the schnauzer in Eight West meet in the elevator —not exactly scrapping, but on their guard. Since it was such a festive occasion, Gran broke down and accepted a glass of sherry and after saying a lot of corny things about the sun being over the yardarm, H. A. decided on a long, strong Scotch. For all of his godliness, H. A. drinks plenty, and Daddy says it's a lot more than most people realize. Then Gran kind of smiled and said, "I notice you've opened the model of the Applegate Arcade." *Notice?* How could anyone miss it, standing up like an iceberg in the middle of the living-room floor?

Ga-ga said, "My God, did *you* give it to them?" And Daddy was about to say something tactful when he stopped with his jaw hanging. There stood Mom wearing Ga-ga's Christmas costume. I say costume because it almost looked like Mom was kidding. The thing was all pink feathers around the top and the bottom and, in between, a whole lot of shiny pink beads sewn onto something that looked like Mom was naked. Now my mother is very nice looking—pretty, even—but she has very definite ideas about the kind of clothes she likes to wear and her choice runs to plain things that show off her figure and no nonsense. This getup reminded me of an old lady called Mae West that Lulu won't let us watch on television. Anyhow, it wasn't the real Mom.

Gran was the first to speak. "Good heavens, child, you didn't go to *church* wearing that?"

"Of course I did," Mom said. "Didn't you see me passing the collection plate?"

"Unfortunately I wasn't able to go, dear. At the last moment I had a twinge of . . . Where *did* you get it?"

"I gave it to her," Ga-ga said. "Isn't it divine?"

"I might have known," Gran said, rolling her eyes.

Then, not to be outdone, Missy appeared. What she'd been doing behind that closed bedroom door I'd hate to tell you, but the results were terrific. Her hair, which is naturally straight and usually hangs halfway down her back, was all of a sudden short and kinky and the color of Mercurochrome. Her face was painted like a clown's and she was wearing long, spidery artificial lashes put on with so much glue she could hardly open her eyes. I got the feeling that Missy wasn't absolutely sure about how great she looked, but, as always, she was going to brave it out. It was hopeless.

"Missy!" Mom gasped. "What on earth . . ."

"Oh, my God," Daddy moaned, "two hookers under the same roof!"

"Darling," Mom said, "what have you done to yourself?"

"I was just playing with Ga-ga's present. It's really keen. It's got scissors and hair dye and . . ."

"She looks *sweet*," Ga-ga said, but not with much feeling.

"You?" Mom said. "You gave a six-year-old child a toy that . . ."

"Disgraceful," Gran said. "Really, Evelyn, this time you've gone too far."

"My hairdresser says it's absolutely harmless. Her little girl . . ."

"Mother," Daddy said, "I don't care if your hairdresser's little girl soaks her head in kerosene and lights it. What are we going to do with Missy? Lulu!" he shouted. "Lulu!"

"She's not here," Mom said. "I gave her the day off."

"You gave her the day *off?*"

"It *is* Christmas, dear."

"Well, of all the . . ."

"All little girls like to dress up," Ga-ga whimpered.

"That dreadful stuff in her lovely eyes," Gran said. "She could blind herself."

"Well, if you'd take a little more interest in your *own* appearance . . ."

"Might as well put a loaded gun in her hand," Daddy said.

"Speaking of loaded guns . . ." Mom began.

Missy started to cry and so did Ga-ga, streaks of blue and black running down their cheeks. I got the feeling that I wanted to laugh, but something told me that it would be a very bad idea. So I decided to play it cool and make myself scarce for a while. "I think I'd better take Maxl out," I said to nobody in particular. "He needs to wet." He already had, but since it was against the Applegate Arcade, it hadn't been noticed.

Cold and miserable as it was, I kept poor Maxl out until my new Timex (which is waterproof and anti-magnetic and a lot of other things) told me it was almost time for lunch. When we got back inside the apartment, most of the gook was off Missy's face. Her hair was wet and hanging in strings, like it had just been washed (which it had—several times), but that crazy red color was still there. Ga-ga was pretending to look through an old fashion magazine and sniffling every time she turned a page. Gran was sitting as far away from Ga-ga as possible, without being in another room. Mom, still in her beads and feathers, was looking like a thundercloud. Sir Rupert had dozed off, which showed more sense than I would have suspected. Daddy was sitting on the floor with H. A. trying to put the Decline and Fall of the Roman Empire Battle of the Visigoths together. He had a full drink at his side and he seemed to shudder with every blink of the Christmas tree lights. "No, no, no, H. A.," he kept saying, "read the instructions. 'In assembling the Ballista, hold the frame (Part A) in the left hand and the trough (Part B) in the right hand. With the other hand, thread retractable arms (Parts C and D) through flexible eyes (H, I, J and K) through . . .' No, H. A., Part A in the *left* hand and . . ."

"H. A. is trying," Gran said coldly.

"That's not all he is."

Mom said, "You'd think that a man who calls himself an architect could at least assemble a toy that any child could . . ."

"Well, if *you* think you can do it so damned well, why don't . . ."

"There was such a nice young colored man at Schwarz," Ga-ga said. "He assured me that an idiot could put it together in . . ."

"Negroes at F.A.O. Schwarz?" Gran said. "I don't believe it."

"Well, if you think I'm lying, just go down to Fifth Avenue and Fifty-eighth Street and . . ."

"I did *not* imply that you weren't telling the truth, Evelyn, although there have been times when . . ."

"Does anybody else want another drink?" Daddy asked, finishing off his own in a single gulp. He was kind of unsteady.

"Well, now that you mention it . . ." H. A. said.

"I think lunch is almost ready," Mom said darkly.

"Luncheon is served," the cateress said.

In his rush to get off the floor and offer his arm to a lady, like he was going to help her over the Alps instead of across the living room, H. A. kicked over the whole Decline and Fall set. It scattered across the floor in pieces and Daddy just held his head and moaned.

"Oh, I say, old man, I'm awfully . . ." H. A. spluttered.

"Oh, H. A., why don't you go and . . ."

"Dear!" Mom said. *"Lunch!"*

Sir Rupert, more or less awake, got to his feet and started huffing and puffing in the general direction of the dining room. He was getting there just fine until he came alongside the Applegate Arcade, then his elbow struck a corner of it. A big cloud of dust came out of the chimney, there was a rattle and a whirring and then a music box started playing "The Battle Hymn of the Republic."

"Oh, I forgot to tell you," Gran said, "the old Swiss cabinetmaker who made the model of the Applegate Arcade also built in a music box. I used to love to turn it on when I was a girl."

41

"Do you think you know how to turn it off?" Daddy asked.

"Well . . . I *think* . . . I mean it's been such a long time . . . but it seems to me that you simply take this lever and . . ." Gran gave it a tug. Whatever it was that she did, the invisible music box must have loved it, because "The Battle Hymn" started playing about ten times as fast—"Ohmineeyeshaveseenthegloryofthe-comingofthelord!" And I will say for this music box that it was no slouch like the modern ones that play Brahms's "Lullabye" inside a stuffed lamb. This one had real pizazz. Daddy grabbed the lever and yanked. There was a sound of splintering wood and the lever came off in his hand. The music kept on louder and faster than ever.

"Please, madam," the cateress said, "the *blinchiki* are getting cold."

"De-ar," Mom said to Daddy, "the cateress says the *blinchiki* . . ."

"You can tell the cateress to take her goddamned *blinchiki,* one by one, and . . ."

"Luncheon everybody!" Mom shouted.

Lunch was one of those great big heavy meals that nobody likes but everyone pretends to because it's a holiday tradition—roast goose, chestnuts, Brussels sprouts (echhh!) and all the rest of it. There was champagne and when Missy and I were offered half a glass each Gran carried on like the A.A. ambulance was waiting downstairs. Then, as though she hadn't caused trouble enough that day, Missy started in on a long spiel (mostly made up) about how she always shared Lulu's beer and how she and her sappy friend Mary Courtney Rogers poured gin into their Cokes at Schrafft's, while Ga-ga giggled and said wasn't it adorable and Gran moaned and suggested an early appointment with Bishop Demorest and Mom trailed one of her feathery sleeves through the goose gravy and said the same word she'd been so sore at Daddy for saying. The music box kept right on playing.

Over the endive salad, which I happen to hate, things were peaceful and very quiet except for Sir Rupert's wheezing and the rattle of Ga-ga's bracelets. Both

Mom and Daddy looked like they'd sell their souls to get finished with all of this and hit the sack. Daddy winced every time the music box started in again, but otherwise he was under control. It was then that the doorbell rang and in trooped the building staff on a cloud of Rheingold, twenty-one strong, singing "O Little Town of Bethlehem."

"Oh, my God," Daddy said, "their Christmas tips!"

"I've taken care of it. All their envelopes are in a big vanilla [?] folder on your desk," Mom said.

"Thanks," Daddy said. "Stop singing, please, fellows. I'll be right back." The building men didn't stop singing any more than the music box in the Applegate Arcade stopped playing. Daddy made his way unsteadily across the living room, stepping on quite a lot of pieces of the Decline and Fall of the Roman Empire with a terrible crackling sound. In less than a minute he was back.

"There's a strange smell in the hall," Daddy was saying. But he said no more. He stepped on a piece of the battering ram from the Roman Empire toy. His feet shot out from under him and the folder he was carrying flew into the air. Poor Daddy landed flat on his back surrounded by two hundred Christmas cards, neatly addressed in Mom's best Miss Farthingale's handwriting.

"The Christmas cards!" Mom screamed. "I gave them to you to mail more than a week ago and now . . ."

Whatever it was that Mom wanted to say about Christmas cards, she never got a chance. There was an explosion from my bedroom that shook the whole building. It was the result of my first experiment with H. A.'s old chemistry set and that is all I care to tell about Christmas Day.

Three

So on the day after Christmas our parents split up. Mom didn't pack her things and go home to mother, the way they do in cartoons. She wasn't crazy enough to do anything like that. Besides, there was the apartment and us kids and Maxl to think of. It was Daddy who did the moving out and you can be pretty darned sure that he wasn't fool enough to go home to *his* mother, either.

By the time Daddy came home from wherever he'd spent Christmas night, he and Mom had got down to a kind of frosty dancing-school manners like they hated each other's guts but would only get into trouble if they let on. I know because I was tuned in on the whole conversation.

Our apartment in New York is laid out so that the living room and the dining room are way up in front facing the park. Missy and I aren't allowed there except on special occasions, which is okay with me as the furniture is very breakable and everything is white and pale green—just begging for fingerprints—and there's no TV. Next comes more interesting territory— the kitchen, the maids' rooms, the front entrance and the service entrance—where you can see who's coming and going and what's in the refrigerator and read Lulu's dream books and (if Lulu's in a good mood) maybe play a hand of poker. Then comes a string of bedrooms: Mom and Dad's, which is very large with a bed big enough for the whole four of us to get into, which we sometimes used to do; Missy's room is straight across the hall from theirs so that they can hear her if she falls out of bed or has a nightmare or

44

some boob trick like that; then comes my room, which survived the explosion just fine except that all the windows were blasted out; and finally, across the back of the whole apartment, a great big sunny room that's for everybody. It's not exactly a library or a playroom or a guest room, but a combination of them all. I mean it's really cool.

Like I said, Daddy's an architect and he designed the room to be what he calls "childproof." Everything in it is older and tougher than we are. It's got books and magazines and records and television and Coke and liquor and a big desk to put bills on and Daddy's drafting table for when he has to do homework and a big, comfortable leather sofa and Maxl's bed (except he usually sleeps with Missy or me) and you can't hurt anything no matter how hard you try. The Room—it's got no other name—also has a thick cork floor to spare the people downstairs and a special kind of ceiling so we won't bother the people upstairs, who are deaf anyhow. But from my bedroom you can hear perfectly if you hold a drinking glass up to the wall like I saw this detective do in a movie. Try it sometime. It works just like a telephone receiver.

It was this way—I mean with the glass—that I once found out that I didn't have to join the Knickerbocker Greys because I could hear Daddy answering H. A.'s sales pitch by saying that he didn't approve of anything that was "pretentious" or "militaristic" or "archaic" and in his opinion the Greys were all three. I haven't looked up the words yet—not when they've got words like "copulate" and "vagina" in our dictionary. (You just ought to *see* some of the words they print!) But for all of H. A.'s spluttering about a family tradition, the Knickerbocker Greys are getting along without me and vice versa.

When I was out of school with my tonsils a year ago I heard Mom's best friend, Liz (her name is really Lispenard of all things!), telling Mom how her first husband was really a "laden homo sapiens" (I *think* she said) who was secretly in love with his own brother, for cripes sake, and "impudent in the hay" [?] except when Aunt Liz was wearing men's pajamas. Well, it didn't make any sense at all, but then I wasn't

45

using my regular listening glass. Besides, I was sick.

Anyhow, it's there in The Room where all the most interesting conversations are held and I had the right glass the day Mom and Daddy decided to say good-by forever. Missy was off at the barbershop with Lulu getting her Antoine-ette Junior Miss dye job hacked off right down to the roots. (And here *I've* been begging for a crew cut ever since I was five!) After the men replaced the windows in my bedroom, I was confined to quarters. First, to clean up the mess the explosion had made and, second, to think about my crime. The cleaning up didn't take very long and from the very beginning it seemed to me that H. A. was much more to blame for blowing up the place than I was. That's what Daddy said, too, just before he hauled off and socked H. A. at the lunch table.

So there really wasn't anything to do but put my glass up to the wall and listen. It's very good practice for becoming a detective. Mom was on the telephone with Gran for about the millionth time that day when Daddy finally came back home. Of course I could only hear one side of the conversation, but it wasn't hard to imagine what Gran was saying on the other end.

"Yes, Mummy, yes. Of course," Mom said. "I *am* sorry. I've told you that. . . . I didn't sleep very well, either. . . . Yes, Mummy, it was disgraceful and I hope H. A.'s eye is better. But, Mummy, anyone who would put dangerous explosives in the hands of a ten-year-old boy . . . Mummy, H. A. had that chemistry set before I was *born*. The things in it must have gone stale or whatever *happens* to chemicals. . . . Yes, I'm sure it was a very good set, when it was new, but it could have killed someone. Just a dollar bill in an envelope would have . . . Mummy, I don't know why you say 'poor H. A.' He has his half of the money Father left and a good job and no living expenses and . . . Yes, I know. I pay taxes, too. Everyone does. . . . I'm not trying to excuse anyone, but you must remember that he's been working terribly hard lately and the shock of having the house blow up on top of everything . . . Mummy, I don't *know* where he went and I haven't heard from him all day." Then she said, "The telephone has been tied up," but Gran didn't seem to get the hint. "Mummy, what's the point in calling the club? He doesn't *belong* to the club. He doesn't believe in clubs. . . . Yes, I know that's where Father always went whenever he had a row with you. . . . Mummy, I'm *not* speaking ill of the dead. All married couples . . . Mummy, I don't *know* what I'm going to do. Probably nothing. I'll have to wait until we talk it over and . . . Mummy, I am *not* defending him but . . . Mummy, that's sweet of you, but why should the children and I leave a comfortable apartment and move in on you, when . . . But nothing *has* been decided. I haven't even seen him this morning and . . ." The front door slammed. "Mummy, I think he's here now. I'll call you later. . . . Yes, Mummy . . . Yes, I'll tell him that if I get a chance. . . . Yes, Mummy . . . Yes. Good-by, Mummy, and do tell H. A. how sorry I am. Good-by, Mummy."

Daddy went into The Room and closed the door. "Good morning," he said.

"Good morning," Mummy said coldly. "Feeling better?"

"I feel like a pile of . . ."

"That hardly surprises me. You must be very proud of yourself—striking my brother, insulting my mother and marching out of here like a madman."

"Oh, stop it! My God, if we could only be left alone once in a while . . ."

"Any more conduct like yesterday's and I can promise you that we will be."

"I suppose your mother's been on the phone all morning haranguing you about . . ."

"Certainly not. Mummy would never intrude her opinions into affairs she feels are no concern of hers."

"Just what affairs would those be—Far Eastern?" It was a good question and a nifty way to get Mom started on a real tantrum. However she let it pass and changed the subject. "If you've been trying to reach H. A. at his office, don't bother. He's at Lenox Hill Hospital having his eye treated."

"Why would I want to reach your brother at his office—or anywhere else?"

"Why, to apologize, naturally."

"*Apologize?* Apologize to that fathead after he nearly killed Kerry and blew up the whole house! I wish I'd broken his . . ."

"My brother was only trying to impart to Kerry his own interest in science."

"Balls! Your brother's so stupid he can hardly mix a Bromo-Seltzer and such a tightwad that he wouldn't even buy the poor kid a . . ."

"At least my brother has some feeling for the family."

"Especially if it doesn't cost him anything."

"Whereas *you*—an only child—spoiled rotten by a frivolous, gadabout mother who was so busy buying clothes and going to parties that she never saw you . . ."

"If she didn't see me, how could she spoil me? I suppose *your* mother sat by the cradle every night and . . ."

"At least she saw to it that I was put in competent hands."

"You mean that old limey bitch who locked you in the bathroom until you . . ."

"What I mean," Mom roared, "is that I have had enough. Either you apologize to poor H. A. for your drunken, loutish, beastly behavior or else . . ."

"Or else what?"

Mom didn't answer right away. When she did, I could hardly hear. "Or else get out."

"Get *out*?"

"Well, I suppose you *could* put the children and me on the street. The lease is in your name. You pay the rent—that is, I *suppose* it's paid."

"Are you out of your mind?"

"I was never more serious in my life."

"You mean just because I lost my head and took a poke at your half-wit brother . . ."

"*And* insulted my mother. *And* nearly shot the children. As for the Christmas cards you promised faithfully to mail . . ."

"I'm sorry. I *said* I was sorry."

"Your being sorry—if true—doesn't get the cards delivered in time for Christmas."

"Are a couple of hundred lousy Christmas cards really so important? Couldn't we send them out next year?"

"No, *we* couldn't because next year there's going to be only one name on them—*mine*."

"Do you mean to sit there and tell me that after twelve years and two kids you want . . ."

"I suppose it's a little late in the game, but I'm doing my best to rectify what Mummy said at the time was a terrible, terrible mistake."

"Your mother is full of . . ."

"Abusing my mother will hardly improve matters. I've seen this coming for a long time and . . ."

"Since when?"

That seemed to stump Mom, so instead of answering, she just went right on. "The choice is up to you. Either you can move out or I can take the children and leave. I suppose I can always find a cheap little apartment somewhere and go back to work . . ."

Mom's business career is a big joke and nobody tells it any funnier than she does. It was at a place upstairs on Madison Avenue called the Junior League Leftovers and it was run by a man who said he was a Sicilian Duke. The shop sold slightly used dresses and furs and the name of it made Gran think that it was all for charity. The Duke was going to pay Mom and her friend Liz fifty bucks a week and commissions on everything they sold. During the first week they bought much more than they sold, but they liked working for their livings just fine. Then on payday (Saturday) Liz asked Mom to have lunch with her and her boy friend and a strange man at the Ritz. Since Mom didn't think she looked just right for the Ritz, she borrowed a whole French outfit (which she was planning to buy, anyway) from Junior League Leftovers and a very fancy fur coat to wear to lunch. She was making a big hit with the strange man (who turned out to be Daddy) when all of a sudden a woman screamed "That's my coat and my hat and my dress!" She was pointing straight at Mom. Well, it turned out that everything Mom had on her back was stolen, like all the stuff at Junior League Leftovers; and her boss, while he *was* a Sicilian and his name *was* Duke, was also a crook. Daddy was very chivalrous and went to the police station with Mom and called a lawyer he knew to get her off, but Gran always connected him with the Mafia after that. That's the story of Mom's career, but she wasn't making any joke of it the day after Christmas.

"Stop talking like a soap opera," Daddy said. "Naturally I'll go on supporting you and the kids. But can't we discuss this like two rational adult people?"

"When you happen to be neither? I expected you to hit me or get that gun of yours and shoot it out."

Then Daddy blew up. "Oh, for God's sake! There's no point in trying to talk to you at all, is there?"

"None!" Mom snapped. "I'll be back in a couple of hours. By then I hope you'll be packed up and gone." I heard her heels clicking on the floor out in the hall. Then I heard the front door slam.

I got my glass put away just in time. Then the door of my room opened and there stood Daddy. "Kerry?" he said. "What are you doing here?"

"You ought to know, Daddy. You sent me here—to think things over. Don't you remember?"

"Oh. Yes. I'm sorry, Kerry. You can come out of your room. It wasn't really your fault. I kind of lost my head."

"That was nothing, Dad," I said, hoping to make the poor guy feel a little better. "There's this kid in the class ahead of me at St. Barnaby's—Dexter Bradshaw? His father really went off his rocker. He did it at Shepheard's . . ."

"I don't blame him," Daddy said.

"And they put him in an ambulance and took him to Pratt-Whitney . . ."

"Payne Whitney, Kerry. It's a mental hospital."

"Yeah. That's what I was going to tell you. And three times a week—except holidays, of course—they'd strap him down on a table and put this big kind of bit in his mouth and shoot about a million volts of electricity through him so he couldn't hardly remember anything. . . ."

"Could hardly, Kerry. Not couldn't hardly."

Well, the story didn't hardly seem to be cheering him up at all so I ended it up kind of lame. "Well, anyway, Mr. Bradshaw's just fine now and bought a big Chris Craft cabin cruiser. It's keen."

"That's nice, Kerry. Where's your sister?"

"She's . . . she's . . ." I didn't want to get him started on Missy's hair again, as he'd also sent silly old Ga-ga home in tears after he'd polished off Gran and H. A. "She's just out with Lulu and Maxl."

"Do you mean to say that your mother went dusting out of here and left you all alone?" Daddy said hotly.

"I'm not alone, Daddy. You're here."

"Oh. So I am. Want to come in and watch me pack?"

I didn't want him to know that I'd just happened to overhear him and Mom, so I said, "Taking a trip?"

"Well, yes and no," Daddy said, leading me down the hall to his bedroom. The glass men had finished replacing the mirror in his bath and a smudgy-looking bill for all their work was perched on Daddy's chest of drawers like a dirty butterfly. "Your mother decided —that is, your mother and *I* decided—that maybe you'd be happier if I moved out for a little while."

"I'm happy all the time," I said. "Except in Latin. As for Missy, she's too young to . . ."

"Well, we thought we'd try it. At least for a time. Hand me that pile of shirts, like a good boy, would you, Kerry?"

"You mean we're not going to see you again, Daddy?"

"Why, of course you are. I'm sure your mother wouldn't keep you from . . . Why, certainly we'll see each other as often as you want."

"That's going to be pretty often," I said. "Where will you live?"

"W-well, I don't exactly know. Some hotel, I guess, until I find a . . . Well, we'll see. Anyhow you know my office number."

"Sure I do: two-one-two-six-three-seven-five-one-oh-two. It's about as easy to remember as . . ."

"I know, Kerry. It's a crazy world we live in."

"Crazy," I said. "C-can I mix you a drink or any-thing?"

Daddy gave me a hug and mussed up my hair—not that it was combed to begin with. "You're a good kid, Kerry," he said, sort of husky-like. "Now would you mind getting that roll of plans off my drafting table?"

When I got back Daddy was blowing his nose.

While he filled up his suitcases we talked about St. Barnaby's Lower School basketball schedule for the winter. I couldn't imagine that he cared very much about exactly what date we played against Buckley or St. David's or Trinity, but he looked kind of down in the dumps so I talked away about whatever he seemed to be interested in.

Like he does everything, Daddy packed his clothes neatly and quickly—not all of them, but quite a lot of things. On top of the pile he put a picture of Missy and Maxl and me taken at Ga-ga's silly little pink house in Southampton. "There," he said, snapping the suitcase shut. "That's it."

"Is that *all* you're going to take, Daddy?" I'd hoped he'd spend just a *little* longer. "You've got golf clubs and your architect's stuff and . . ."

"I'll send for the heavy things if we really . . . I mean when I find a place." He picked up the two suitcases and I walked out into the hall with him.

"Can I help you carry anything, Dad?"

"No thanks," he said in a kind of muffled way. Then he got down on his knees and put his arms around me. It was kind of babyish for two men of our age, but nobody was looking and I wouldn't have cared anyway. "Well, Kerry, it looks as if you've got to be the man of the household now. You'll probably do a better job of it than I did."

Right then and there I realized that I wouldn't. "No, Daddy," I said, hugging him hard. "I won't do a better job. I'll try but I won't be anything like as good at it as you." For cripes sake, I was practically bawling! "Daddy, don't leave."

"I've got to, Kerry. I don't want to, but your mother wants me to go. It won't be forever. We'll see each other a lot—the circus, the hockey games. Maybe you and Missy and I can take some sort of trip together in the spring. We'll have a big time, Kerry. Really we will."

"Daddy, if you could only go on living here and . . ."

"I wish I could, Kerry. But now you're in charge. You've always wanted to be grown up and . . ."

"But not just now, Daddy. Not all of a sudden. I . . ."

Then I got the feeling that I wasn't making anything

any easier for anybody. So I let go of him and said, "Okay, Dad. See you around. Keep in touch."

Daddy got up and wiped his eyes. "Will you be all right alone here in the apartment until your mother or Lulu gets back?"

"S-sure. Sure I will. Like you said, I'm the man of the house now."

"That's right, Kerry. Be a good boy. Help your mother all you can and kiss Missy good-by for me." Then he was gone.

Alone in the apartment, I wandered into forbidden territory—the living room. The Applegate Arcade was still in the middle of the floor, but the music box had run down. The Christmas tree stood in front of the middle window, but with the lights turned off it looked kind of bleak and not very cheery. So I went back to my room and lay down on my bed to have a good cry. I haven't cried since *The Dog of Flanders*—not even at *Oliver!*, which was kind of a drag, anyway. But I hardly got started when I heard the front door slam and Maxl yapping and Missy yelling "Kerry! Kerry! I got all my hair cut off and Lulu says I look like a bull dike." She came busting into my room (without even knocking, if you please). "What's the matter, Kerry?" Missy yelled. "You look funny."

"*I* look funny? Get a load of yourself!"

Michael, the barber, had had to clip Missy's hair almost down to the scalp to get the red out of it. "Ain't it a pisser!" she said happily. "Go ahead, feel it. It's like a door mat." Pain in the ass that she sometimes is, Missy's a pretty good kid.

"I like it," I said. "It looks kind of cute." Then we both had a good laugh.

Mom came home and sort of peeked into every room of the apartment, as though she'd lost something and was looking for it. Then she told Lulu to take Missy and I—Missy and *me*—out for lunch and to the movies, like a divorce was some kind of big celebration. We went to the Eighty-sixth Street Automat where a lot of dirty old men hang out. Missy made quite a stir with her crew cut and her stretch pants and her ballet slippers. And whenever some old bum would come up to her and say, "Are you a ballet dancer, sonny," then Missy would bat her eyelashes and dimple and act real sissy and say, "Yes. Are you a dirty old man?" It slayed me, but Lulu got all huffy and East Side and made us move to a table in the section that's roped off for women and children.

Back home that night, though, I knew that our life had really changed because we ate dinner with Mom in the dining room, which is also kind of a celebration thing. Usually Missy and I ate off trays in The Room at seven o'clock in our pajamas and Mom and Daddy— and any company they had, which was quite often— did things up grand in the dining room at eight. This was kind of a compromise. We had dinner at half past seven with Lulu serving and candles and finger bowls and all the rest of that jazz. Mom was kind of dressed up in a long sort of bathrobe and smelling very good. When Missy said, "Where's Daddy?" Mom said, "Well, that's what we're going to talk about after dinner," and the meal went on.

After dinner we all went into the living room and sat in a row on the long white sofa—Mom in the middle and one of us on each side. "Et-gay our-yay ig-bay eet-fay off-ay e-thay ofa-say," I said to Missy.

"That's right, Missy darling," Mom said. "You're in the grown-up part of the house now. In fact we all have to be very grown up tonight. I've got something to tell you and I hope you're going to be able to understand it—or at least to understand most of it. And that is that your father and I have decided not to live together any longer."

"Why?" Missy said.

"Well, dear, we just thought it would be better."

"But why would it be better?" Missy asked. I tried to catch her eye and give her a For-cripes-sake-shut-up look. Missy is too young to realize that you've got to be very careful when you're talking to grownups. I mean they're awfully mixed up to begin with and then they don't expect kids to be bright enough to understand very much. In fact, they don't even *want* kids to understand much of what they're saying, and they get all flustered and embarrassed if you ask them to lay it on the line. Since I had all the inside information anyway, I was able to play it cool the way adults want you to, but not old Missy.

"You mean you're going to get a divorce like Mary Courtney Rogers' mother?" Missy asked.

"Well, not *exactly* like Mrs. Rogers, dear."

"Her name isn't Mrs. Rogers any longer, Mom. It's Mrs. Parkhurst and Mary Courtney says she's going to get rid of him very soon because . . ."

"Darling, what I mean is Mrs. Rogers or Mrs. Parkhurst has had a number of husbands. . . ."

"Three: Mr. Rogers; Mr. Boyce; and Mr. Parkhurst. And she's not even thirty yet."

"Well, dear, Mary Courtney's mother has always been more spectacular about marriage—and about everything else—than I've ever wanted to be. . . ."

"What's spectacular mean, Mom?"

"Missy!" I said. "For cripes sake stop interrupting and let Mom talk for a while."

"Well, children, that's about it. Your father and I have simply decided that we'll be better off—*happier* —living apart. And I suppose a divorce is more sensible—tidier anyhow—than just going on. . . ."

"Don't you love Daddy any more?" Missy said.

Mom waited for a long time before she answered. "I'm very *fond* of your father. I always will be and I want you to be, too."

"Doesn't he love you any more? Doesn't he love Kerry and me?"

"Missy," I said. "*I'm* supposed to be the big talker in this family."

"That's all right, Missy," Mom said. "I expect you to ask questions. Of course your father still loves you. You can see him as often as you want."

"But I want to see him all the time."

"Missy!"

"It's all right, Kerry. Missy's younger than you are. She doesn't understand."

"Sure I understand," Missy said. She can be just like Maxl when he gets hold of one of my slippers and won't let go. "You and Daddy are going to get a divorce. But if everybody loves everybody else so much, why are you going to?"

"Missy, I can't explain it all tonight. You're tired and . . ."

"I'm not tired." If Missy were halfway dead she wouldn't admit it.

"Well, *I'm* tired. You'll understand a little better when you're older. I just wanted you children to know that nothing's going to be any different. We're going to be just the way we always were."

"But *everything's* going to be different," Missy said. "If Daddy's gone away and you get a divorce and . . ."

"It's past somebody's bedtime." It was Lulu and I swear she'd been listening from the dining room. If there's anything I can't stand, it's a snoop.

"Thank you, Lulu," Mom said with a big sigh of relief.

"It's Christmas vacation," Missy said, "and I can stay up as late . . ."

"It's near nine o'clock, child," Lulu said, "and you got a big day tomorrow. Ingersoll girl's birthday party and I don't know what all."

"That's all," Missy said. "Just Tracy Ingersoll's old party and that isn't until . . ."

"Lulu's right, Missy," Mom said. "It is late. Now kiss Kerry . . ."

"Do I have to?"

"Don't have to if you don't want to," I said. "It's no skin off my . . ."

"Kerry!" Lulu said. A kiss for Mom and one for me, and Missy was gone, thank God.

"Well, Kerry," Mom said. She sounded real worn out. "Is there anything you want to ask about . . . about your father and me?"

"No, Mom. I guess I know everything. Now I better take Maxl out."

"Oh, Kerry. No. It's so late and . . ."

"Daddy isn't here to do it any more. I'm the man of the family now. He said so."

"All right, darling. It's sweet of you and I *am* tired. But don't go where Riley can't see you every minute of the time and come right back."

For some reason I couldn't get to sleep that night

and it was almost eleven by my Timex when I began to feel drowsy and then who should come barging into my room? You guessed it. Missy!

"Kerry?" she whispered. "Kerry! Are you asleep?"

"Yes," I said.

"You are not! Can I get in bed with you?"

"For cripes sake you've got your own bed and it's newer than mine and it's a Simmons Beautyrest."

"Aw, please, Kerry. Just this once. I wanted to get in bed with Mom, but she's in her room crying. I could hear her all the way through the door."

"Yeah?" I said, moving over. Missy crawled in and I could feel that her face was all wet. "What's the matter? What are *you* crying about?"

"Nothing."

"Nobody cries about nothing. Come on. You can tell me."

"Nothing, Kerry. It's . . . it's just my hair. I hate my hair this way." I can always tell when Missy's lying and this was one of the times.

"I think it's kind of cute," I said. "It's different. You've got to say that. It really is different."

"It . . . it makes me look like a boy."

"So what? You always wanted to be a boy. It's what that hotshot psychiatrist says. You've got 'penis envy.' All girls are jealous because . . ."

"Well, I'm not jealous of *yours!*"

We didn't say anything for a while, then Missy said, "Kerry, are Mom and Dad *really* going to get a divorce like she said?"

"Sure. I guess so. Why would she say so if she didn't mean it?"

"Kerry! I don't *want* them to!"

"Well, for cripes sake, who does? But you know what grownups are like—crazy."

"Crazy," Missy said.

"And everybody gets divorced nowadays. Just look at the people we know—Aunt Liz, twice; Mary Courtney's mother two times and another one coming up; Mr. Ingersoll before he got married this time and had Tracy . . ." It made up quite a list but it didn't seem to give Missy much comfort. Finally I said, "Aw,

Missy, be a good kid and please stop crying like a God-damned baby."

"But, Kerry," she said, "you're crying, too."

"Oh, shut up," I said. Then we both cried ourselves to sleep.

Four

The next day Missy was ramming around the apartment about 6:00 A.M. and I felt like ten miles of bad road. I threw up at breakfast and so Dr. Fischer came in to look me over. He said I had a virus exetera, exetera, exetera and there was a lot of it going around exetera, exetera, exetera and put me to bed with tea and toast and ginger ale if I wanted it (echhh!) exetera, exetera, exetera and Missy looked fine only keep her away from me.

Wouldn't you think that with three solid months of school between New Year's and Easter I could manage to get sick some time *except* Christmas vacation? So I wound up in bed with the television set and my listening glass.

For somebody who really wasn't very sick, I drew visitors in swarms. But it didn't take long to see that they were using me as a handy excuse to get into the apartment and spend a long time shooting off their mouths to poor Mom.

The first was Daddy, who didn't even know I was sick. He showed up right after Lulu got back from delivering Missy to her birthday lunch party. Only by now everything was different. Instead of letting himself into his own apartment with his own key, he had himself announced from downstairs and rang the doorbell a few seconds later like he was some kind of guest instead of our father. I heard him telling Lulu that he'd come to pick up some things from his desk, then I yelled, "Daddy!"

Daddy stuck his head into my room and said, "What are you doing in the sack?"

"Sick," I said. "It's a virus. There's a lot of it going around."

"That's tough, Kerry. Can I send you anything like candy?"

"You can send it, but I can't eat it. The virus is in my gut."

"Well you'd better get over that in a hurry, Kerry, so you can come down to my apartment and I can cook for you."

"Can you cook?"

"No, but I can try."

"Gee, Dad, that would be swell," I said, although the thought of eating anything made me want to throw up all over again. "Where are you going to live?" It sounded funny to be asking Daddy where he was going to be living.

"Why, in a place I'll be renting from a young architect who's going to Brazil to work. He takes off today. So tomorrow I move in to Number Nine Minot Mews." For cripes sake, he said it like it was the Empire State Building or something anybody had ever heard of.

"Minot Mews," Daddy explained, "is down in the Village."

New York is a very orderly city. I mean all of the streets and most of the avenues are just numbered and if you can count you can find where you're going. I'm even fairly familiar with kookie addresses like Henderson Place, Sutton Square and Riverview Terrace, but they're *uptown*. "How will we ever find you?" I asked.

"Oh, you can't miss it," Daddy said. "It's a row of old stables—all of them nearly two hundred years old."

"With horses?"

"No, not with horses, Kerry. They've all been done over into studios. And I'm lucky to get this one. You'll like it."

"Sure I will," I said.

Then Daddy said, "Is your mother in?" just like he was saying something about the weather.

"Sure, Dad. She's in The Room, writing thank-you notes."

"Well, I'll just stop in and see her for a minute. I'll

60

ask her if you and Missy can come down for lunch on New Year's Day. How will that be?"

"That'll be great, Daddy. I'll be fine by then."

Daddy mussed up my hair and said good-by. I don't know why grown men are always messing a kid's hair one minute and then yelling because it isn't combed the next. But Daddy saw to it that *his* hair was smooth and adjusted his necktie before he tapped on the door of The Room. It was open anyway.

"Are we speaking?" he asked Mom, kind of embarrassed.

"It would be foolish not to be. I'm sure we'll be having a great deal to talk about. Come in."

"I can only stay a second. I'm taking Mother to lunch. I suppose someone has to spring the news on her."

"You deal with yours, I'll cope with mine," Mom said.

"I'm afraid it's going to break Mother up," Daddy said.

"Somehow I doubt that."

"You never did like her, did you?"

"Nonsense," Mom said, "I'm very fond of your mother." She said it the way I'd say "I'm very fond of eggplant," when some kid's parents invite me to lunch. Only Mom didn't add, "But I've had enough."

"She's crazy about you. *And* the kids."

"She can see them any time she likes. It would be bad for the children to have their whole lives changed in one fell swoop."

"You could hardly say that a divorce is going to be exactly beneficial to them," Daddy said.

"If you don't mind, I'd rather not discuss it. You said you were in a hurry?"

"Yes. I just wanted to get some things out of the desk and leave you my new address and telephone number."

"Oh?"

"Yes. I'm moving in tomorrow."

"That was fast work."

"Well, I have to live somewhere."

"Yes, I suppose you do."

"I'd like the kids to come to lunch on New Year's Day—that is, if it's all right with you."

"Perfectly all right. Until we get some sort of definite arrangement worked out, you're free to see the children whenever . . ."

"Do we *have* to have a definite arrangement? I mean couldn't this thing . . ."

The telephone rang. "Excuse me," Mom said. "Hello? . . . Yes, Mummy . . . No, Mummy, I haven't seen a lawyer yet. . . ."

"Oh, for God's sake!" Daddy snapped and then he marched out of the room.

"Wait!" Mom called. But it was too late. I heard Daddy's heels pounding down the hall and then the front door slammed.

"Mummy," Mom said, "could you hold the line just a minute? . . . Yes, I'm afraid it *is* rather important. . . . Mummy, *I'll be right back.*" She ran down the hall after Daddy, but by the time she got to the front door he was gone.

The next visitor was Ga-ga. Even though it was cold outside with snow on the ground, Ga-ga was got up like the breath of spring. She brought me a whole, great big mocha cake from Passy (one of her two favorite restaurants). It must have been delicious, but the very sight of a cake almost made me throw up the tea and toast I hadn't quite been able to eat for lunch. She came chirping into my room like some kind of crazy canary, spilling ashes all over my bed. "Kerry, darling, I was lunching with a beau"—I knew that it was with Daddy, but what was the point in spoiling her fun?—"and when I heard you were sick, I just *had* to run in and see you. So I said to Hans—you know, he's that nice captain who always looks after me at Passy; so tall!—I said, 'Do you think you could let me have a mocha cake for my favorite grandson?'" Since I'm the only grandson Ga-ga's got, that's not a hard record to make. Well, she went through a long conversation—as made up as one of Missy's—about what she said to Hans and what Hans said to her (you guessed it; it was *impossible* that she could be a grandmother); and how Mario, the headwaiter, had called her "Mademoiselle," when he'd known her for at least thirty years but it must have been her new hairdo (meaning wig); and how her "beau" had been so chivalrous that he insisted on paying for the cake (which meant Daddy must have socked out about fifteen bucks for it if I know Passy); and how she'd run into her old friend Lorraine Titweiler in the powder room and how poor Lorraine had had a partial stroke and looked at least a thousand years old; and how she'd ridden over to Gracie Square with a taxi driver who'd flirted with her so much that she very nearly took down his number to report him except that he was a young Italian and so attractive that she didn't have the heart; and how she could have sworn that our doorman had winked at her (poor old Riley's so boozed up most of the time that he can hardly open either eye, let alone wink). Then she said, "Darling, it's naughty of me to make you talk so much and wear you out." I hadn't said a word, but she *was* wearing me out. "Is your mother in?"

"Sure," I said.

Just then Mom came into my room. She looked sad and tired and the sight of Ga-ga, got up like a Kewpie doll, didn't do very much to cheer Mom up. "Darling!" Ga-ga said. "I've just heard and I'm simply *sick* about it! Now, sweetie, in spite of this awful thing you and I are still going to be f-r-e-i-n-d-s, aren't we?" Even if Ga-ga couldn't spell it, I knew what she was talking about. But with grownups it's usually smart to play dumb.

"Yes, of course we are, Evelyn," Mom said without much spirit.

"Remember, darling, I'm an old hand at d-i-v-o-r-c-e. Why, practically every living soul I know has been through it and they've *always* turned to *me*. I mean, darling, who knows, if poor Charlie hadn't had that ghastly heart attack that took him off like *that,* even he and I might have ended up in R-e-n-o, not that he wasn't a living saint."

"Yes, Evelyn."

"And of course the last thing in the *world* that I'd dream of doing is to take s-i-d-e-s. In fact, I never think of you as a daughter-in-law, but more as a

63

sister. Oh, and I blame myself a good deal for this, don't think I don't. I know now that I made a dreadful mistake in choosing a boarding school where they take boys as young as twelve. I mean they're just babies. I should have kept him at home with me where he would have had some feminine influence and learned how to act with a woman, but I was too busy being an alluring wife to Charlie—not that he ever appreciated it—to be a mother to . . ."

"Evelyn, Kerry is quite sick and . . ."

"Yes, the poor little tyke. Ga-ga's been so upset about it. Really, darling, I could hardly finish my lunch. But, as I was saying, those practical French have always said, a good wife must be a hostess in the salon, a chef in the kitchen and a mistress in the bedroom." I don't know what kind of a wife Ga-ga was, but she can hardly make a cup of Nescafé. "And, darling, I fully intend to pitch right in and take a hand with the children or do whatever I can to help you. This is a trying day or night. That reminds me, what time is it now?"

"Two-thirty," Mom said. "Kerry really ought to have a nap."

"*Zut alors!* I had no idea it was so late. Don't I envy people who can take naps! With me it's rush, rush, rush all day long. I've got to have all my Palm Beach things fitted and then I've promised to run in and have a drink with Blanche de Lunésy, who's had such a bout with gout, poor dear. And tonight I'm playing bridge with a new beau and his roommate. They've opened this little shop on Fifty-sixth Street and they make the dearest hats. Of course there's nothing serious in it. . . ."

"Of course," Mom said. "Well, if you really must tear yourself away . . ."

"Alas, I must. And such a bore! The holidays just wear one out. Parties, parties, parties!" The front doorbell rang. "Kerry, darling, kiss Ga-ga—but just on the cheek, dear. Whatever it is you've got . . ."

I glanced toward the door and there stood Gran. "Do you realize," she said, "that you left me hanging onto the telephone more than two hours ago? Oh, Evelyn! If I'd known you were here . . ."

"Now there's no need taking that tone with me,

darling. It's not *my* fault that they can't get along. We've already discussed it and we've decided the only sensible thing to do is for everybody to remain as friendly as possible—if only for the sake of the c-h-i-l-d-r-e-n. I mean this *is* the twentieth century, darling. Isn't that right, sweetie?"

"Yes, I guess so," Mom said. "Wait while I go and hang up the telephone. I'm terribly sorry, Mummy, but with Kerry sick and . . ."

"Well, if he's sick I'm certainly not going to stay in here and run the risk of catching whatever it is that he's got. Too much Christmas, I suppose."

"Ah, there's a day that will live in infamy!" Ga-ga said, putting on her fur coat.

"Poor little Melissa," Gran said, "her beautiful hair simply ruined by that wicked frivolous . . ."

"Well, at least *I* didn't put something in the hands of a child that could blow the whole building to kingdom . . ."

"And as for that *outré* pink feather wrapper . . ."

"I notice that the hideous old Applegate Arcade is still cluttering up the living room. I mean really, haven't you ever heard of the Goodwill Industries?"

"Now you listen to me, Evelyn, that son of yours . . ."

"Darling, I've told you, it's not *my* doing and there's no need to get upset about . . ."

"Anything that harms my child upsets me—naturally. What kind of mother are you, anyhow, Evelyn?"

"Well, darling, at least *I* was conscientious enough to come and visit poor Kerry when he's sick and not just to make trouble."

"Make *trouble?* Well, if you think that I'm going to stay here for one more minute and be insulted by you . . ."

"Don't bother, darling. I know when I'm no longer wanted and I'm going. *Au revoir,* Kerry, dear; call Ga-ga when you're better." Ga-ga marched out with her nose in the air.

"Impossible woman!" Gran said with a sniff. "Always was. Well, Kerrington, I'm sorry you're ill, but if I stay in here I'm bound to pick it up and Miss Fitch will be so cross with me. You're sure he's not in a draft?"

"Yes, Mummy," Mom sighed. "I'm *certain* he's not in a draft. Try to get some sleep, Kerry. Then maybe you and Lulu and Missy and I can all play a game." She led Gran into The Room and Gran said, "Close the door, please." So I got out my listening glass.

You must have figured by now that Gran is a strictly no-nonsense type, except about things that concern Gran. She started out by saying that Ga-ga was a nosy, bossy, talkative old fool and then she settled down to be just as nosy, bossy and talkative herself.

"Well, my dear, I gather that you've decided on a divorce. The first in our family and a pity, but I think you're being wise."

"It seems to me, Mummy, that you and H. A. have done most of the deciding so far," Mom said.

"H. A. has been a great help. We talked about getting old Judge Spencer to arrange it for you. Hewlett, French and Spencer have always handled our affairs—and very capably. However, H. A. points out that the judge is close to ninety and quite hard of hearing. Now while Hewlett, French and Spencer don't *usually* take divorce cases . . ."

"Mummy, I . . ."

"Please don't interrupt, dear. I've had a very taxing day. This has bothered me more than I can tell you. Not only that, but it's forced me to call off lunch at the club. Harry Emerson Fosdick was going to speak. Now, as I was saying, H. A. feels that while they don't usually handle divorces, they *will* make exceptions for their older clients and it would be better to have a conservative old firm that we *know* takes care of things, but *best* to use one of the younger partners."

So Gran went on and on and on about that. Mom seemed to have lost most of her fight except when Gran got to talking about Daddy's money and Mom's money and Mom said, "He's never touched a penny of my money and you know it." Otherwise, Gran did all of the talking. She went into changing wills and trust funds and guardians and alimony and settlements and all sorts of stuff like that while Mom hardly said a word.

Finally Gran finished her business—which took quite some time; so long that I was really cramped leaning against the glass against the wall. She drew a breath and said, "What are your plans for New Year's Eve, dear?"

"I really haven't any. We were supposed to go to a lot of parties, but nobody wants an unattached female and I don't much feel like it anyhow."

"But of course you're coming to my affair."

Gran's "affair" is a great big reception she gives on New Year's Eve. Everybody who goes to it is over a hundred, except for Mom and Daddy and a few younger people who are sucking around for favors from the old folks—or so Daddy says. Our parents never stay more than half an hour and from their descriptions of those thirty minutes I'm almost glad I'm not a grownup, because then I'd have to go, too.

"Mummy, if you don't mind, this year I'd rather just stay at home."

"Nonsense. You've got to begin going about alone and what better place to start than your own mother's house? You'll know everybody there and besides, H. A. is asking some single men for you."

"Mother, I would simply rather . . ."

"I'll expect you for dinner at half past seven. It's a terrible chore for me to have people in for dinner first, but I thought if I kept it down to eight or ten, I could get through it."

The front doorbell rang again and I heard Aunt Liz's breezy voice saying, "Hello, Lulu, I suppose she's cooped up back in that room. I'll find her." She went clattering along the hall, knocked on the door of The Room and burst in without waiting. "My God! Every old frump you can think of chose today to come into town and . . . Oh, how do you do, Mrs. . . ."

"How do you do, Lispenard," Gran said. Mom's best friend Liz is no favorite of Gran's and never has been since the first day Mom and Liz met at Miss Farthingale's. Gran more or less puts up with Liz because, like Gran says, she comes from a "good family" (her mother was a Bleecker); but there is also "bad blood" (her father drank) and Liz, according to Gran, is "unstable" (she's been married twice and is shopping around for Number Three). Also Liz is a "bad influence."

The conversation kind of came to a standstill and then Gran said, "Well, I was just leaving." Gran always seems to be just leaving whenever Liz shows up.

"Oh, don't dream of going on my account," Liz said, all phony politeness. She doesn't care for Gran any more than Gran cares for her. "I just came in to deliver an invitation for New Year's Eve."

"Well, I . . ." Mom began.

"Isn't that a pity, Lispenard," Gran said smoothly, "but I've just engaged my daughter for my *own* party. I find it so difficult to entertain alone nowadays. But I do hope that you'll stop in at some time during the evening."

"Well, if I can . . ."

"Yes. If you can. Well, good-by, dear. Don't bother to see me out."

After the front door closed on Gran, Liz said, "Difficult to entertain! A house full of servants and all the money in the world. I'd like to see her try to swing so much as a round of drinks on the alimony I get—or *don't* get—from . . ."

"Mummy's getting on, Liz," Mom said. "You don't seem to understand that those older New York women are so accustomed . . ."

"Don't tell me, my dear. Bone selfish, every last one of them. Really, the knock-down, drag-out I had with *my* mother on Christmas! Won't I go to Florida with her? Won't I take a cruise with her? Can't we spend next summer in Europe together? Can't she buy a new apartment and have me move in with her? No amount of money is too much if it's spent on *her* pleasure with me along as an unpaid companion. But just let me ask for a couple of hundred bucks to keep body and soul together and you'd think Mother was in the poorhouse."

"I suppose they're just lonely, poor old things," Mom said.

"And speaking of mothers, my dear, not half an hour ago there I stood in my half-slip trying to find something decent to wear that I could afford and from the next fitting room I heard that idiot mother-in-law of yours telling the saleswoman all about it."

"All about what, Liz?"

68

"Oh, come along, my dear, don't play coy with me. Is it true that you literally ordered him out of the house at gun point? Now tell Liz all about it."

"Liz, wouldn't you like a big, strong drink?"

"Wouldn't I just! And then you can tell *all.*"

By New Year's Eve I was out of bed and able to take a little nourishment like hamburgers and hot dogs and chili and pizza and Coke. In less than a week Missy had become one of the biggest things in New York and half the girls she knew had taken manicure scissors to their hair. In fact, the first grade at Miss Farthingale's looked like Sing Sing until about March, when all the bristles started growing out. The mothers were pretty sore, but Missy was in solid as a style-setter.

New Year's Eve isn't much if you're not grown up and even Mom, who is, didn't seem any too crazy about it. But she got all dolled up in an evening dress and her new fur jacket and came in to kiss us good night and wish us a Happy New Year while we were eating dinner. And on account of it being New Year's Eve she even said that we could stay up until midnight to hear all the bells and sirens, but no later. Then she went off to Gran's party like it was the electric chair. Missy and I spent the evening in our pajamas playing Monopoly with Lulu and drinking ginger ale out of champagne glasses while we watched a whole lot of mental re-tards on television wearing funny hats and throwing paper at each other and screaming "Happy Nooo Year!" like they were actually enjoying it. The midnight bells and sirens were hardly worth waiting up for. In fact, Missy had been dozing for more than an hour. So after the racket died down and the TV had shown a few million more morons blowing horns and yelling in Times Square, I was ready for bed.

I'd hardly put the lights out before I heard the front door close gently and Mom was home. I was about to call out to her and find out exactly how terrible Gran's reception had been when I heard her say to someone, "We could sit in the living room, but since all the liquor is at the opposite end of the apartment, why don't we just settle back here?"

"Wherever you say," a man's deep voice said. "It's a beautiful apartment."

"Why, thank you," Mom said. Everyone tells her it's a beautiful apartment but she still acts sort of surprised. Through the open door of my bedroom I could see Mom drifting along the hall in her new dress. She was followed by a big sandy-haired man—taller even than Daddy—in white tie and tails. They went into The Room and left that door open, too, so I could hear just fine without even using my glass.

"What would you like to drink, Mr. Reynolds?" Mom asked.

"Scotch, please. And I wish you'd call me Sam."

"All right, Sam."

"Whoa! Not too much."

"Sorry. I felt the least I could do was give you a decent drink after what you've gone through at my mother's."

"Oh, really? I thought your mother's party was kind of interesting."

"Interesting?" Mom said.

"Yes, I enjoyed seeing Old New York all gathered together."

"Old is right. But I'm not sure how enjoyable."

"It's a sight I've never seen before. I thought it was refreshing."

"Well, it's a sight I've seen once a year in those very rooms ever since I was born and I can assure you it's not. Of course a lot of them are dying off."

"Was all that jewelry real?"

"I'm afraid it was."

"Amazing."

"Amazing that they don't have it cleaned after all these years. A lot of the evening dresses you saw to-night are antique, too. I can remember Mrs. Spencer's from the time I was twelve."

"A wonderful old gentleman, Judge Spencer."

"Oh, do you know him?"

"I work for him. *With* him I guess you might say. I've just been made a partner of Hewlett, French and Spencer."

"Oh, yes. I guess H. A. did tell me you were a lawyer."

"A remarkable man, your brother."

"H. A.? Well, he's remarkably stuffy."

"That's not quite true. He's more a gentleman of the old school—a true aristocrat."

"Have you known H. A. for very *long?*"

"A little over a year. I play backgammon with him at the club sometimes. I'm a new member. H. A. was very nice about writing a letter for me and introducing me around. I'll always be grateful."

"But why on earth did you want to join it?"

"It's a very old club. The oldest."

"Don't I know! My husband would never go near it."

"From what I gather, your husband and you didn't see eye to eye on a great many subjects."

"We did about clubs—that one in particular. I mean what I can't understand is why an active, intelligent young man would want to join it. It seems such an anachronism."

"It's different for someone like you. Your grandfather was one of the founders."

"My great-grandfather, I think. But I absolve myself of any blame. Women aren't permitted beyond the front door, thank God."

"It's easy for you to laugh. You see, you and your brother were born into that sort of world. I come from plain working people. I had to make it myself."

"Yes, but now that you've made what a jerk like H. A. was born into, do you find it worth the trip?"

"Yes. In a funny way I do. It's like that party at your mother's tonight. It was novel."

"And when the novelty wears off? Make yourself another drink, Sam, while I take a look at the children."

"Do you mind if I come with you? I'm crazy about little folks."

"They'll be sound asleep—at least they'd better be —and my daughter had to have all of her hair cut off for reasons I won't go into right now. But come along if you like."

They did Missy's room first and Mr. Reynolds said how cute exetera, exetera, exetera the sleeping princess was. Next came my turn. Well, I was so curious to

71

see what this complete square looked like at close range that I decided to pretend to be asleep and to have a beautiful awakening like the ones Shirley Temple has on old TV movies. So when Mom put on the night light in my room, I stirred, stretched, yawned, batted the old baby blues and mumbled, "Mommy dear?"

"What's the matter with you, Kerry?" Mom said.

"Nothing. I just woke up. Did you have a nice time at Gran's?"

"Naturally not, Kerry. Are you sure you're all right? Oh. Mr. Reynolds, this is my son, Kerry."

I did some more blinking, yawned, stuck out my hand and said, "How do you do, Mr. Reynolds?"

"How do, sonny," he said. "Doesn't he have blue eyes!" Of course I'm used to this so I don't even bother to answer any longer, but it seems to me that eyes only come in a few colors and blue is pretty usual. Now if mine were orange . . . Well, there's no sense in going into that. Grownups just naturally say boob things to kids, like we weren't bright enough to talk about anything intelligent. His next question proved what a real square he was. "Where are you going to school, sonny?" They always ask that. They really don't give a damn, but they think they're "showing interest." Once when some dizzy dame Ga-ga knows asked me the same question, I answered "Elmira Reformatory," and she said, "Isn't that lovely!" and went right on yakking away until Lulu gave me a crack and said, "You tell your grandma's friend where you *do* go to school and stop acting so smart, hear?"

Knowing how big this Mr. Reynolds was on tradition and all that jazz, I did the baby-blue bit again and said, "St. Barnaby's, *sir.* Daddy went there, too."

One thing I will say for Mr. Reynolds, when he asks a child an idiotic question, at least he listens to the answer. My answer impressed him, just the way I knew it would. "Isn't that wonderful! Father and son in the same school." (Actually it isn't wonderful at all. You can go to St. Barnaby's cheaper if your old man went there too.) "It's a fine school," he said. (It isn't. St. Barnaby's rates lower than Allen-Stevenson, even in divorced parents, and any school that rates under that *can't* be fine.) I knew he was going to say it and he did. "I believe that your uncle went to St. Barnaby's, too." Then I let him have it. "Yes," I said, with a lot of eye business, "until he flunked out." Old Sambo's jaw dropped so far that I thought he'd have to pick it up off the floor. I will say for him that with his mouth open or closed, he was real nice looking. Big, like I said, with wavy hair and eyes that kind of crinkled. He reminded me of the Good Guy in any TV Western.

"Kerry, it's late," Mom said. "Go back to sleep."

"Yes, Mommy dear," I sighed. "I *am* sleepy." Then I stretched out my arms to be hugged and kissed. Mom gave me the fish eye, but she didn't say anything. "Good night, Mr. Reynolds," I said as I nuzzled into the pillow.

"He's a fine little fellow," Mr. Reynolds was saying as Mom closed the door of my bedroom. For cripes sake, if any kid tried an act like that with me I'd give him a root in the stones, but some people will fall for anything.

I'd meant to get out my glass and tune in on what was going on in The Room, but I guess I really was sleepy. Next thing I knew it was New Year's morning. Missy was sitting on my stomach and Maxl was licking my face.

Five

We've been in East Haddock a week now and about the second thing Gran had to say to us after we got here was that we were never, never ever to go up to the attic so, naturally, that's about the first place Missy and I went. As soon as Gran was "well" enough to put on her hat and her visiting jewelry and get into the back seat of her big old Packard with Miss Fitch to go out and call on other old ladies, we were up to the top of the house before the car got out from under the porte-cochere. What a letdown!

The attic is big and hot and smells of mildew and mothballs. All the junk that isn't downstairs is up there and none of it—absolutely nothing—is interesting. There are lots of old trunks and suitcases covered with stickers from such jazzy ships as the *Berengaria, Lusitania, Normandie, Rex,* the White Star Line—I mean no boat you've ever heard of—and all labeled things like "Spring coats," "Evening dresses," "H. A.'s uniform," "Fans," "Baby clothes" and like that. There are at least two million empty boxes and a kind of toy department filled with stuff the Salvation Army wouldn't even take away. One of these antique items must have belonged to H. A. a century ago. It's called an Erector Set and it turns out to be nothing but a lot of odd lengths of metal that you put together and make a lot of useless things like Ferris wheels and that sort of stuff. I only mention it because it made me think of Daddy's apartment the first day Missy and I were taken to visit him.

Like Daddy said, his new place was down in Greenwich Village (this is not pronounced Green-witch, like it looks, but Gren-itch, for cripes sake!) and it is territory that I am not familiar with. I mean the guy who laid it out must have been a real creep. There is a West Fourth Street and a West Eighth Street, but whatever happened to Fifth, Sixth and Seventh? Fourth Street also *crosses* Tenth and Eleventh! How do you like that for neat planning? Then there are streets named things like Charles and Perry and Waverly Place and Patchin Place and McDougall Alley. Minot Mews is someplace in the middle of all this mess, but don't ask me where. Lulu wasn't exactly great about getting there, either. I mean she knows Harlem like the back of her hand, and that's pretty confusing, but the Village was just too much for her. As for the cab driver, he wasn't much better. "Now, if it was Brooklyn . . ." he kept saying. Finally, after going around and around and around all kinds of kookie little streets, Missy, who can hardly read "the cat sat on the mat," spotted Minot Mews tucked away between a dump called Advanced Stage (some kind of theater, it looked like) and a hole in the wall with some nursery-school pictures hung up in the window called Galerie Demain (French for "tomorrow"). Minot Mews was so narrow the taxicab couldn't even turn in, so Lulu said, "You wait right here, hear? You'll be taking *me* back."

Once inside, Minot Mews wasn't so bad—kind of cute, really. It was a row of old stables, just like Daddy said, that weren't good enough for horses, so they'd been fixed over for people. There were a couple of gas street lights and some of those New York trees the caterpillars like to eat so much. The stables all had fancy front doors painted bright red or yellow. Number Nine was right between Number Three and Number Six, naturally.

After quite a long time Daddy answered the door. He was in his robe and his hair was hanging all over his face. Lulu kind of pushed us inside and said, "Here they are. And you're going to bring 'em back?" Without waiting to hear what Daddy answered, she turned around and ran for uptown.

"Happy New Year, Daddy!" Missy yelled. Daddy kind of staggered.

"C-come in," he said. "I seem to have overslept."

Daddy led the way in and right away hit his head on a whole lot of crazy tin shapes hanging down from the ceiling. "Christ!" he said. Like I said, H. A.'s old Erector Set made me think of Daddy's place in Minot Mews. Most of it was two stories high with all kinds of crazy steel beams across the ceiling—except that a lot of the ceiling was also a window. There were some more steel things holding up the roof, some winding steel stairs that went up to a little balcony that was Daddy's bedroom and some pictures made out of nuts and bolts hanging on the brick walls in steel frames. Daddy's kitchen was under the balcony and there were some steel bookshelves dividing it from the rest of the room. There were tables with steel legs and a few steel chairs with all kinds of like steel wire criss-crossed underneath and big fur cushions. There were a few statues made out of old hunks of iron and steel coming up from the floor and a whole lot of steel lamps hanging down from the ceiling at different heights. The man who owned the place must have been quite short because Daddy kept banging his head on them and swearing.

"Like it?" he asked.

"It's crazy, Dad."

"It's functional, Kerry."

"Oh, I see." I sat down on the edge of one of the fur chairs and Missy hiked up her skirts and plunked down on the sofa and then giggled because the fur cushion tickled her rear end. Even if it was Daddy and it was his place and we were his children, it was all sort of strange, and I felt kind of funny, like the first time I had to go all by myself around the corner from St. Barnaby's to visit the school's psychiatrist on Park Avenue. You know what I mean—formal, like. To make conversation I said, "Did you have a late night?"

"Well, yes, rather," Daddy said. "How did you know?"

How did I *know?* His black coat with the velvet collar was tossed over the drafting table, the white silk muffler Mom gave him was draped around what I guess should have been the shoulders of a naked statue made out of scrap metal. His pants kind of

76

hung off the balcony where he slept and the toe of one patent-leather shoe was peeping over the edge. Like I said about Christmas morning, I can always tell. "Oh, I don't know," I said, "New Year's Eve and all."

"Just a couple of parties," Daddy said. "Nothing special. Did you kids have a nice time?"

"We played Monopoly and ate brownies and had champagne and stayed up all night," Missy said. The big liar! She'd conked out before it was even twelve. "And Mommy got all dressed up and went out—I don't know where to—and she was still asleep when Lulu brought us down here." Well, that was partly true.

"I see," Daddy said. "Well, if you kids can amuse yourselves for a couple of minutes, I'll put on some clothes and then we'll have lunch."

"Are you going to cook it, Daddy?" Missy asked.

"Of course I am."

"I didn't know you could cook."

"Any fool can," Daddy said. "If you can read you can cook."

Daddy reads very well, especially when he reads things out loud to Missy and I—and *me*—but maybe he counted too heavily on it for cooking or maybe the meal was too fancy. Well, I don't know what, but it didn't work out just the way he planned.

In one corner of the room was something that looked like a steel toilet with a big, old steel funnel that came down from the ceiling and hung over it. At first I thought that it might be some kind of hair drier for ladies but it turned out to be a brand-new type of fireplace, also very functional, as Daddy said. "I thought we'd just cook a steak over the fire and roast some potatoes," he said, "just as though we were out in the woods." Missy and I had never been out in the woods and I don't have any reason to think that Daddy ever had, either, especially now. But it sounded fine.

Daddy got a lot of wood and some charcoal and the New York *Times* and also a big splinter in his hand. Then he got a needle and a match and some vodka, because he didn't have anything like iodine, and got the splinter out. After that, he put on the white gloves he'd worn the night before and sort of laid the fire. It looked great, but it didn't much feel like burning.

After he went through a couple of books of paper matches, he squirted the whole thing with lighter fluid and then lit it. That worked so he poured out some Coke for us and a drink for himself and said, "Now we'll just wait until we get a nice, steady blaze." We did. I mean we waited. All of a sudden Missy, the big ham, started coughing like she'd been gassed and said, "Daddy, my eyes are running so much I can't *see!*" Well, she did have a point. The room was getting kind of smoky, even if it wasn't all that bad.

"I'll open a window until the chimney starts drawing properly," Daddy said. The whole front of the place was one big window large enough to drive a car through, but there didn't seem to be any way to open it, so we settled for the front door and a couple of windows up in the balcony where Daddy slept. A fine wind blew through and the place got pretty cold but nothing much happened with the smoke. It just got thicker and thicker. Before long I was spouting tears like a fountain and even Daddy was coughing and hacking away. "Maybe there's something I haven't done about the flue," he said with a laugh that didn't sound like he was very amused. "I've never tried to use this fu . . . this fireplace before." He bent down and reached up the big steel funnel, then he jumped back and said a really terrible word. Missy giggled and from the way her lips were moving I knew she was memorizing the word before she forgot it. But poor Daddy! One of his white kid gloves was as black as coal and he'd scorched his sleeve. "Well, I guess we're ready to cook the steak now, kids. Everybody hungry?" We said that we were.

Daddy got out something with a long handle that looked like two tennis racquets stuck together. Then he went to the kitchen, which was also all made of steel only not much bigger than a closet and got a great big thick steak, three large potatoes and a book that told all about cooking out-of-doors. At least the room was cold enough by then to be the North Pole.

The steak—it really was beautiful, if you care for the looks of raw meat—was so thick that Daddy couldn't get the tennis-racquet thing locked around it, but he said he'd just squeeze the handles together good and hard and that should do it. He tossed the potatoes into the middle of the blaze, sprinkled on a whole lot more charcoal, said something about a fine bed of coals and asked me to mix a drink for him. Before I got back from the steel kitchen there was a terrible commotion that gave Missy a whole lot of new words to memorize. Poor Daddy! He'd squeezed the handles so hard that the steak had shot halfway across the room. He picked it up off the floor, took it to the kitchen sink, gave it a good rinsing, sprinkled on a little Ajax for sanitation, and rinsed it again. Then back to the flames. From what I could see through the smoke, the steak seemed to be foaming a little, but by this time it was getting the general idea and beginning to cook. The only trouble was that the steak was spitting big bullets of hot grease all around the room—especially at Daddy. He was pretty brave about it until one got him square in the eye, then he dropped the whole steak into the fire and let fly with a real stream of swear words. I've got to admit I admired anyone who knew so many and never repeated even one. But if you think I was impressed, you should have seen Missy. "Missy," I told her, "if Lulu ever hears you using any of those words she'll snatch you bald-headed."

"Who cares," Missy said. "I haven't got any hair anyway. What does blue-balled mean?"

"Missy!" Daddy shouted, as if he hadn't used that very expression just a second ago. He put on his gloves and tried to fish the steak out of the fire and said it again, along with some other real beauts. After quite a long time he got the steak out, said it was probably cooked and put it onto a big steel platter. It slipped right off the other side and the steak went all down Daddy's front before it hit the rug. (The rugs, by the way, were fur and white. At least they used to be.) Once again, his language was a masterpiece. I had to hand it to him. He dusted some of the animal hair off the steak, got it back onto the platter and, with the fire tongs, fished the potatoes out. One of them—mine—turned out to be a piece of charcoal, but it didn't make much difference. Then he banged three

plates down on the table—one broke—and said, as cheerfully as he could, "Come and get it!"

The meal didn't look awfully good, but when you actually got your teeth into it you knew it was something really terrible. And the potatoes were even worse than the meat, except for mine, of course, which had never been a potato at all. "Good," I said, trying my best to encourage Daddy's first try at cooking. "Mmmm," Missy said, but not with her usual gift for play acting.

"Is it all right?" Daddy asked.

"Yes," we both said.

Then Daddy dug in. Let me tell you, his face was a study. "For God's sake, you poor kids," he said, "it isn't fit for pigs!" He swept up the whole meal and tossed it into the garbage can. "Wait till I shave and put on something presentable," he said. "Then we'll all go out and have a *real* meal."

We ended up at the Ritz.

I had never been to the Ritz before and I couldn't, for the life of me, see what all the shouting was about, unless this one isn't as nice as the old Ritz that grown-ups still talk about like they'd lost their best friend. To me it was just a room with too many waiters, too many mirrors and not enough customers. Missy and I were the youngest things in the place, including the Christmas decorations, which looked kind of raggedy-assed by New Year's Day. However, two of the people there are worth talking about.

The first person we bumped into was none other than old H. A., coming out of the bar on his way to the can. Like Christmas Day, he was got up in striped pants and a cutaway, only today he had a big black patch over one eye. He looked handsomer than ever, like maybe he was selling shirts in a magazine ad. Since I'd been on hand at the big dustup that was the reason he was wearing the eye patch, I tried to melt into the checkroom behind Daddy and be as invisible as possible. But do you think old Missy could play it one bit cool? Not on your life!

"Hi, H. A.!" she screamed at the top of her voice. "What happened to your eye?"

Ooba-dooba! He looked like he'd been goosed with

a cactus. "Fake out!" I muttered to Missy, but after her big ace play there wasn't much anybody could do except become visible. "Happy New Year, H. A.," I said. "Happy New Year, Kerrington," he said like he was handing me a life sentence. But at least I rated better than Daddy. When he said, "Hello, H. A.," our boob uncle stuck his beautiful nose into the air and marched into the men's room, coattails flying. The thing that wrecked it was that with only one working eye, and that one focused on the ceiling, H. A. bumped smack into some poor old geezer who was busy straightening his pants on his way out of the john. Missy had a great yak over that. I've got to admit that it was funny, but sometimes it seems to me that Missy hasn't got any poise at all.

The second meeting took place upstairs in the restaurant. Since Missy looked like such a freak in her velvet coat and fur muff and a crew cut, for cripes sake, the headwaiter said, "I'll put you at this nice table back here. The little . . . uh . . . the little one in the corner." I noticed that he didn't light the red candles on the table, either.

"I feel like a drink," Daddy said. "Are you ready for another Coke?" We always are.

I really wanted steak, but I didn't want to upset Daddy with any reminders of our first lunch, so I settled for roast beef. Having made up my mind so fast, I had plenty of time to look over the place while Daddy was reading the menu aloud to Missy and she was asking all kinds of boob questions like what are *côtes de porc* and what's a *fricassée de poulet,* when she usually acts like she's invented the French language. I couldn't help noticing the lady at the next table. She was a looker in a kind of fashion-magaziney way. She was all by herself and she kept staring at our table and smiling. Well, with Missy's hair chopped off the way it was, you could hardly blame her. The lady was cuddling a tiny little cup of coffee and giving us the eye for fair. After about an hour, when Missy had made up her mind and chanted it a million times, Daddy gave the waiter our order. By then the lady had finished her coffee and the next thing I knew she was on her feet and heading our way.

Like I said, she was very pretty except she wore those ugly clothes that other women think are so great. Females are very funny. I've noticed it when I've gone out with Mom and Aunt Liz and even with Ga-ga, who is nearly blind. A real dish will come along wearing a dress that makes her stick out in the places women are supposed to stick out and go in in the places that women are supposed to go in and they all act like she was a nun or something. But let some dame show up with her hair hanging every which way and a lot of stuff on her eyes and a big homely hat like a bucket on her head and a dress that's made like the bag on a vacuum cleaner and ugly stockings and shoes that look like she was on skis, and they practically have a spasm. "Oh, Liz, isn't that divine!" "Isn't she heaven!" "Don't you wish you *dared* to look like that!" Of course if someone ever passed a law that said all ladies *had* to dress that way, there'd be a revolution. But that's women for you.

This one had really made it, pretty as she was underneath it all. She had on a shaggy fur hat that came down almost to her nose and a big old coat made of some kind of fuzzy stuff that hung like a teepee with a floppy belt just under the butt and high-heeled boots like she was some kind of cowhand. Every woman in the place took her in and you could tell that they thought she was just gorgeous.

"I'll bet you don't remember me," she said in kind of a husky man's voice when she got to our table. I could tell that Daddy didn't. But he jumped to his feet. So did I, only I knocked over my Coke and that gave Missy a great big boff. She has no poise, like I said.

Then, without waiting for Daddy to say whether he did or didn't remember her, she said, "I'm Dorian Glen. We met briefly at the Atwoods' party last night."

"Oh, yes," Daddy said. "These are my children, Melissa and Kerry. Miss Gray."

"Glen," she said, stretching out a big, long glove for us to shake. "Dorian Glen. So many people make the same mistake." Then she lamped Missy. "I adore your hair. It's positively chic! Don't I wish I had the courage! Do sit down, please." We didn't.

"The hair happened by accident," Missy said.

"We won't go into it right now," Daddy said. Then, for nothing better to say, he said, "Won't you join us, Miss . . . uh . . . Miss *Glen*."

"Just for a moment." The waiter slid a chair under where her seat should have been and then helped her off with the big fuzzy coat. Underneath it she was wearing a sleeveless sweater that came all the way down to her knees and about a million strings of beads around her neck. All the ladies in the room took in the dress, the thin, bare arms, the ton of beads, sighed, and went back to their eating.

With a little coaxing, Miss Glen agreed to have a drink. "Well, just a *digestif*." Then she rattled off some order in French with R.s.v.p. [?] at the end of it all. It turned out to be an eye-dropperful of brandy in a glass as big as her head. Then she opened up a purse the size of a postman's bag and dug out a lot of smoking equipment—cigarette case, holder, lighter, special filters. Gadzeeks, I've never seen such an operation just to smoke one lousy cancer stick! Then Miss Glen kind of took over the whole conversation all by herself, which was just fine as I was busy eating and couldn't think of anything much to say to her.

Well, according to Miss Glen, the Atwoods' party —whoever the Atwoods happened to be—was ra-ther amusing after Daddy left. Some big Spanish artist had shown up and a man named Dicky or Nicky, who took photographs for Miss Glen's magazine, arrived wearing a brown velvet "smoking" (I couldn't help getting a picture of his clothes all on fire, like the steak) jacket and a "heaven shirt" made of the sheerest lawn (*grass?*) with dozens of tiny tucks. And this Dicky or Nicky had brought Burma, the most gorgeous half-assed [?] model—a beautiful slant-eyed "your agent" [?] who was going to be on the cover of *Harper's* next month. St. Barnaby's library subscribes to *Harper's* and I haven't seen anything like *that* on the cover before or since. But yes, it *was* an amusing party except that Johnny and Bart had got into one of their ghastly spats [?] and a hideous space-man from *Vogue* and his vulgar wife had crashed. (*That* sounded kind of exciting.) And why had Daddy left so early? I thought

83

I knew. But what I couldn't understand was why he went in the first place.

Then she turned her guns onto Missy and said again how she admired Missy's "coiffure à la Gertrude [Zair-trude] Stein" and how much she liked Missy's dress. "I'll bet it came from Dimanche Sœurs on Madison Avenue, didn't it, darling?"

"Nope," Missy said, "Stern Frères on rue Quarante-deux." I got a good laugh out of that. So did Daddy. And so did Miss Glen—only just a little bit late. Then Miss Glen asked what schools we were in—*naturally* —and congratulated Daddy on choosing schools with "true *chicté*." She focused on me for a little while and asked if I knew a kid at St. Barnaby's whose mother was the Foundations Editor (whatever that is) on Miss Glen's magazine. As a matter of fact, I did. He's a real mess. But I just said, "Yes, I know Christopher. But not very well. He's a class behind me."

"Well, I'll see to it that you young men get to know each other a lot better."

Echhhhh!

Then Miss Glen launched into her favorite subject —Dorian Glen. "Yes," she said, spinning the brandy around in her glass. "There's something about the dear old Ritz."

"Except that this isn't the old one," Daddy said.

"Oh, of course. I know that. But they still maintain a standard of style and service that's all but gone in this day and age. The last of the true French *délicatesse*." She was interrupted by a terrible crash. Two busboys had run into each other carrying trays loaded with dirty dishes. "Pork or madonna," I think one of them said. The other yelled, "Fun ghoul," I believe. Their conversation didn't make much sense to me, but then it didn't sound very French or very stylish, either. Miss Glen went right on. "It's a tradition in our family to have New Year's luncheon here at the dear old Ritz and now that I'm the last one left—well, I simply lunch here by myself." Gadzeeks! Close your eyes and you could be hearing H. A.! And Miss Glen's voice was just as deep.

"You remember I was discussing with you last night the doing-over of our offices."

"What?" Daddy said. It seemed to me that there were a lot of things he wasn't remembering about the night before. And of course it was just possible that Miss Glen was some kind of nut who'd mistaken Daddy for another man. But that didn't seem very likely, as she knew his name and that he was an architect and some of the work he had done. Suddenly Daddy was all ears. Like he's always said, there's no such thing as an architect that's too busy and since he's been on his own, he has to hustle to find enough jobs to pay all those assistants he's got. "Oh, yes," he said. "You wanted your offices remodeled."

"Just the editorial offices," Miss Glen said. "But I'm to have a good deal to say about the work. I'm frightfully interested in spatial concepts [?] exetera, exetera, exetera." Gosh, you'd think she was Frank Lloyd Wright, to hear her carry on. "Of course," she wound up, "you understand that these are the offices of a *high*-fashion magazine."

"High fashion or low fashion," Daddy said, "it's just about the same thing—cubicles, desks, chairs, filing cabinets. You could do about as well at an office supply house. And a lot cheaper. That's what I did for my place. Unless, of course, you want structural changes." I never saw him turn down business so fast.

"But I do want structural changes—quite a lot of them," Miss Glen said in a now-hear-this tone of voice. "If you're interested, that is."

"Well, sure I'm interested. But this kind of thing is expensive, while just redecorating—a coat of paint, some new furniture . . ."

"No. This is to be a *thorough* renovation. Naturally the publicity would be invaluable. . . ."

"Practically useless," Daddy said. "I've never had a job of mine appear in print without getting five hundred letters all asking for free plans or how a fifty-thousand-dollar job can be done with a hundred bucks' worth of plywood." I got busy with the rest of my chocolate declare and didn't pay much attention to what was being said until I heard Miss Glen saying, "Heavens, look at the time! I promised Monica—that's our editor-in-chief—that I'd stop in to a little 'do' she's having this afternoon. If you'd like to come along and discuss a bit of this with her . . . Of course it would be a fearful bore for the children. . . ." (Amen!)

"I've got to take them home. I promised their mother that . . ."

"You're divorced? Separated?" I didn't like her tone.

"We're *apart*. Nothing official."

"I see."

"But if I could drop them off first . . ."

"Of course."

Daddy called for the check and got not only ours, but the bill for Miss Glen's lunch, too, which she finally allowed him to pay. Going down the stairs to the street we saw H. A. kind of weaving to the can again. Gran says he suffers from the Applegate bladder.

" 'Bye, H. A.!" Missy called.

"Isn't he that fabulously good-looking Heathcote Ap . . ."

"He isn't anybody," Missy said. "He's just our uncle."

"*Really?*" Miss Glen cooed. "Here, darling, let Tante Dorian help you on with your coat."

When Missy and I got back to the apartment we found Mom having tea with Mr. Reynolds, the man she'd met at Gran's the night before. They were in the living room and Mom was pouring out of the big silver set, which is never used since nobody in the family likes tea, and Lulu says is such a pain in the A-double-S to keep polished. Mom was all dressed up and old Sambo was looking pretty sharp, too, and the whole thing reminded me of some English movie on TV. I said Happy New Year to Mr. Reynolds again and was about to take off, but not Missy. She was all over him, sitting on his lap, playing with what he said was a Phi Beta Kappa key (not a key at all, really, but a piece of jewelry that looks very much like an earring Ga-ga lost) and being so adorable you could barf. No wonder Daddy says she's a recipient nympho-something. She just can't leave men alone.

"Did you have a good time with your father?" Mom asked.

"Sure," I said. I wasn't certain whether we had or we hadn't.

"Good lunch?"

"Great."

"That's nice. Well, you two can run along and . . ."

"Oh, let them stay for a little while," Mr. Reynolds said. "I'm crazy about little folks."

"And I love men," Missy said.

"That's what's been worrying me ever since she was born," Mom said. "Does your father have a nice apartment?"

"It's very interesting," I said. "It's really a little house."

"And did he *really* cook lunch?"

"Yes," Missy said, "only he . . ." The telephone rang.

"Excuse me," Mom said and went into another room to take the call.

"I'm just crazy about little folks," Mr. Reynolds said again. "Now tell me, Missy, how old are you?" Missy was only too happy to.

When Mom came back she didn't look exactly sore, but kind of upset.

"Kerry," she said, "I thought you told me that you went down to your father's new apartment for lunch and that he did the cooking."

"I did, only . . ."

"Only you neglected to tell me that you actually had lunch at the Ritz with your father and some woman and you were both very rude."

"We weren't rude at all," Missy said. "I'll bet H. A.'s the one that told you. He was very rude. And he was drunk, too."

"Missy! Go to your room this instant!"

"Why should Missy have to go anyplace?" I said. "We were very polite and H. A. *was* rude—he didn't even speak to Daddy—and he was also drunk."

"H. A.?" Mr. Reynolds said. "I find that very difficult to . . ."

"And he's got a big black patch on his eye, Mr. Reynolds," Missy said. (She was halfway to the door —just in case.) "He looks like a pirate."

"Please, Sam," Mom said, "let me handle this."

"Sorry."

"Kerrington, Melissa, it doesn't make any difference

87

where you had lunch. Your father can take you any-place he likes. What *is* important is that you can't tell me the simple truth about it ten minutes after you get home."

Cripes but grownups can be difficult! In the first place I hadn't had time to tell Mom anything. In the second place I didn't want to say that Daddy was living in a spider web and make him look like a mental re-tard in front of a stranger just because he couldn't cook a steak. As for that big sneak, H. A. . . .

"I was going to tell you, Mom, only nobody gave me a chance. Lulu took us to Daddy's new place like you told her to . . ."

"*As* I told her to."

". . . *as* you told her to, only the lunch didn't turn out very well. . . ."

"The meat was all covered with hair and the po-tatoes were like . . ."

"Shut up, Missy. So we went to the Ritz, instead, and that's where we saw H. A. and met Miss Glen."

"This may be important," Mr. Reynolds said. "Tell me, Kerry, who is this Miss Glen?"

"I don't know. I never met her before."

"We don't know her and Daddy didn't even know her," Missy said. "But she knew him and she came to our table in a great big fur hat and . . ."

"Really, Sam," Mom said, "I don't think it's right to ask the children to spy on their own father."

"I'm not asking them to spy on their father, my dear, but any lead we may be able to get . . ."

"I don't care. It still doesn't seem right. As for H. A. . . . Well, it was a little sneaky to get right to the telephone to report and he did sound a little . . ."

"Your brother is a gentleman," Mr. Reynolds said. For cripes sake, if he was so crazy about old H. A., why didn't he go over to the Ritz Bar and leave *us* alone?

"The lady knows H. A., too. She said he was good looking and Daddy said he's a big pain in the . . ."

"That's enough, Missy," Mom said. "Children, I think you'd better run along and get ready for your supper."

"We just finished *lunch,* Mom," Missy said. That

was true, too, but this was one of those days when a kid just couldn't win.

"Please do as I say."

"I'm very interested in this woman," Mr. Reynolds said. "Kerry, you say that she . . ."

"Sam, *if* we're going out, I think we should go right now. Good night, children."

And that was the beginning of the New Year.

Six

Everybody's always talking about how terrible divorce is for kids, but let me tell you right here and now that the most terrible part is trying to cheer up the people who are trying to cheer *you* up, if you see what I mean. To begin with, you feel like you're being watched every time you want to do something as natural as take a leak and all of a sudden things that nobody ever paid any attention to before have a new meaning. Of course the great one for this was Dr. Epston, the school psychiatrist.

Divorces don't count for much with the kids at St. Barnaby's. I mean it's not like, say, St. David's, where everybody's Catholic—only not very—and about all that ever happens at home is a new baby to hand your blazer down to. I never stopped to figure before, but I guess about half the guys at St. Barnaby's have got a divorce somewhere in the family. As a matter of fact, Timothy Brooks (he sits ahead of me) turns up on Parents' Day with two mothers and three fathers—his own mother, his stepmother, his real dad, his present dad and a stepfather from in between who just likes to see how Tim's doing. And all five of Timmy's parents laugh and snicker and gas it up in the back of the chapel until the headmaster has to remind them that they're in a place of worship. And the haul Timmy gets on his birthday! Ooba-dooba! What I mean is we don't pay much attention to an everyday thing like divorce. But you ought to see the headmaster and Dr. Epston go into action whenever some kid's parents split up. It's like he'd got straight A's for the whole year.

Now that it's happened to me, I can tell you all about it and, from what I hear, it's the same with every kid whose parents get divorced. The headmaster sends for you right out of the blue at about three in the afternoon so you miss athletics but not anything you'd like to get out of like Latin. Well, naturally, you're sweating bullets because you can't figure out what you've done to get in trouble. Or if you *have* done something, you can't imagine how the headmaster found out about it. So you go to his office and tap on the door and say, "You sent for me, sir?"

His office is all wood, like being inside a cigar box, with a fireplace and big old leather chairs and about as cheery as a morgue. The Head looks at you from across his desk and sucks on his pipe (slurrrp!) and smiles like a shark (only with dimples) and says, "Why, yes, Kerry." (At all other times you're just called by your last name.) "I thought we'd have a little chat. Get to know each other better. With so many boys to look after I sometimes feel that I don't have enough chance to . . ." (slurrrp!), blah, blah, blah. "Like a cup of tea, Kerry? I always like a cup of tea about this time of . . ." blah, blah, blah. "Helps sweep the cobwebs out of the old . . ." (slurrrp!), blah, blah, blah. "Sit down, Kerry." Then you sit in one of the leather chairs on one side of the fireplace and the Head comes around from his desk and sits in the other leather chair and you know that it isn't going to be a chewing-out but, worse, one of his chummy times. So Miss Lardass (that's his secretary and her real name is Gertrude Lazarus— Dirty Gertie Lardass—and she weighs about ten tons) clumps in in her Space Shoes with Girl Scout cookies and clattering teacups. "Thank you, Miss Lazarus" (slurrrp!). Knock-knock-knock! He's always thumping his damned pipe against the mantel. "Habit I picked up in England when I was doing graduate work at Oxford—tea in the afternoon . . ." blah, blah, blah. "Sugar? Milk? Lemon? I'm very pleased with the way your grades are holding up, Kerry. Mr. de Vilbiss says you're getting a real grasp of Latin if only he could read your writing . . ." blah, blah, blah. I'd just as soon grasp a rattlesnake as Latin, but, as a matter of fact, my grades *are* pretty good. Not that I care, but it helps to kill the time in school if you do a little work once in a while.

Slurrrp! Knock-knock-knock! "And how are things at home, Kerry?" Then there's a tap at the door and in comes Dr. Epston from his cave around the corner on Park. "Well, Larry, this *is* a pleasant surprise! Come right in!" If it's such a surprise, why did Miss Lardass bring in *three* teacups instead of only two? I mean I plan to be a detective when I grow up, but any idiot that can count to three could see that somebody else was expected. "That would be very refreshing, Barry," Dr. Epston says, getting out *his* pipe.

"And of course you know Kerry, Larry. Kerry, Larry and Barry, heh heh heh, that's quite a trio of names, eh? Sugar, milk, lemon, Larry? Here, take my chair. I've been sitting all day." Then the Head gets up and drapes himself over the mantel like he's crucified. "Kerry was just telling me about the situation at home, Larry." I wasn't, but it didn't make any difference.

"Oh, yes, I was very sorry to read about that, Kerry," Dr. Epston says. That's something else that really grabs me. Here these jerks are always talking about "good newspapers," like the New York *Times* and the *Christian Science Monitor,* without even any funnies, for cripes sake, but let a one-line mention of Mom and Dad breaking up come out in the *Daily News* (that only maids are supposed to read) and they know all about it. I'll bet if it was splashed all over the air-mail edition of the London *Times* they're always cheering about they wouldn't even see it.

"Read about what?" I said.

"Could I kindly borrow a pad and pencil, Barry?" Dr. Epston said.

"Surest thing, Larry," the Head said.

Dr. Epston wrote down "hostility." I know because when he and the Head went out to Miss Lardass' office for "a word in private," the dumb spaz left the whole thing behind for me to read—or try to read. Talk about lousy penmanship!

"The trouble at home, Kerry."

"What trouble?" Then he wrote down "evasion."

Then there was a long interruption while they

gouged a lot of crud out of their pipes and rammed some fuzzy wires into them and hammered them against the fireplace. "Try some of my tobacco, Larry, I have it sent over from this little shop in German [?] Street."

"Thanks, Barry, I'd like to try it. Hmmm, very aromatic. Nice!"

Nice? It smelled like the time Missy burned up a whole box of marshmallows trying to toast them over the kitchen stove.

"Kerry," the Head said, "we were all awfully sorry to hear about your parents."

"To hear what?" Dr. Epston wrote down "flight from reality?"

"Barry, perhaps if you would permit me . . ."

"Very well, Larry [slurrrp!], but as head of this school I was only trying . . ."

"Yes, I know, Barry, but this sort of thing is my line of country. The sympathetic layman is one thing, but . . ."

"Very well, Larry." Knock-knock-knock. Slurrrp!

"Now, Kerrington, I understand that your father has moved away from home."

"That's right. Nine Minot Mews. It's down in the Village and is it ever kookie! It's this old horse barn that's been turned into a studio and everything in it is iron or steel or tin or like that. I mean it's a real hardware store. And Daddy was tossing this big steak around the room and cussing a blue streak. . . ."

"Your father was *throwing* a steak?"

Well, after about an hour of telling Dr. Epston about Christmas and Daddy shooting at us and the Applegate Arcade and Missy's hair and the explosion and socking H. A. and Miss Glen at the Ritz and like that, just trying to explain to him that it was perfectly natural, he was writing faster and faster. Boy, you should have seen those notes! I can't remember all the words I wanted to look up. There must have been a hundred of them. Anyhow, after the Head and Dr. Epston had a little talk outside the room, they came back and said, "Kerry, we've decided that you are to be excused from athletics every Monday, Wednesday and Friday and consult with Dr. Epston."

"Consult about what?" I said. Dr. Epston made another note, but I didn't get to read it.

"Now it's nothing to be worried about or ashamed of," the Head said, thumping his pipe into a big old ashtray. "Divorces hit children kind of hard."

"You're divorced yourself, aren't you, sir?"

"Well, yes. But to get back to your problem . . ."

"What problem?"

"Kerry, Dr. Epston can't help you if you don't want to help yourself."

"Help me what, sir?"

"All right, Kerrington, enough of this horsing around. Dr. Epston will be expecting you at three tomorrow and at three on every Monday, Wednesday and Friday. If your mother is at home now I should like to telephone her."

I met Lulu at the stationery store on Madison Avenue a block away from school. Like I said, it's embarrassing for someone my age to have a nurse. The stationery store is very practical for both of us. It has magazines and comic books and school supplies and a Coke machine for me and the owner also puts bets on horses and on the numbers for Lulu. Lulu was about the same as ever—grumpy. If I couldn't ever pick the right horse, I'd give up wasting my money on them. Only try to tell Lulu that.

But when I got home Mom was entirely changed. She was all dressed up and waiting at the front door. Before I could put my schoolbag down she had both arms around me and was covering me with kisses. "Hey, cut it out, Mom," I said.

"I just wanted you to know that I love you very much, Kerry."

"Sure, I know, Mom. What's for dinner?"

"Something you like a lot. We were just going to have lamb chops back in The Room"—I hate lamb chops—"but I've changed my mind. After I help you with your homework, we're going to get all dressed up and have a party."

"Yeah? Who's coming?"

"Nobody, darling. Just the family."

"You mean Daddy, too?"

94

"No, dear. Not your father. You know that's impossible. But I'm going to try to be both mother *and* father to you and Missy."

"Yeah?"

"And now, darling, let's get right at your homework."

"I can do it," I said. For cripes sake, I always have. "There isn't much anyway."

"What is it, dear?" Mom asked, all interest. I mean how can anybody be interested in some cruddy old homework?

"It's math. I did the rest in study hall."

"Oh," Mom said. Her face kind of fell. Mom can hardly count and when it comes to balancing the checkbook every month she almost has a spasm. In fact, things got so bad with the bank that Daddy finally turned over the checkbook to his secretary, who does it just fine if Mom remembers to write down all the checks. "Well, you go into your room, dear, and I'll be right in."

I looked in on my way past Missy's room. She was wearing (backward) a slip that was all lace and ruffles that Ga-ga gave her and Missy hates and trying to pull a blue silk party dress over her scalp. The language she was using could curl your hair.

"You better pipe down," I said, "or Mom'll wash your mouth out with soap."

"Oh, go shit in your hat! She will not."

"Hey, what's the matter? What gives around here?"

"Don't ask me. Mom caught me brushing Maxl's teeth with your electric toothbrush and she was just about to give me a spanking. Then the phone rang. It was that nut that runs St. Barnaby's and after Mom talked to him for a while she got all mushy and pulled me up on her lap and kissed me about a million times and told me how much she loved me and made me put on this damn dress. I'd rather have the spanking."

"Crazy!"

"Crazy is right. And you know what we're having for dinner? The pink tablecloth and beef whateveritis with all the icky sour cream."

"Hey, keen!"

"Well, I hate it—and wild rice, too. Why can't we

just eat in The Room and watch 'Magilla Gorilla'? Here, do me up the back."

"What's the magic word?"

"Up yours!" So I hit her and Missy let out a yip and Mom came running and instead of doing something intelligent like giving each one of us a clip, she sat down on Missy's bed and put her arms around us and told us about how we'd all have to love each other twice as much as ever before. I mean crazy!

So Mom sat there on the bed (you can bet your boots she never lets *us* sit on a bed when the spread's on it) with one arm around each of us for about an hour, which was hot and which crumpled Missy's dress. I got all sweaty and had to go to the john something terrible and Missy was sore as a crab because she was missing "The Mighty Hercules." Really, I couldn't imagine what got into Mom. She's usually very sensible.

After *that* was over, Mom took me to my room to help me with my homework. It was just math and even if St. Barnaby's does have a pretty good mathematics course, it isn't really hard at all. So I opened the book to the first problem (there were only ten to do, I'm happy to say, or I'd still be shut up in that room with Mom) and we started in. Well, it was as simple as this:

$$\frac{2}{9} = \frac{x}{13\frac{1}{2}}$$

"Let me help you, darling," Mom said.

"You don't need to, Mom, it's real easy."

"Well, that's good. Now, dear, perhaps if you'll explain the problem to Mother."

"There isn't anything to explain, Mom, we're supposed to isolate the unknown on the opposite side of the equal sign."

"What, Kerry?"

"I said we're supposed to isolate the unknown on the opposite side of the equal sign."

"Kerry, don't joke with me, please. Education is a very important thing. If you just kid around you'll never amount to . . ."

"I'm not kidding, Mom. This is what we're supposed to do. Maybe if you'd go and help Missy do whatever it is she wants to be doing . . ."

"Kerry, you're old enough to understand most of . . . most of what we're all going through and I want you to know that at least your mother is here to help you. Now, let's see, two-ninths equals x-thirteenths and a halfs. Halves? It seems awfully complicated for the fifth grade. When I was at Miss Farthingale's, Mummy had me excused from . . ."

"Yeah. I'm getting excused from athletics to go to that kookie. . . ."

"I know, darling. I had a long talk with Dr. Epston this afternoon. Don't worry. I want you to know that whenever you need me, you're not to feel . . . What are you doing?"

"My homework. See, Mom, you multiply two times thirteen and a half and that's the same as nine x."

"No, darling, I don't see why it is at all. Kerry, are you sure that you're not terribly upset about all this business with Daddy and just not telling me?"

"I'm getting terribly upset about not doing my homework, Mom. So then you work it out that nine x equals twenty-seven. . . ."

"But why would it equal twenty-seven, dear? You just said it was the same as . . ."

"Because two times thirteen and a half is twenty-seven, Mom."

"Oh? Oh, yes."

"And so twenty-seven divided by nine is three and x equals three. It's very simple."

"Kerry, don't be rude."

"I'm not being rude. The answer is three. It's easy."

"Well, I'm going to call your Aunt Liz."

"What for?"

"Well her new . . . I mean she knows a man who's a physicist and I'm sure he can help us."

"I don't need any help, Mom. Now, if you want to look at the next problem . . ."

"Just let me take this first problem you've done to the telephone and call Liz."

"Be my guest."

I could hear Mom on the telephone in The Room.

"Liz? Dear, I hate to bother you, but I don't suppose Jim's there by any chance is he? . . . Oh, marvelous. Thanks . . . Jim? . . . Well, I'm just fine, thanks. And you? . . . Listen, I've got this kind of problem. If two-ninths equals x over . . . I said, Jim, if two-ninths. You know, a two and then a little line under it and then a nine and then two little dashes and then . . ."

Mom was on the phone with Liz and with Liz's boy friend and then with Liz again and then with the boy friend again for more than half an hour. She came back into my room looking kind of wild. "Kerry, darling, don't worry. Mr. Young—that's this important scientist who's a friend of Liz's—has a friend at the Institute for Advanced Studies at Princeton and he's going to call him long distance and they'll take care of everything. And tomorrow I'm going to telephone the school and have a good, straight talk with your arithmetic teacher. The idea giving a ten-year-old boy problems like this! I mean they don't make sense. No wonder so many young people have severe mental breakdowns. But darling, you're not to worry. As long as I have a breath left in my body . . ."

"But, Mom," I said, "I'm not worried. I'm all finished. When do we eat?"

I guess that whatever got into Mom also got into Daddy. We saw him once a week and sometimes more, and while he never came up to the apartment or saw Mom, they did talk on the telephone quite a bit and Mom was always saying things to him about being civilized and making the best of a difficult situation and not creating added problems for Missy and I—*me*—by any "display of open animation [?]" and the importance of love to a child. I mean why couldn't they just have loved each other, the way they were supposed to in the first place before we were even born, and left Missy and me be?

But they couldn't. Of course they never came right out and said, "Your father's a bastard" or "Tell your mother she's a fink," and they never said anything mean about each other. But in little funny ways Missy and I were always in the middle. For instance one day when we were going out with Daddy, Mom told Lulu to get us all dolled up—me in my new blue suit from De Pinna's and Missy in a whole lot of ruffles. Then Daddy took us on a boat ride around Manhattan Island and dopey Missy spilled a hot dog with mustard all over herself and I tore my pants on a nail. Don't think we didn't hear plenty about that when we got home, plus Gran's calling up and talking about *mal de mer* and several famous disasters at sea about a hundred years back where children drowned like rats. So the next Saturday afternoon, when Daddy asked us out, I got sent off in my last year's St. Barnaby's blazer and some old, old flannels while Missy was a picture in one of *my* old camel's-hair coats and a dress so short that her rump showed every time she bent over. And where did we go *this* time? Some restaurant so fancy only Miss Dorian Glen (she was along, too) knew where it was and so expensive they don't even put prices on the menu and some old French fart with a chain around his neck talking about the "bouquet" of the wine like it was a dozen roses. I'll admit the food was pretty good, but my zipper kept slipping down and when Missy reached for the pepper mill her dress split all the way up one side, it was that old. Oh, I tell you, we were a pair! Even Daddy, who hardly ever pays any attention to such things, said, "Can't Lulu or your mother or *somebody* see to it that your clothes aren't falling off your backs? From the amount that's spent on dressing the two of you . . ."

Then Miss Glen started talking about some people she knew who had "such a chic little boutique" called Jeune Fille, for cripes sake. Everything was imported and simply exquisite and while Miss Glen's friends only saw customers by appointment, Miss Glen was certain that they'd make an exception for Miss Glen. They would. Jeune Fille was a joint on Fifty-seventh Street done up with miniature fitting rooms and copies of the Babar books in French. Miss Glen's two people, if that's what you call them, turned out to be a man and a woman but you couldn't tell which was which. They thought Missy was simply "dolling" and *"très* droll" and before anybody knew it, old Missy was fitted out from the shoes up—pants, slip, dress, hat, coat, gloves, everything. She looked kind of cute, I will say that, but gadzeeks, when it came to paying for it all, Daddy nearly passed out. It's vulgar to talk about money, but let me tell you, Miss Glen's friends were real robbers.

"Isn't she dolling!" the woman (she wore a tweed skirt) said.

"Simply adorable," Miss Glen said. "I'd love to run a full-page picture of her in the March issue."

"Oh, Dorian, dolling," the man (*she* wore tweed pants) said, "we'd love a plug in your magazine. So few parents have any appreciation of *haute couture* for the young."

"I'd have to ask her mother about it," Daddy said.

"You *would* like to have your photograph in my magazine, wouldn't you, Melissa, dear?" Miss Glen said.

Then Missy yawned and said, "No thanks. I've already had a page in *Vogue* and that's enough." Boy, sometimes I've got to hand it to my baby sister. When it comes to being a real bitch she leaves the experts behind. Then she said, "Would you just put my old things in a box and send them, please." Ordinarily Daddy would have cuffed her, but he put his arms around her and said, "All right, sweetheart. Whatever you say."

"Daddy, you're tickling me," Missy said.

"Poor little thing," Daddy said. "She's having a tough time. They both are."

"Of course," Miss Glen said, "the trauma." (This is one of the words Mom learned from Dr. Epston and the two of them used to bat it around like it was as simple as yes, no or maybe.)

So to get Missy over the trauma of having just been bought the most expensive lunch she'd ever eaten and the most expensive outfit she'd ever worn, Daddy took us to Rumpelmayer's for some more expensive food; very good but awfully rich. Maybe he should have bought Missy a stomach pump instead, because she puked all night long, and not on purpose either. Mom blamed it on that old trauma, when any fool could tell that it was from *vol-au-vent,* asparagus with hollandaise sauce, salad, baba au rhum, and, an hour later, two French pastries, ice cream and hot chocolate. But I'm getting ahead of the story.

After we were dropped off at the front door and all but squeezed to death by Daddy and even offered Miss

Glen's bony cheek to kiss ("you must call me Tante Dorian") we went up to the apartment and there was a silk hat on a chair in the hall, just begging to get sat on. From the living room we could hear a man's voice. "That's the list: Idaho six weeks, Nevada six weeks, Wyoming sixty days, Arkansas ninety days. Good recreational facilities in all four states if you wanted to take the children. But I still maintain that adultery in New York State . . ."

"No, Sam! The children are going through enough without having their father on the front page of every cheap tabloid in town." I was getting kind of interested. But do you suppose Missy could just shut up and listen? No, indeed. "Mom!" she screamed. "We're back!" Then she went pounding into the living room. There was nothing for me to do but go along, too.

"Well, well, well," Mr. Reynolds boomed. "Just look at my little girl. My, don't we look nice!"

"Why, Missy," Mom said, "what a lovely red coat! And a dress and . . . Where did you get all the new clothes?"

"Daddy and Tante Dorian."

"Daddy and who?"

"That's Miss Glen. They said I looked like a ragamuffin." That Missy! Her middle name is Tactful.

"Oh, really?" Mom said. "Well it's all very smart, I'm sure. What's that hanging down from the coat, dear?" It was a tag of some kind. "My God!" Mom said. "One hundred and forty dollars for a coat that won't fit you a month from now!"

"I like it," Missy said. "They say I look like a sheik in it." (She meant *chic,* Missy that big French expert!) "And that old dress you had me wear . . . gee, it just ripped into about a hundred pieces at lunch."

"Is insanity grounds for divorce in any of those states? He's lost his mind. One hundred and forty dollars just for a . . ."

"And you ought to see how much Daddy paid for *lunch!*" Missy said. "It was this real fancy French place with real orange trees growing . . ."

"Dear God! The Orangerie! He never took *me* there. Too expensive. But for two children and this Miss . . . Miss . . ."

101

"Glen," Missy said helpfully.

"I was thinking of dining there tonight before the opera," Mr. Reynolds said.

"No thank you," Mom said. "The most expensive restaurant in New York for two children and . . ."

"You oughta order this dessert they have. They pour rum on it and then light it and . . ."

"It's a very common failing," Mr. Reynolds said, "for fathers who are extranged [?] to overindulge their children in an attempt to buy infection [?] . . . competition with the former souse [?] exetera, exetera, exetera." I don't know how *he* knew so much about it, being a bachelor. But then, like he was always saying, he was crazy about little folks.

"Well, you children run along now," Mom said. "Mr. Reynolds and I are talking business."

"You're awfully dressed up for business," Big Mouth said. "Are those Gran's diamonds you're wearing?"

"We're going out later. I'll be in to say good night, children."

So, like I said before, we kids were kind of caught in the middle, and nothing that either Mom or Daddy ever did ever seemed right to the other one. If Daddy just had us down to Minot Mews for a meal (he learned to cook, more or less, but in the kitchen) and a movie, Mom acted like it hadn't been much of an outing—even though she never came right out and said so. If he took us to a restaurant and then a matinee or the circus or like that, then he was shooting the wad and once Gran even said, "A fool and his money soon part." It worked the other way, too. If we told Daddy that Mom had given a dinner party he'd say, "Living it up, eh?" But if Missy would tell him something like, "I'm hungry, Daddy. We only had sandwiches for lunch," then he'd say, "As long as I'm still paying the bills around there I don't know why my children can't be properly fed." It seemed like nobody could win.

And then both grandmothers got into the act. In the days when Mom and Daddy were together, Gran used to ask us all to her house on Eightieth Street for what Daddy called a "tribal write" [?] about once a month. It was like trying to plan for an eclipse of the sun because it had to be a day when H. A. wasn't invited any place else (my guess is that he's free about 365 days a year) and a day when both Eustace, the butler, and Nellie, the cook, were on duty and also a day when the McGuire sisters (no kidding, that's their name, only they don't sing) weren't off. And it also had to be a time when Miss Fitch would be visiting her married sister in Jackson Heights because seven people would "throw out the whole table." So with four people all bumping into each other in the kitchen and the pantry, six of us could sit down to a meal of creamed-everything with service plates and wine glasses and finger bowls crashing around like flying saucers while Gran gave orders like "No wine for the children, Eustace," "I hope that sauce is not seasoned, Eustace," "Eustace, please cut up Miss Melissa's veal," and poor old Missy, trying to be polite, would be saying, "It's delicious but I don't care for any," while no one listened.

After some terrible dessert that's supposed to be good for kids, like prune whip or tapioca, the females would "withdraw" and leave Daddy and me to put up with H. A. and the booze decanters while he said interesting things like "Port doesn't travel" and complained about the sentiment [?] in the Madeira. For cripes sake, it looked like there was a raisin pie in the bottom of the bottle. But sentiment or not, it was something to see how much of the stuff H. A. could put away while he carried on about drink being the curse of the working-man and the gall of Alcoholics Anonymous wanting to use the church auditorium for meetings, exetera, exetera, exetera. It was good that he had plenty to talk about, because Daddy and I never had anything to say to him. But he'd keep on gabbing and guzzling until Gran would have to send old Eustace with a message that we were to join her in the drawing room P.D.Q. Then we'd all get into the creaky old elevator and jiggle upward a full ten feet to a dark green room to sit on dark red chairs with bright white light bulbs blazing and hear about how punk Gran was feeling. I'd feel pretty lousy, too, living there. After a bit of that, H. A. would jump to his feet (once he fell flat on his

103

face and Gran gave Eustace and the McGuire sisters a big chewing-out for having the floors too waxy) and suggest that Mom and Dad might care for a drink, like he'd just discovered alcohol and hadn't slapped back about a gallon of it down in the dining room. That always put Daddy on the spot. If he said, "No, thanks," H. A. would glare at him and sulk all night. If Daddy said, "Yes, please," then Gran would say, "Well, if you really think you *should*," and sulk all night. But old H. A. could do no wrong. While he was off in the library clanking ice cubes and, as I happen to have seen with my own eyes, helping himself to an extra gulp or two right out of the bottle, Gran would say, "H. A. is such a perfect host. I wonder why he's never married." Well, if she could see him in the locker room at the beach club she'd know. He's got the littlest one this side of nursery school. Anyhow, that's the way our big evenings used to go and if Missy didn't fall asleep, I'd pretend to just so we could all get out of there and go back home where things were fun.

But at least we had Mom and Daddy to run interference for us in the days when everybody treated us like plain everyday kids and there wasn't all this jazz about showing us how much we were loved. The minute Daddy moved out of our apartment, Gran got real busy with Mom and the way every minute of her life was being spent. Like Mom said to her friend Liz, "She hasn't shown this much interest since she got me into the Junior Assemblies." Anyhow, you'd think Mom was coming out or getting married all over again for the hustle and bustle that was taking place on Eightieth Street.

For a woman who held a funeral every New Year's Eve and called it quits for the next twelve months, Gran really went into action. She tottered off to the vault and got out *all* of her jewelry, including a big diamond thing she clamps over her head like it was earmuffs, and called the dressmaker in to turn out six more shrouds in black velvet or silk or lace or like that, and sent H. A. to the tailor's and bought *him* some new evening duds (can you imagine that, he still lets his mother buy his clothes; I've been picking mine out—with Daddy having the final say, of course—since I was seven and a half). Then Gran got out her "list of young people." Gran knows the oldest young people in the world. To begin with, they're all in their thirties and forties and hardly what you'd call adolescents. But they might as well be. They all live with very old mothers or fathers. They never get married. They don't seem to do anything like work and they sure don't play much either, unless you count going to some old folks' dinner party every night. Nobody ever sees them out in the real world except maybe at the Colony Club or church or steering someone like Gran to the opera or the Philharmonic. They all call each other "Mr." and "Miss" even if they've been friends for like twenty years. Aunt Liz gives a real funny imitation of them. She says they're a rare New York breed that's dying out fast, but not fast enough. Anyhow, they're Gran's idea of a real fun bunch. So, at the rate of about two dinner parties a week, Gran started up what she called "a suitable social life" for Mom with people "we know something about."

Mom will put up with almost anything—unless it happens to be Daddy or Missy or me—in order not to have a scene, but she used to go off to every party like it was the dentist and come back home like she'd played four quarters of football. Aunt Liz says that that embalmed bunch are the biggest dead beets [?] in New York and a dame's lucky if she gets a ride home in a taxi that she doesn't have to pay for, but after a few big evenings at Gran's one of the fifty-year-old "young men," who also had a rich mother, decided to do the big thing and throw a house party at his mother's big old place in Tuxedo Park. And can you believe it, *his* mother wrote to *Mom's* mother to ask if Mom, who's a mother herself, could come—like it was a birthday party in Missy's crowd! Gran said that Mom could and poor Mom almost hit the ceiling.

Then the ax fell. "No sacrifice is too great, dear. So as not to spoil your fun, the children can spend the weekend here with H. A. and me." Echhh!

So while Aunt Liz was saying all kinds of kookie things like in that atmosphere the last thing any girl would have to worry about was her diaphragm and the place would be full of queens (but I guess not Elizabeth II or that Dutch one or any I ever heard of), and Mom kept snapping, "Oh, shut up, Liz!" everybody got packed for the weekend.

I didn't know what kind of time Mom was in for at Tuxedo Park, but the weekend looked pretty grim for us. Old Eustace met us at the top of Gran's brownstone stoop, took our overnight bags and led us through all the sets of glass-and-iron doors that mark off the entrance, the vestibule and the rickety old elevator. Missy was let out on the third floor, which is where Miss Fitch sleeps and kind of the women's floor. It has a couple of guest rooms (never occupied) that are more or less pink and lavender (that is, the few things like curtains and bedspreads that aren't black or brown). Missy drew the lavender one that's got a bed with a big ruffly tent over it and a portrait of Gran with her hair done up on top like a bird's nest that was painted a couple of hundred years ago and stares at you wherever you happen to be, unless you go into the closet and shut the door. It made Missy real nervous and I didn't blame her. There was a bay window that looked out at the back of a big apartment building on Seventy-ninth Street and Gran's gritty little garden with the bare branches of a dirty old tree scraping against the windowpanes. "We're putting you back here, Miss Melissa," Eustace said, "so it will be quiet." *Quiet!* It couldn't be quieter if we were buried!

Eustace and I rode up one more floor and he said, "You'll be up here with Mr. H. A." The men's floor has H. A.'s sitting room and bedroom (this is so he'll be so comfortable he won't want to move away from Gran, although I can't see a tightwad like H. A. giving up free room and board if he had to sleep on a bed of nails) and a kind of bleak, black room with too much furniture in it and a picture of a mean old man in a white wig. That was for me. Eustace—he's very nice in a kind of formal way—hobbled around raising the shades and turning on lights, not that any of it did much to brighten the place up. "There's only one bathroom on this floor," Eustace said. "I know you won't mind sharing it." He opened a door and there was a great big white tiled room about the size of the science lab at school. Everything in it was oversized and old.

106

There was a great big marble sink—dripping—with all of H. A.'s soaps and mouthwashes and shaving stuff on it. There was a tub a block long and half as deep up on feet and also about a million doors all alike. Eustace started opening the doors. "This one leads to Mr. H. A.'s bedroom. This one is the shower. The toilet is in here." He opened that particular door and there was the can hidden under a kind of wicker chair, for cripes sake. There was a big box up over it and a long gold chain hanging down. I pulled the chain and the toilet coughed a couple of times and then flushed. "The wonders of science!" Eustace smiled and then opened another door. "You'll find extra towels and linen in here." The next door was just a lot of shelves where H. A. kept all his pills and stuff like that. From the looks of his "drugstore" he was twice the invalid Gran was. Eustace opened another door and there was a tall white scale with a lot of weights and stuff like in a doctor's office. There was a calendar on the wall with numbers written in for every day. I figured that H. A. weighed himself twice a day and wrote down the results, like he was a race horse. "Very particular about his weight," Eustace said. "Very particular about everything."

"Crazy," I said. Eustace snorted and then pulled a straight face. "Any other doors?" I asked.

"Only the one back to your bedroom. If there's anything else . . ."

"What goes on above here?" I asked. Can you believe it, in ten whole years I'd never been any higher in my own grandmother's house than her sitting room-bedroom-chapel deal on the second floor! We see all these lovable little old white-haired grandmas on TV all the time, always baking apple pies and like that, but with a pair like Gran and Ga-ga for grandmothers, the television set is as close as Missy and I ever get to that kind of "Land sakes alive" old lady.

"The maids live on the top floor," Eustace said.

"With you?"

"*I* have an apartment in the basement," he said, like maybe I thought he slept under newspapers in Central Park. Then he messed up my hair—*naturally*—and

107

said, "Your grandmother should be waking up soon. Don't get lonely."

Don't get lonely! That was a hot one. I unpacked as slowly as I could, but how long does it take to put away a suit and a couple of shirts and your pajamas? There wasn't any sound from Missy on the floor below, so I looked around for something to read. If I were going to ask somebody to sleep over at *my* place, at least I'd put out a couple of copies of *Mad* or like that for them to read in bed. But not Gran. So I wandered across the hall to H. A.'s quarters, which spread across the whole front of the house, not really snooping, you see, but just looking for something to read. The sitting room was very he-man and leathery with a big portrait of—you guessed it—H. A. in his white Navy uniform looking like "Full speed ahead and damn the torpedoes!" Daddy always said that H. A. spent the whole war dancing at Delmonico's, but *I* figured that he'd passed most of the time having his portrait painted or his picture taken, as there were also three photographs of H. A. in still-different uniforms. He sure was a looker, but didn't he just know it! There was a big kind of cabinet that looked like it was full of books behind gold chicken wire. But when I tried to open it, all the books turned out to be fake and the thing was full of liquor bottles. But that's not all! Down in the bottom was a whole stack of magazines and I mean the kind of magazines that Lulu won't even let me *look* at in the stationery store. They were every last one of them full of pictures of naked people—mostly ladies, but some with men *and* ladies and a few with just men. "Ooba-dooba!" I said to myself, "there may be some hope for H. A. after all." Most of the magazines were in English, so I could at least tell what they were about, but the really hot ones were in all kinds of kookie foreign languages. There were a couple in French called *Nus* (that means nude), which I earmarked for future reading. The others, though, were really crazy, and in languages I couldn't tell what they were, with dots over some of the letters and lines drawn through the o's (like this: ø) and I don't know what all. I was starting in on one called *Läder* that had a real wild picture on the cover. It was this fat lady wearing high boots and long gloves and that's all, cracking a big old whip over some guy's tail end, while the stupid spaz grinned away like he was loving it, for cripes sake. But before I could even get the magazine open, Missy was yelling up the stair well. "Kerry! *Kerry!* Where are you?"

Well, this just wasn't the kind of stuff a six-year-old girl ought to see, so I stashed it all back in the cabinet and looked as innocent as an angel by the time she got to the fourth floor to say that Gran was up and ready for tea.

I've already told you about Gran's teas in the country, but you ought to see the ones in town. There's twice as much silver and twice as much food and Gran sends three times as much back because, like she always says, she eats like a bird, and the "ozone of East Haddock" gives her an appetite that she just doesn't have on Eightieth Street. While Gran was wasting enough to feed a family for a week, H. A. came in, all very brisk from Wall Street, kissing Gran and tucking all sorts of little "dears" into his conversation with her. (He never did have much to say to Missy and me and the better we all get to know each other the less talk there is.)

Well, I mean to tell you, H. A. was the perfect son, right out of some old etiquette book written about a million years ago. He had a long to-do with Gran about all the money he'd made for her that week by messing around with her stocks and bonds. I guess Gran must be pretty well off because whenever grownups hear that she's my grandmother they all say "Oh, ye-ess," and treat me like I'm better than I really am. But to listen to Gran, you'd think she was heading for the Peabody Home tomorrow. I told H. A. that our math class had all chipped in and bought a share of Xerox at seventy and that it had already split four ways (which it had) and we were going to wait until it hit a hundred (which it did) and then sell it (which *we* did—at one-thirteen, if you want to know, in May). He said, "It never will, Kerrington." And then he excused himself, saying that he had a lot of reading to do. I'll just bet he had!

Miss Fitch gave Gran a lot of different pills which

must have put new life into her because she got groaning up out of her chair and said, "Now let's do something amusing, children."

Gran's idea of something amusing was to get into the elevator and ride down one floor to the library and read to us—backward—out of a big old book that told all about the Heathcote Family ("My mother's people") all the way back to some guy called Norman Conquest. We could have cared more. I guess I sound like kind of a fink griping this way. Gran's real old and she really was trying to be nice and entertain us, but it's been such a long time since she was little like Missy that she must have forgotten what a bore things like that can be. When Missy suggested that it might be a camp to play department store in the elevator, Gran knew down to the last fraction just how much it cost to run the lousy old thing round trip from the cellar to the attic and said a lot of things about its not being a plaything and waste not want not. But she *was* trying.

At seven we changed for dinner (I know how Gran kills the time now; when she isn't sleeping, she's changing her clothes) and after we'd done the Eustace–McGuire sisters plate-changing bit (it's always fish on Fridays because all the help, except Eustace, is Catholic and Gran almost is) and Missy choked on a bone, the "ladies" finally "withdrew" and I was left all alone with H. A. Gadzeeks! H. A. is supposed to have such wonderful manners (even Mom, who ought to know better, says so) but he didn't say word number one to me for a solid hour while I sat there and watched him guzzle. And he sure wasn't any too polite to the help, because when I asked if I could have a glass of water he got up and kind of swayed to the pantry door and barked, "Water!" Just one word. No please, no thank you, no nothing. Lulu would have clouted me if I'd ever dared to do anything like that to her. Moira, the pretty McGuire sister, came in with a whole tray of silver pitchers and ice bowls and like that, and giggled. Then H. A. went all red and poured out another big glass of port. After about a million years, Gran sent Eustace down to fetch us. By then Missy was nodding and we were sent to bed. That ended our first happy day visiting Gran in town.

But if you think Friday was bad, you should have spent *Saturday* on Eightieth Street. Breakfast was at eight, with silver egg boilers and covered dishes and Eustace and the McGuire sisters hopping around the table and all the rest of that jazz, while Gran read the *Herald Tribune* out loud and H. A. grumbled. The Democrats, I found out, were the reason why Gran and H. A. were so poor.

H. A. took off for his club about ten and Gran went back to bed. That left the whole day for Missy and me to kill. Since we didn't want to send Gran to the poorhouse, we used the stairs quite a lot (stairs were kind of a novelty to us—even at St. Barnaby's and Miss Farthingale's they have elevators) but hiking up to the fifth floor and then going all the way down to the basement, flight by flight, on your butt gets to be kind of a drag after six or seven times. Besides, it hurts. Missy is much younger than I am, so while she was trying it—bump, bump, bump, bump, bump—for the *eighth* time, for cripes sake, I kind of bombed out and futzed around up on the fifth floor, where the maids live, along with the empty boxes and wrapping paper and the old sewing machine and Gran's body (no arms or legs) that her dressmaker uses. Pretty soon one of the doors opened and there was Moira McGuire, the pretty one, like I said before, with her red hair all coiled up in what looked like Lincoln Logs. "Faith and you gave me a start, Mr. Kerry," she said. (She talks like some kind of comic on TV. "Fay-ith" and "Mist-herr" and like that. But she is kind of pretty.) "Cuminta me room for a minute, would yez?" Well, you ought to see the rooms Gran keeps them in. Reform school! Lulu's got TV and her own princess phone and a chaise longue. She'd quit otherwise and she gripes about the view as it is. Gran's maids make do with an old iron bed and a dresser and a hard chair and one old light bulb swinging down from the ceiling. Maybe it's because they don't know how to talk English and can't complain.

Anyway I went in. "D'ye like this?" Moira said, holding up a kind of dress that was black and you could see clear through it.

"Sure," I said. "What is it?"

111

"It's a genuine Se-ductress Robe de Noot. I ordered it from a maggyzine. Six dollars it cost, almost. And hahdaye like this." She squirted some stuff into the air. I coughed. Lulu only wears a perfume called Arpège, which is very expensive, as I found out when I tried to buy her some for Christmas. This stuff smelled like whatever they put in the urinals at St. Barnaby's. "It's called Lye-ason," Moira said. "Liaison" was what the label said. It could have been Lysol for all of me.

"Very nice," I said.

Then old Missy got me off the hook. "Kerry," she screamed up the stairs. "Eustace says we can go out."

Have you ever tried to play in a New York back yard? Grownups that buy town houses are always saying how wonderful it is to have a garden for the kids, but I'd like to see them try to enjoy one. Except for a big apartment building at each corner, Gran's block on Eightieth Street is still solid houses, although Gran's is the only one that is still lived in by just one family and hasn't been turned into little apartments and doctors' offices. Out in front the houses all look very grand. Most of them are brownstone like Gran's, only not so wide, and some are limestone and even marble. But whoever built them all sure stopped caring when he got to the backs. Instead of fancy stone, the backs of the houses are brick painted all different colors about a million years ago because it's mostly peeling off. There are a lot of fire escapes and built-on additions of all different heights that jut out every which way, so what little light and air there should be is all gone. Gran's garden has a high brick wall built around the whole thing so that it's like being in the bottom of a well. With her garden, like with entertaining us kids, Gran *did* try. There's this big tree growing out of the grit and the gravel and dead vines on the wall and a few sick bushes and a statue of some Greek god with his pecker chipped off. But the results are pretty sad and it doesn't help to have a big apartment building right behind Gran's house. It's supposed to be one of the "best" buildings on Seventy-ninth Street and filled with real classy people. But I wish the doorman out in front could see what those classy tenants live like when they think nobody's looking. They toss cigarette butts and funny-looking rubber things and even empty whiskey bottles right into Gran's garden. Can you imagine! And during the two hours Missy and I sat out on a rusty iron grape sofa, I counted four different maids shaking their dust mops over our heads and then some old cow on the third floor with a bird-feeding station on her window sill threw a whole loaf of stale French bread out and then slammed her window down. I guess it was meant for the pigeons, but it hit Missy. I was so damned sore that I picked it up like a football and sent it right back through the window, glass and all. There was a terrible squawk and then she stuck her fat face through the hole and started screaming "You little brats! I'm gonna call the police!"

"Go ahead and call 'em. And be sure to tell 'em you've been throwing your garbage out the window like the slob you are."

"Fresh little bastard!"

"Neurotic!" Missy yelled.

"What did you say? You cheeky little . . ."

Then Eustace came bustling out, chops jiggling, in his silver-polishing apron and he got into it, too, until Miss Fitch stuck *her* head out of one of the upstairs windows and in a voice that would cut through steel screamed that we were disturbing Gran's rest. That ended our playing in the garden. Besides, it was starting to snow anyway.

Somehow we got through lunch and the afternoon with Missy asking me what time it was every five minutes and not believing that it wasn't at least an hour later than I said it was. H. A. missed tea (poor guy) but showed up in time for dinner, looking kind of glassy-eyed, if you ask me, and I went through the silent treatment after dinner with him just like the night before, with Moira McGuire switching her tail around the table and smelling a lot stronger of Liaison than she had when Gran was in the dining room. There was no "Jackie Gleason Show," no "Defenders," no "Gunsmoke," because Gran doesn't keep a television set—except in her bedroom. So at nine o'clock when Gran said that we were ready to go to bed she was one hundred and one per cent right.

I got into my pajamas and sat in the window practicing a little bedroom astronomy with the people in the apartment building behind Gran's house. But there wasn't much to see—just a dame slapping cold cream all over her face and a fat old man brushing his teeth, which I mention only because the teeth were in the palm of his hand. Finally I went to bed and fell asleep. But around midnight I woke up with a terrible thirst from the tongue—echhh!—we'd had at dinner, I guess. The light was on in H. A.'s big bathroom, but I couldn't find a drinking glass. I knew I'd seen one—several—in H. A.'s bathroom the day before when Eustace was showing me around, but where? With seven big brown mahogany doors in the place, I was pretty certain that the drinking glasses would be behind one of them. I pulled the first one open.

The next thing I knew I was smelling Liaison perfume stronger than ever. There was a kind of frantic scurrying sound and then a big thud and a voice saying "Oooof!" "Holy Mary, mother of God!" another voice said. A light was switched on and there, right before my eyes, was Moira sitting up in H. A.'s high old bed, her red hair all wild and her lipstick smeared all over her face. The new black nightgown she had showed me was all ripped and she kind of held the sheet up to her front and whimpered like a sick puppy.

"Excuse me," I said.

"You little devil," a voice growled.

I looked down and there was H. A., buck naked, sprawled on his bedroom floor.

"Gee, H. A.," I said, "I'm sorry. I must have got the wrong . . ."

"Faith and I'm ruined!" Moira blubbered. Then she leapt out of the bed and, clutching the shreds of her "robe de noot" around her, went racing out of the room.

"Well, good night," I said. I started to go back through the bathroom to my own bed. The next thing I knew I was flying through the air and landed with a plop in the middle of H. A.'s rumpled bed. Before I could catch my breath he was on top of me, pinning me down, the thick black hair on his chest tickling my nose. He may have been a boob, but he sure was strong. "Ouch," I said, "hey, H. A., let go."

114

He did but just a little. He grabbed both my arms with a pair of real steel claws and pinned them behind my back. Then at last his chest fur was out of my nose and his own nose was there instead. "Ow," I said, "you're breaking my arm! Let go!" Then I added, "Please."

"Listen to me, god damn you, if you ever say one word about this . . ."

"Say one word about what? Ouch! For cripes sake, you're hurting me."

"You know."

"I know what? Owwww!"

"About Moira being down here."

"Well, what about it?" I said. Suddenly he let go. "For cripes sake, H. A.," I said, wriggling out from under him. "What's so interesting about that? I crawl in with Lulu all the time. So does Missy. Mom doesn't care. Do you suppose Gran would?"

"My God!" H. A. said. He got to his feet, kind of unsteadily, put on a robe and sort of smoothed his long hair back out of his face. Then he changed entirely—like a mad scientist I saw once on this show on TV. "Like a ginger ale or anything, Kerrington—Kerry?"

"N-no thanks," I said. I'd have loved one, but not with him. "Well, I'll be saying good night."

"What's your hurry, Kerry boy? Sit down." I kind of had to since he'd got hold of both my shoulders again and was pushing me down into a chair. "There. That's better." He lit a cigarette and poured himself a big, stiff drink—no ice, no water, no nothing. I noticed that he was shaking like an aspirin. "Moira's a very nice girl, Kerry. Attractive."

"K-kind of fat," I said.

"And you know she's very lonely in this country."

"Why? She's got her sister Bridget right upstairs and a married brother over in Brooklyn."

"That's not quite the same. She likes to come down here sometimes and just—uh—talk."

"Sure," I said, getting up.

"But your grandmother might not understand. She's old fashioned and not as democratic as you and I are."

"What's there to understand?"

"Well, I wouldn't mention it to her, if I were you. Or anyone else."

"Okay," I said. "Well, I think I'll be hitting the . . ."

"Wait a minute, Kerry." He went to his wallet and got out a five-dollar bill. "Here. Buy yourself something. And this will be our secret—just yours and mine."

"And Moira's, of course."

"Of course. Well, time for bed. Got to be up bright and early in the morning. Church, you know."

Boy, I got out of there fast. And you know, I wouldn't have thought a thing about it if he hadn't put on such a scene.

Seven

So January turned into February with everybody working overtime at loving us. Ooba-dooba! When I think of
the murder Missy and I could have got away with if
only we'd wanted to! I mean if we ever hadn't wanted
to go to school—and we never much did—we could
have thrown a slight tantrum about eight o'clock in
the morning and Mom and the Head and the old dame
that runs Miss Farthingale's would all have been so
busy *understanding* that we could have spent the whole
day at the movies. Or we could have wet our beds—
after we got out of them, of course—and the whole
world would have stopped turning. But like a couple of
real chumps, Missy and I didn't do much of anything
that was out of the ordinary, except that I had to spend
three hours a week with Dr. Epston.

Everybody nowadays is so big on psychiatry that
there must be something to it but, for the life of me, I
can't figure out what. Or maybe it's just Dr. Lorenz
Epston. Dr. Epston specializes in kids. My appoint-
ments were at three o'clock just after a nutty little guy
in a Buckley School cap who stuttered so bad that I
was always in Dr. Epston's torture chamber with both
parts of the double door closed before the poor kid
could finish saying "H-h-h-h-h-h-h-h-i." Just between
you and me, I think Dr. Epston made his stuttering
worse. We go to dancing school together and he talks
as plain as anything, except when they make him get
up and dance. The patient that came after me was a
regular giant of a girl in a green Chapin School uniform. It wouldn't be ethnical to tell you their names.

Well, anyway, Dr. Epston's consulting room is small

117

and dim with a couch to lie on; two easy chairs; Kleenex, for crying into, I guess; a desk and a bookshelf with about a million copies of *Tensions in the Metropolitan Adolescent* by I. Lorenz Epston. I guess it wasn't exactly what they call a best seller, but he's getting rid of the supply bit by bit by making each patient's family buy a copy (at ten bucks a throw). There are also some pictures on the wall that look like Missy painted them and a framed photograph of Dr. Epston's three daughters. One is in the upper school at Dalton, one goes to Rudolf Steiner and the littlest one is in the School for Nursery Years—if that gives you some idea of what kind of kids *he's* got. They also look like Eskimos. In fact, Dr. Epston's first question was always "What are you thinking about right now?" And my answer was always "Eskimos." But when he'd ask me why, I just couldn't tell him, because even if he is kind of a boob, I didn't want to hurt the poor guy's feelings. So I'd hem and haw and talk about igloos and blubber and wasn't it interesting that the French spelled Eskimos *Esquimaux* and like that. So I always got kind of a demerit for being what Dr. Epston called "evasive" (when I was only trying to be polite) and at the end of the first week Mom sent off to Wakefield-Young Books for copies of *Nanook of the North* and *Inyuk* and some other suitable reading about the North Pole, when I didn't care much one way or another.

The first day Dr. Epston made me lie down on the couch and darned if I didn't drop right off to sleep while he was droning away about trusting him and telling him everything that came into my mind, no matter what. After he woke me up he kept asking me what I was trying to escape from and he wouldn't believe me when I told him that I'd stayed up late the night before watching "The Nurses" (it was all about this dope fiend) and it would have been rude to say that also he was kind of a bore. But after that he let me sit up straight in a chair.

He kept telling me that everything I said or didn't say or did or didn't do or remembered or forgot was for a reason deep down inside of me. It seems to me that lots of times people just plain forget things and I said

118

so. But he told me I was dead wrong. You're always wrong with Dr. Epston. Then one day, right in the middle of my appointment, his wife called up and gave him a terrible chewing-out for forgetting to meet the Miami plane with her mother on it. (What a set of pipes that Mrs. Epston has! I could hear every word clear across the room. And they were *some* words!) When I asked him what the real deep-down-inside reason was for not remembering to meet his mother-in-law, he said "*Ver geharget*, you smart little goy!" Golly, that psychiatric lingo!

I suppose you've figured by now that it's not hard for me to make conversation with anybody. I know the things that adults don't like to hear about. But one thing Dr. Epston wanted to do that I just plain couldn't manage was to dream a dream every night. "I almost *never* dream," I told him. Then he said, "Nonsense, Kerry, everybody dreams every night. And if you don't remember there's a reason for it." He also told me about some outfit—the Institute of Dreams or some such name—where these dream experts stuck a lot of wires into people's heads before they went to sleep and found out that they dreamed practically every minute of the whole night—except the people couldn't remember any of it. I guess that's my problem. But if you can't remember dreaming, why bother to dream at all? Anyhow, it was another black mark every time I showed up without a dream to talk about. However, Missy dreams a lot and recalls everything, so I solved the problem just fine by asking her what she'd dreamed and then fixing it up a little to make it sound more like my own original work. And whenever Missy let me down there were always Lulu's dream books. I don't like to sound stuck-up, but between Missy and the dream books and what little I could add, I went into that office with some material that made Dr. Epston absolutely flip. A few of my dreams were so cool that he got out his tape recorder and made me tell them again for this new book he's writing. And when he played them back I sounded great. Maybe instead of a detective I could be like a commentator on TV. "Good night, Kerry." "Good night, Chet."

So even if it was kind of a drag, I really didn't *mind*

119

spending all that time (*and* money!) with Dr. Epston. The only times it ever made me feel bad—or feel *anything*, when you get right down to it—was when the old blabbermouth would telephone Mom. Then she'd look awfully worried and unhappy and telephone Daddy and he'd start looking like one of his buildings had just caved in and they'd all get busy at loving me more, which was a terrible nuisance. Missy had all the luck. Her school is much more old fashioned than St. Barnaby's. The feeling there is that once you're a Farthingale girl you're a lady for life and that's that. They don't have any truck with any head-shrinkers at all. From a couple of things I told him about Missy, Dr. Epston was itching to get at her (and Lulu and Maxl, too, I'll bet) and even made an appointment for the one-to-two-o'clock shift, which ruined everybody's lunch plans. It was a close call, but Missy came down with chicken pox instead and by the time she was better, Doc was all wound up with a big bruiser from the Brearley School, where they grow the girls rough and tough. Like I said, old Missy was just born lucky.

After I caught on to the sort of stuff Dr. Epston enjoyed hearing, things were much easier and I was on my way to being a real star in child-psychology circles. I used to take real pride in my work and whenever Doc's mouth dropped open and all those gold fillings flashed at me, I knew I'd scored. Don't think I'm bragging when I tell you that I was one of just three patients who got Dr. Epston's private phone number. One day after I'd told him a really gross dream which I'd kind of cribbed from this movie, *The Man with the X-Ray Eyes*, his pipe fell right into his lap and he put his hand on my shoulder and said, "Kerry, I'm going to give you my home telephone number. Write it down because it's unlisted. But if you want to call me at any hour of the day or night—Saturdays, Sundays, it doesn't matter when—I *want* you to do it."

"Sure," I said, putting the slip of paper into my blazer pocket. For cripes sake, what would I want to call *him* for?

As a matter of fact, I was getting a list of numbers that would put the Manhattan phone book to shame. Missy can dial just fine, but we kind of discourage her from using the telephone ever since the day she was playing around with it and had a long talk with a strange Chinaman in San Francisco. But everybody was so busy loving us that they all acted like we didn't have anything better to do than gab on the phone all day. Daddy wrote down the number of his office and also his pad in Minot Mews. Gran told me to call her any time I needed her, except when she was resting—whatever time that would be. Miss Glen got into the act with the numbers of her magazine and her apartment and so did Mom's lawyer, Mr. Reynolds. Even Aunt Liz, who is practically famous for not liking children, told us to call her whenever she could do anything for us. And of course Ga-ga wasn't going to be outdone, although if she wasn't out, her line was always busy.

Ga-ga was kind of miffed about our having spent that gay weekend at Gran's and she practically drove Mom out of town so that we could move into her place for a couple of days.

Like I said, Ga-ga hardly takes up any space at all. When Daddy was a boy and Ga-ga's husband was alive, they lived in a great big old duplex. But now that Ga-ga is what she calls "all alone in the world," she keeps moving into smaller and smaller apartments. "Just give me a bed at a good address," she keeps saying, and she's practically down to that now.

Her new place is on Sixty-fourth Street in an old building. Ga-ga likes the older places "because the rooms are so gracious." But for someone who talks about "gracious" all the time, you'd think there'd be more in the refrigerator than yoghurt and No-Cal ginger ale. When she isn't eating a lot at Passy or Voisin—or in the Regency Club dining room while she's dummy at some bridge game—Ga-ga is always on a diet. In fact her kitchen is really a closet and she doesn't even have a dining room any longer. But everything else is as gracious as all get-out.

I guess I told you that she's very fond of the color pink. Her living room is all pink and very pretty, but we can't ever go into it because she's got this Audubon [?] rug that she won't let us walk on. It seems kind of old and threadbare to me, but Ga-ga keeps talking about this big French queen, Marie Antoinette, who used to own it. And since she carries on the same way about all the furniture in her living room, it's just asking for trouble to *look* in there.

Her bedroom is pinker than the living room—even the light bulbs and lamp shades—and everything in it that isn't pink is a mirror so that Ga-ga can see herself from every whichway, except that she can't see to begin with and all the lights are so dim and rosy that it's like being inside somebody's stomach. Ga-ga lets us come into her bedroom, but not with our shoes on because the rug is a mess of rosebuds that a whole lot of Frenchwomen sewed by hand until they went blind and it's very delicate. But when Ga-ga wakes up about eleven in the morning, she likes to have a little company with her breakfast—especially if the company knows how to make a cup of instant coffee and brings it in on a tray along with her mail and the newspapers like Missy and I do. Then Ga-ga puts on a kind of jacket that's all lace ruffles and props herself up on a couple of hundred little pillows that have things like "Never Complain, Never Explain" and "*Bonne Nuit*" and "*Vive l'amour!*" stitched onto them. "I'm holding a real levee. You be Madame Royale, Missy, and Kerry will be the Dauphin. Isn't this *fun*, darlings?" The answer is no, especially when you've been tiptoeing around all morning with nothing to eat but No-Cal and Melba toast.

With all the pink and the mirrors and the bowls of flowers and the little china knickknacks around the place, you'd think that Ga-ga's place would be a lot cheerier than Gran's. It isn't. To begin with, it's awfully small. Daddy says it's just part of what used to be a really decent apartment—and the back part, at that —that some crooked landlord divided into fourths so he could get ten times as much rent. (If I told you what Ga-ga pays for that "good address" you'd pass out.) The living room—Ga-ga says *salon*—faces the street, which has terrible traffic jams all day long and most of the night, too. The rest of the rooms look out at a brick wall, and it's on a low floor anyway so the place is always dark as your pocket. But even if the aurora borealis was going on outside it wouldn't make any

122

difference as Ga-ga keeps the windows covered with about a hundred layers of stuff. First come thick, dark green window shades, then Venetian blinds, then some kind of fancy shades that are all scallops and catch a lot of dust, then some very thin white material to pick up even more crud, then heavy pink silk and over the top of it all three shades of velvet and fringe all looped around to collect whatever soot gets through the rest of the fortifications. New York isn't the cleanest city in the world and when Ga-ga talks about "dusty rose" she sure says a mouthful. Ga-ga doesn't like anything to be too bright and she lives mostly with lamps and candlelight and complains to Daddy about her electric bill.

But if you think the main rooms sound dark, you should see the one Ga-ga puts us into. It's off the entrance hall, where some "extremely talented beau" of Ga-ga's has painted a lot of elderly French people with white hair having a picnic outside some palace (Marseilles, I think). Ga-ga calls it the Card Room and sometimes "my gambling den." I can't imagine what it was to begin with, but now it's like being in a submarine. It's all dark gray with an air conditioner droning away in the window. Right in the middle is a very modern white table growing like a mushroom out of the floor and four white swivel chairs, all set up for a bridge game. A big bright light hangs down over the card table like somebody's about to get the third degree from the F.B.I. Another "extremely talented beau" has painted the doors to look like playing cards. Ga-ga, as the Queen of Diamonds, leads to the hall. The painter himself is the Jack of Hearts and that door goes to a closet that's crammed full of Ga-ga's old evening dresses. On the walls are a lot of little French pictures called "Jeu des Cartes" (game of cards) with the ladies' knockers all but falling out of their dresses—not that you can see them in the light. There are two little love seats that open up into beds and that is Missy's and my happy home—when we can get into it.

Ga-ga wasn't in on Friday when Lulu dumped Missy and me at her building and her cleaning woman had gone for the day. So we sat down in the lobby for more than an hour waiting. Finally Ga-ga came charging in like a marathon runner, covering us with kisses and excuses. "Ga-ga is *désolée*, but I was at the Regency Club and we just *couldn't* finish the rubber and Myra—you know Mrs. Forsythe, darlings" (we didn't)—"well, Myra kept bidding on absolutely nothing, my dears, just to try to make game and we kept going down, down, down until finally I took the bit between my own teeth and bid three spades on a count of eleven but since Myra had a void in clubs, I was *finally* able to make it and then I simply could *not* get a cab" (the distance is three blocks) "and I had to take the Madison Avenue bus and I had nothing smaller than a ten-dollar bill and . . ." Oh, Ga-ga leads a hard life. Just ask her.

Her entrance hall was so full of packages that we could hardly get in and Ga-ga thought it would be a big treat for Missy and me to watch her try on all the new clothes she'd been buying. "Ga-ga's going to give you a little fashion show." Her duds all looked kind of young to me, but we said they were very pretty as Ga-ga put on lots of pairs of tight bright-colored pants and said, "Don't my hips look just like a boy's?" (Not like any boy I knew, except maybe that fat Throckmorton kid in the seventh grade who eats so much that he's got boobs, for cripes sake, and is hung like a doughnut.) "Ga-ga found this marvelous masseuse down in Palm Beach and she simply took tons off my rear. And isn't Ga-ga *brown*?"

A while later this Italian guy—Count something; most of Ga-ga's pals have got handles to their names—came in. He had a lot of black hair slicked up and back and black suède shoes and a black suit so tight that it looked like it was painted on. He was a jewelry designer and just happened to be carrying a few samples—"Not to buy, *carissima*. Only to admire." So Ga-ga admired and bought a bracelet. We went to Passy for dinner and then to see some real old silent movies made by this Charlie Chaplin who Ga-ga says is just a scream. He was such a scream that she fell sound asleep and so did Missy. But the Count was full of pep and kept his hand on my leg until I managed to spill a bag full of hot, greasy popcorn all over *his* leg. A big evening!

Saturday, after no breakfast, we had no lunch because Ga-ga had too many things to do. For somebody that old she can get up and down Madison Avenue like a guided missile. We went to a place to pick up Ga-ga's wig from being cleaned and pressed. Then we went to another place and waited while Ga-ga had her missing eyelashes filled in. Then we went to a corset store and waited while Ga-ga tried on a whole lot of underpinnings. Then we went to another place and waited while Ga-ga got fitted into some "little nothings" that looked like pillowcases with holes cut out for the head and arms. For nothing they sure took a long time, which was good because I was able to sneak out and buy Hershey bars for Missy and me to keep from fainting of hunger. Then we went to an art gallery because one of Ga-ga's beaux had a lot of terrible pictures he'd painted hanging there. Since none of them had been sold, Ga-ga bought two. Then we went to a jewelry store where Ga-ga got into a big fight with a foreign lady who had sold her some black pearls that were really white pearls dyed black, exetera, exetera, exetera. The prices were really scary. Lulu has lots more jewelry than Ga-ga or even Gran and she never pays more than a dollar for anything.

We got back to Ga-ga's place just in time for her to take a bath and change all of her clothes. About eight o'clock the doorbell rang and there was one of Ga-ga's Palm Beach chums—a leathery old lady in a white fur coat—with two kind of sissy men that ran an antique shop. One of the men must have been pretty young because he was worried about being drafted into the Army. But the old lady—she had a voice like a tuba—would only laugh and say, "No danger, dearie," and the other man kept saying that if they took the baby away he was going to become a camp follower and do over the barracks in louie cans [?]. Crazy!

We took two taxis one block to Voisin for dinner and the two men got into a row about the way it was decorated. It looked just fine to me—blue—and the menu looked even better. The food was good; very rich, but Missy and I would have eaten Maxl's Doggie Delight (it's not bad, at that) by then. There was a big argument over who was going to pay the check. I just had a feeling that Ga-ga would win and of course she got it. Then the doorman hailed two more taxis and we all went back to Ga-ga's.

"Ga-ga's going to let her babies stay up late tonight," she said. Hell, it was eleven-thirty even then. So she took her pals into the Card Room and told us to entertain ourselves in her bedroom, but please be quiet as they were all cutthroat bridge players and she had to concentrate extra hard. For entertainment she gave me this book called *In the Swim*. "It's by darling Tony," she said. "He was this heavenly lifeguard at Cap Ferrat and so madly beautiful that nobody could resist him. A dear, dear friend of mine. They say I'm in it, so you can read it for me and save me the trouble." Then she was gone.

Missy sprawled out on Ga-ga's bed under the lady's coat and konked out, so there wasn't much for me to do *except* to lie down next to her and read darling Tony's book. I couldn't make much sense out of it. It seemed to be his life story from the time he was a poor kid diving for coins through about ten marriages to rich old women. He was always talking about Gertie and Daisy and Emerald and Elsie and Elsa and Elissa (ladies who all seem to be dead, and no wonder) and I almost gave up trying to find Ga-ga in it. But he did write a few words about her and I guess what Ga-ga says about her hips must be true. He spoke of her as "the consummate ass of the entire Côte d'Azur." Then I fell asleep because the next thing Missy and I knew it was morning and we were still in Ga-ga's bedroom. Ga-ga was kind of cranky from having slept on the chaise longue, but she said that no sacrifice was too great to make for her babies.

Eating breakfast, though, was just more than Ga-ga could face. There had been talk about going to some "fun place" like the Plaza and then, if it was a nice day, doing the Central Park Zoo or even taking a ride in one of those old handsome [?] cabs, which is something we never have done—probably because we live in New York. It was beautiful weather—what you could see of it through all the curtains—but Ga-ga said she was just too *hors de combat* to budge before lunch. "Darlings, *je suis absolument morte de fatigue*. They

126

didn't leave until after four and Ga-ga has just the teeny-tiniest little twinge of hangover. So why don't the two of you go into the Card Room and amuse yourselves while Ga-ga has a little siesta? Then we'll all go out for lunch."

"Okay," I said. What else was there to say?

Ga-ga gave us a box of *marrons glacés* to keep body and soul together, opened the door to the Card Room and had a pitiful coughing spell. "Zut! The smoke!" Ga-ga gasped. "Here, let me put on the air conditioner and just clear the air." She lurched around the place kind of emptying ashtrays and tossing out old score pads. "I can't *look* at all those dirty glasses," she said. "But Ga-ga will give you some old decks of cards and you just help yourselves to anything you want. Do whatever you like—as long as you do it quietly—and if the telephone rings, for God's sake answer it."

"What'll we say?" Missy asked.

"Tell them I'm dead, darling. Wake me up at two and we'll go to someplace for a little bitey. *À bientôt,* darlings."

We started out playing Russian bank but that's never a good idea because Missy is so young she doesn't see half the moves she can make and she gets sore when I stop her. Then we tried slapjack and go fish until Missy got bored from the card games and thirsty from the *marrons*. So I started playing solitaire and the next thing I knew, that kookie Missy had snuck into the closet and came out wearing one of Ga-ga's evening dresses and a frowsy old wig.

"Hoo doo yoo doo, dolling," she said—just the way Ga-ga talks—then she groped her way around the room pretending to be half blind like Ga-ga. I nearly split. That Missy's a real comic when she doesn't overdo it.

"That's really cool, kid," I said. "But you'd better take it off. I'm sure that dress cost a lot—everything of Ga-ga's does."

"Ooo, noo. This old rag, dolling. Ooo, *je suis morte de fatigue.* Shopping, shopping, shopping! I think just a little drinkie." Then she picked up a glass that was more than half full of *something* and belted it down. She damned near choked.

"Missy!" I said, "that's liquor!"

"What did you think it was, *chéri,* horse piss? And now a little bitey." She gulped down another *marron.*

"If Ga-ga sees you in that rig she's not going to think it's half as funny as it is," I said. But Missy comes on strong and once she's on she stays on.

"Have you met my dolling friend Count to Ten, dolling? Isn't he dolling?" Then she took a big gulp out of another stale drink.

"Missy! You'll get drunk."

"Shut up. Didn't Ga-ga say to help ourselves to anything we wanted? Ooo, dolling, do let me give you a little drinkie."

"No, thanks."

"Well, if you insist, dolling." She polished off that glass, too. Just then the phone rang. I got up to answer it but Missy was there first. "Hellooo," she said, just like Ga-ga. "No, dolling, it isn't Evelyn. Evelyn's dead." Then she hung up.

"Melissa!" I said. "You're really going to get your ass in a sling for fair."

"Ooo, I've already got it in a sling, sweetie. There's this movelous little corset woman on Madison Avenue. She says I'm just like a boy." Then she stuck her tail out and switched across the room kind of unsteadily like Ga-ga. Well, I couldn't help laughing.

"Ooo, the smook in this room! It *absolument—comment dite en français*—stinks." She kicked her train and went into the bathroom. In a minute she was back with a bottle of rose geranium bath oil and before I could stop her she poured the whole thing into the air conditioner. *"Missy!"* I yelled, but it was too late. There's some kind of poison gas that's supposed to smell like geraniums and, boy, now I know what war is like. The air was thick with it.

"Look what you've done. The place smells like a candy factory. What are we going to do now?"

"Ooo, dolling, I think we'll go to Pussy and have a little din-din." She picked up another glass. There wasn't much in it but it looked strong. "Chin-chin," she said, just like Ga-ga, and emptied it—only most of

128

it went down her front. Suddenly I realized that she was drunk! I mean she's only six and not having any breakfast . . .

The telephone rang and she reached out kind of unsteadily and got it again. "Helloo . . . Noo, dolling, Evelyn's . . ." Then Missy snapped out of it. "Daddy? This is Messy. . . . I mean this is Missy. . . ." She was right the first time because she started to barf right into the mouthpiece and keeled over onto a love seat.

Nasty as it was, I grabbed the telephone away from her. "Daddy? It's Kerry. . . . Why, we're just fine, thanks. . . . Ga-ga's d . . . I mean Ga-ga's asleep." There was a long, low moan out of Missy and then she started to get sick all over again all over herself and the wig and the dress and the love seat. "Missy? Well, something seems to have disagreed with her. . . . You're coming up *here*? . . . *Me*? Call a *doctor*? Well, gee, Daddy, it's just a little . . ." But he'd hung up.

Within fifteen minutes Daddy and Dr. Epston arrived together.

Well, I think I felt even sorrier for Ga-ga than for Missy that day. Poor old Ga-ga never did get her beauty sleep. Daddy yanked her out of her bedroom with her sleep mask still on and kept shouting "What have you done to my child?" It was quite a scene and I was kind of sorry that Missy wasn't able to hear it, lying there like she was, with the wig over one eye. Dr. Epston seemed to be very interested. He took a lot of notes and said later that Daddy wasn't edible [?] at all. In fact, he'd never heard anyone lay his mother out so thoroughly.

When Daddy finished with Ga-ga he turned on Dr. Epston and said, "Well, where's your bag?" And Dr. Epston said, "What bag?" And Daddy said, "What the hell kind of doctor are you?" And Dr. Epston said, "Sir, I am a psychiatrist but alcoholics aren't in my line. Now, Dr. Fox . . ." And then Daddy blew up again and said, "*Doctor*? I don't know what you can do that a vet couldn't do better. Now get the hell out of here, you goddamned charlatan, and let me try to flush this poor baby out."

It was about an hour before we got Missy sponged off and onto her feet. Daddy said he was going to take us down to his place to sober Missy up before he dared to let us go back home. Ga-ga had locked herself into her bedroom for a good cry and kept moaning things through the door about ingratitude and how the dress had been a real Paris cremation [?] and how she was going to throw herself out the window. (It's only three flights.) That was the last of our visits to Ga-ga.

Eight

Out here in East Haddock, where we have now spent two weeks and where nothing ever happens, New York seems a million years ago and a million miles away. There are a few kids parked around—mostly grandchildren and great-grandchildren of Gran's crowd, but they're not very convenient like back in New York where there are sixteen kids between the ages of five and twelve (four of them creeps) in our building alone and it's just a short elevator ride or a couple of flights on the service stairs to get to them and vice versa. And that doesn't even begin to include the kids we know at school or the millions that live on East End Avenue and Gracie Square.

Here in the wilderness there have got to be all kinds of arrangements made over the telephone—and it's something they call a party line, if you can imagine such a thing, where you can listen in on other people's conversations, only they're not very interesting—by nurses and mothers and grandmothers to get a couple of kids together. It's like trying to see the President or the Pope, for cripes sake. Then there's a lot of driving —either us to their big ramshackle houses in the back seat of Gran's old Packard or them here to Dead Man's Gulch. And let me tell you, it isn't worth the time and trouble. The East Haddock summer children mostly come from Boston and Hartford (two from Philadelphia and three from Washington, D.C.) and they're as square as picture frames. There are a few local yokels in the village, only we're not allowed to play with them.

When I was still young enough to be taken to the park and Missy was still in diapers, for cripes sake, I

131

noticed that a kid's chums depended pretty much on what kind of a nurse he had. The nannies all sat together and knitted and told big lies about how fancy the families they'd worked for back in England all were. The mademoiselles all sat in another spot and talked about money and never let their kids get dirty. The Fräuleins kept to themselves and so did the Irish and the Scotch and the Negroes. The colored were the most fun, I always thought. And if you didn't have a popular nurse you were a gone goose.

Well, we never had any trouble that way because Lulu is a born social leader—the Pullman porters' Elsa Maxwell, Daddy always called her, whatever that means —and I am here to say that when Lulu appears at the beach club in her red Keds and her big red straw hat and her bag of beer and the black underwear under her white uniform, it's "Look out everybody!" Even the old English biddie who used to work for a duke recognizes real class when she sees it. I mean Missy and I could be the biggest things in East Haddock, if we wanted to. But who wants to? We have each other and there's also the help.

Gran talks about "cutting down" in the summertime, but as far as I can see, the cast of thousands—like they say about movies—that she keeps in New York is just the same and even bigger. The only person who's lucky enough to stay behind in New York is an old troll who lives mostly underground and sweeps the sidewalk and polishes the brass. Otherwise, Miss Fitch and Eustace and Nellie and the McGuire sisters are all on hand at East Haddock, beefed up by Lulu and MacKenzie, the old caretaker who also looks after the garden, and MacKenzie's son, Hughie, who's hung like a horse and about half as bright. Hughie's six feet seven and weighs two-fifty and it's all solid muscle—especially in his head. He's twenty-two years old and doesn't smoke or drink or do *anything* and he blushes as red as Lulu's Keds every time he sees a woman—even Gran. Missy gives him a real hard time, always climbing onto his lap or trying to catch him taking a leak or sweet-talking him in French, which he doesn't understand. He hardly digs English.

Besides sitting stock still and staring straight ahead

like maybe he was going to have a vision, Hughie cuts
the grass and messes among the roses with his dad and
drives Gran's car. The Packard is older than Hughie
and Gran says they don't make cars like that any
longer. They don't and it's a good thing, too. Gran
also keeps saying that she's "not long for this world,"
and with a mental re-tard like Hughie at the wheel of
that old wreck she's absolutely one hundred and one
per cent correct. Every time she puts on her visiting
jewelry and feels up to taking a trip down the road to
drink tea with some other old widow, I think it's going
to be her last. And when Hughie gets home alive there's
a whole lot of cheering from the back porch after he's
dumped Gran at the porte-cochere and then driven the
car practically through the barn. I could fly a rocket to
the moon a lot safer than Hugh-boy could get to the
general store and back.

The McGuire sisters have been working on Hughie
ever since they came to Gran two years ago. A lot of
good it does them! He goes all red and blushes and
stumbles around and tries to get away from them as
fast as he can. Bridget, the homely one, is still trying
to make first base with him, but this summer I guess
that Moira has kind of given up on Hughie. In fact
she's more or less given up on everything. She's got
fatter than ever and just moons around and cries a lot
when she thinks nobody's looking. Well, I can't blame
her out here in Lonelyville. The only time she ever
cheers up is weekends when H. A. drives out. Then she
fixes her hair and squirts on a lot of Liaison and makes
eyes at him and then he gets as red as Hughie and
sticks to Gran's side like Gran was magnetized. If he's
such a good friend of Moira's I don't know why he
doesn't at least talk to the poor cow. Missy and I try
to cheer her up all the time and even Lulu, who doesn't
much care for white people, feels sorry for Moira. But,
like I said before, H. A. is a rat fink from way back.

Mom is very good about writing to us, except the
Miss Farthingale's penmanship is very hard to make
out unless you happen to have gone there to school,
like Missy. But then Missy can only manage the easy
words. Daddy sends us a lot of post cards with the

message in architect's printing, which is simple to read. Otherwise, nothing.

You must have caught on by now that life—if you can call it that—out here in East Haddock isn't very interesting, so I guess I'll tell more about the winter in New York, which is at least civilization.

It seemed to me that every time Missy and I saw Daddy, Miss Glen—I just couldn't call her Tante Dorian and neither could Missy, so we just left things at "Hey, you . . ."—was somewhere around, and every time we looked, Mr. Reynolds was with Mom. Of course it was strictly business, I realized that. Daddy was remodeling the offices for Miss Glen's magazine and Mom was all tied up with Mr. Reynolds seeing about the divorce. But it sure ate up a lot of time.

I was especially surprised at Daddy. It seemed to me that he was taking longer to remodel a dozen rooms at Miss Glen's magazine than it took him to put up a whole fifty-story building with a garage in the basement and a swimming pool on the roof. Daddy always said that the worst thing that could happen to an architect was the client's wife and the troubles really began when Mrs. Client and her sister and her mother and her artistic daughter all horned in to change everything once the plans had been okayed. And here was Miss Glen's magazine made up of all women and poor old Daddy knocking himself out to try to please every one of them. Some business!

And Mr. Reynolds wasn't being any supersonic jet, like I said, about the divorce. Oh, sure, I could hear him say things like how unwise Mexico or Alabama would be and like that, but he was always showing up dressed fit to kill to take Mom off to the theater or the opera and you sure can't talk there without having some tough usher come and kick you out, if it's anything like the movies.

But the thing that really made it tough to be around both Miss Glen and Mr. Reynolds was that without knowing anything about us—or about any other children—they both had crazy ideas about what sort of kids Missy and I should be. And let me tell you that kids like the kinds they had in mind just don't exist, except maybe in the minds of people who don't have children. I told you that Lulu always talks about our Upstairs Manners (when we're just futzing around the apartment and being ourselves) and our Downstairs Manners (when we can be seen). But we've got still more sets of manners. There are the manners we have at school, the manners we have with other kids (like when we play), the manners we have at birthday parties and the manners we have with different adults. And they can change a lot, depending on who the grownup is—like we have different manners for both Gran and Ga-ga and they're both our grandmothers and both the same age. Well, I mean I bet everybody has different sets of manners that can be put on and taken off to suit whoever it is you're with. But even when you change what you do or say, you're still the same person. With Mom's Mr. Reynolds and Daddy's Miss Glen, we weren't. Like I say, they didn't either one of them know anything about children, but they sure knew what they thought kids *ought* to be.

The Dorian Glen Child was just like a professional child model in her fashion magazine. (And you know something? That magazine of hers isn't even all that great. Aunt Liz always called it "The Doxie's Digest." I don't know exactly what she meant but it didn't sound good.) Anyhow, Miss Glen's ideal was what H. A. probably must have been forty years ago—nice looking, all dressed up, never a hair out of place and dead. Miss Glen kept calling Lulu our "governess," for cripes sake, and talking about "good" schools (which we happen to go to—only they aren't) and the "best" dancing class (which we also happen to go to and if that one's the best I'd hate to see the worst) and telling us how important it was to speak French *"en famille"* (boy, you should hear some of the clangers *she* could make just on a menu) and how important it was to ride well (like New York hadn't heard of the horseless carriage yet) and get in with the "right set"—whatever that is. Well, it was some order. Oh, sometimes we'd give it a try, just because it was such a camp to put on the Chic Child Act, but sooner or later one of us—usually Missy—would break up and we'd laugh so hard the tears would come. And you know what? About half the

135

time I couldn't help feeling that maybe Miss Glen wasn't exactly certain about the line of bull she was slinging out to us—although I guess she must have been or she wouldn't have had that important job.

The Samuel de Koven Reynolds Child was exactly the opposite but every bit as phony. Old Just-crazy-about-little-folks must have got all his ideas off television, where the children's parts are all written by grownups and (or so this guy at school told me) acted by midgets. He liked us to come bouncing in full of "Gosh, gee whiz, gloriosky, Uncle Sam!" (*Uncle Sam?* Who did he think he was, some old geezer with chin spinach and stars and stripes all over his hat?) He was always talking about Normal, Wholesome, Healthy, Real American Kids (what did he think *we* were, Chinese?) and the Wonderful World of Childhood and Overnight Hikes with the Scouts (overnight hikes to where—Central Park and get mugged?) and the Thrill of Crawling Under a Tent Flap to catch the circus. (Just try crawling under Madison Square Garden, Sambo, if you want a *real* thrill!) I didn't know where he grew up (I do now—it happens to have been Jackson Heights, which isn't exactly in the Huck Finn country) but he sure had a picture of childhood that was about as up to date as *The Young King Arthur*. And we tried our best to please him and do the *Child Life* bit (have you ever tried to *read* that magazine?) but it always made me feel like a real damned fool and even Missy, who doesn't mind how babyish she acts most of the time, would get embarrassed and finally sore and ruin the whole act by saying something like, "The Good Fairy does *not* put a dime under my pillow when I lose a tooth. Mom does—or Lulu, if Mom's out with you—and the price has gone up to a quarter and everybody knows there aren't any fairies anyway." Then Mom would make Missy apologize for telling the exact word-for-word truth. We couldn't win. With Miss Glen I always felt like one of Ga-ga's beaux; with Mr. Reynolds, like I was still in my pram.

Our first outing with Mr. Reynolds was a real bomb. He said he wanted to start early so we could make a long day of it—and we sure did. Mom got us all dressed up and we showed up at Mr. Reynolds' apartment on a sunny Sunday noon. Mr. Reynolds lived in what I guess would have been the parlor floor of an old marble town house in the Seventies. It kind of reminded me of H. A.'s rooms at Gran's, except that everything was new instead of old. But it was all kind of leather and tweed—and so was Mr. Reynolds. He kept saying, "This is just where I hang my hat when I'm in town. My *real* home is my farm in New Jersey—plank floors, hand-something beans [?], Dutch ovens, exetera, exetera, exetera. Can I give you a Bloody Mary, my dear, with just plain tomato juice for the little folks?"

Then he showed us over every inch of the apartment like it was some old museum and kept telling how it had been "the old Morris mansion" until Mom finally said, yes, it had belonged to this cousin of hers until he got so old and nutty that he had to be put away if only for the sake of his housekeeper. You'd think that that would have shut Sam up, but he went on and on about the grand old traditions in New York until Mom finally said that she hoped chasing your housekeeper with an ax wasn't one of them.

So after he talked a little more about how he liked "mellow old things with an air of the past," he suggested that we go on to lunch and said that it was such a beautiful day, why didn't we walk part of the way through Central Park. So we did. Mr. Reynolds was very big on "the lovely old homes up here in the Seventies" and "some of the spellbinding old family histories their walls could tell if only they could talk." Mom said she could talk just fine and she also could tell him some family histories that would curl his hair. He said she had a great sense of humor, but he sounded a little disappointed to me. So then he changed the subject and talked about how a clear, crisp winter's day made you glad to be alive and didn't we wish we were at his place in the country. The answer was Not especially, but nobody said so.

Before Mr. Reynolds had entirely run down we were at the Central Park Zoo. "Well, well, well," he said, "guess where we are now."

"The zoo," Missy said patiently, like Mr. Reynolds was a visitor from out of town or not very bright. I

137

mean she'll answer any idiotic question just to be saying something.

"Just look at all the kiddies," he said. "Aren't they having a wonderful time out here?"

If you want my honest opinion, they didn't seem to be. One was getting spanked; another was having a spasm because a big leopard had roared at him; one was lost; some squirt was in hysterics because he'd let go of his balloon which was about a million feet up in the air by then; and another had just fallen down and skinned his chin. All in all, there were enough tears flowing to fill the seal pond.

So we went into the monkey house, which smells like I-don't-know-what, and Mr. Reynolds got all fatherly and put Missy up on his shoulder and stood in front of a cage that had a crowd around like they were giving away money. "Well, Missy, look at Mr. Monkeyshines," he boomed.

"It's not a monkey. It's an orangutan," Missy said.

"That's right. And what do you suppose he's doing?"

"I'm not sure," Missy said, "but I think he's pulling his pudding."

Well, let me tell you, that really brought down the house. I thought I was going to explode and even Mom, while she made a stab at saying, "Missy! Where did you ever *hear* such language?" broke up. So after that big exhibition of wholesome American goodness, we all fell into a taxi and went on to lunch.

Sunday lunch was another special treat for the little folks. It was this big sort of South American restaurant, all decorated in tile like it was the subway and food that would turn a rat's stomach. I mean nobody likes a good bowl of chili any better than I do—unless it's Missy. But this joint! Chicken in chocolate sauce! Echhh! Even worse than the cooking was the entertainment—some clowns that were about as funny as a forest fire and a dreary old bag with castanets and a lot of ruffles who came out and howled like Maxl when he caught his tail in the elevator door and clattered her heels on the floor and hollered "Oh lay!" Oh lay is right. Oh lay down and die!

Mr. Reynolds kept saying, "Isn't it wonderful the things they plan for little folks nowadays?" And Mom

138

would murmur, *"Isn't* this fun." Somehow she didn't sound very sincere.

Looking around the place I noticed that other kids were whining or squirming or refusing to eat (who could wonder?) or asking to be taken to the bathroom. I didn't see anyone you could swear was having a ball. But the adults were all being childish enough to make up for the kids.

Two-thirty and we still weren't off the hook. "We've got to step some," Mr. Reynolds said, looking at his watch.

"Are we going home now?" Missy asked.

"No. We're all going to the Lollipop Theater."

"To the what?" I asked.

Mom's face kind of fell as he repeated it.

Daddy's got this friend that works for this big publishing company and says that half the people that pick books for kids are elderly bachelors and old maids, but since the kids aren't the ones who go to bookstores and lay out the money for what they really want to read, these people (they are called Juvenile Editors) can get away with murder. Amen! The same goes for the people who put on shows for children.

The Lollipop Theater turned out to be a place on the East Side that was once a very unpopular church. It is still very unpopular. So for like three bucks apiece we were allowed in. About ten other grownups had got the same hot idea as Mr. Reynolds, so there were maybe twenty of us in this big, cold barn of a place all staring at a wiggly curtain with a lot of lollipops painted on it and cute things like "Candy Land" and "For Someone Sweet." Well, we waited around in the draft while the curtain kept on swaying and every now and then this big eye would peep out of a hole to see if any other victims had shown up. No one had. We were the last. Everybody else was too smart. So around half past three an old dame that looked like the music teacher who comes around at St. Barnaby's two days a week trudged in, sat down at a piano and let fly. After getting off to a couple of bad starts, the curtain opened with a terrible ripping sound, then out clumps this big, fat cow done up like an old-time princess in a dress that would have been too tight for Missy and like a

139

dunce cap on her head with some kind of skimpy material hanging down. "Children of all ages," she said, "I'm the Storytime Lady and my tale today is called *The Ogling Ogre.*"

Missy sighed and said, *"Oi veh!"* and somehow we both knew what was in store. Mom kind of settled in with a sigh and some more curtains got torn apart and on with the show! First we got this old guy wearing an oilcloth alligator's tail and a big kind of monster mask with flashlight bulbs for eyes. ("Isn't that clever?" says Sambo, only it wasn't terribly clever or even efficient, as one of the bulbs was burned out.) For all of his huffing and puffing and booming and ho-ho-ing, he had this kind of sissy voice and hissed his s-sounds like a snake.

"Is thisss the prin-sssesss I ssspy ssstrolling in the foressst with her maidssss?"

Well, it was just about then that I shut off my hearing aid for the afternoon. What a drag! I mean if they want to entertain kids, why don't they at least *ask* us what we'd like to see instead of insulting our intelligence and charging three dollars a head to do it? Missy is really young and even she thought it was too babyish to put up with. "How do you spell 'bore'?" she whispered to me.

"The living theater has its enchantment for every age, hasn't it, dear?" Mr. Reynolds whispered to Mom.

"Hmmm?" Mom asked.

So the no-talents of the Lollipop Theater sang and danced and acted for us all-day suckers for about the next ten hours. There were only two funny things in the whole show: a great big piece of scenery that was the Rock Candy Mountain fell down with a crash; and about halfway through the afternoon this real Nancy guy who was playing Good Prince Somebody started to get a hole in the seat of his tights and it got bigger and bigger and bigger every time he'd bend over and bow to the prin-sssesss. Some brat called out, "Oh, Mommy, I can see his bottom!" But even that wasn't enough to save the afternoon. A few kids, who didn't have our poise, absolutely insisted on being taken home. They had all the luck.

"I guess the excitement is just too much for some of the little folks," Sam said. For cripes sake, was he *kidding*?

Finally it all came to a grand and glorious end with everybody out on the stage singing "Go Blow Yourself a Bubble" while they tossed some withered old balloons at the piano player and the Good Prince's bottom all but fell into the footlights. But by then nearly everybody was gone and the dozen people, maybe, who were left were too busy getting into coats and hats and ski suits to notice.

"I don't know how they think of these things for the little folks," Mr. Reynolds kept saying.

Neither do I.

Miss Glen's entertainments weren't much better, but at least they were shorter. Tea at "my little hole in the wall" was about as far as she was willing to go and that was far enough. They generally happened after Daddy had taken us to a good movie or maybe even a matinee where we saw this real funny guy named Bert Lahr climb right up a wall.

Miss Glen lived in one of the big, new apartment buildings that Daddy hates so much. He says they're not nearly as well built as tenements that are a hundred years old and they're the slums of tomorrow and so expensive that honest people can't live in them (Miss Glen's a crook?), exetera, exetera, exetera.

Miss Glen's building is called the Mondrian, after this big foreign artist that painted with a ruler, and I guess Daddy's right. It has a doorman who's dressed up much fancier than our Riley and a lobby with all kinds of modern furniture and man-eating plants and a fountain with changing lights instead of just two hall chairs and this Sheridan [?] table so old it's falling apart like in our building. But for all the music in the elevators and like that, you can still hear other people's television sets and toilets flushing and food mixers whirring and doors slamming. The elevator was not only playing "Let's Twist Again Like We Did Last Summer," but was also decorated with some black lines and red-and-blue squares like a picture painted by this Mondrian and a sign saying that we were on closed-circuit television. When I told Missy that, she got all adorable and even blew a kiss in the direction of the ceiling, the big ham!

Miss Glen's apartment was very high up. As Daddy rang the bell, the door opened and a great big cross-looking woman barged out. She had short, curly black hair and wore boots, a big canvas kind of spy coat and, like I said, a mean expression.

"Hello, Jane," Daddy said.

"Don't worry," she growled, "I'm on my way out." Then she blew a big cloud of smoke at us and yelled, "Hold it!" at the elevator. There wasn't anybody like an elevator man to do anything about it. The door slid closed and I'd hate to tell you what I *think* this Jane said then. Anyhow, she started poking the elevator bell like it was a punching bag and we went into the apartment.

Just the way Miss Glen had said, the place *was* a hole in the wall. It was all white and kind of empty. There was a great big sofa and a big, low glass table and a couple of real modern chairs and a zebra rug on the floor and a kind of beat-up-looking old trunk and that was it, except for a great big picture that I guess was supposed to be a naked lady. For cripes sake, it seems like anybody can be an artist nowadays.

Miss Glen was floating around in big, floppy pants and a dainty shirt. *"Mes enfants!"* she said. "Kiss Tante Dorian." We got the cheekbone again. I also noticed that her hair was a new color—kind of a streaky dark yellow. It was hard to keep up with Miss Glen's hair and sometimes I wondered if even she remembered what color it really was.

Then Miss Glen was on—louder and longer than even Missy when she goes to her own room and starts talking to herself. ". . . so glad you could finally come up to my little place . . ." blah, blah, blah . . . "instead of tea we're going to have *chocolat jamaïque* . . . not just ordinary cocoa but this really soo-pub kind of chocolate our travel editor brought back this winter . . ." blah, blah, blah . . . "cocoa beans, cinnamon, tumeric [?] and add a jigger of ve-ry dark rum . . ." blah, blah, blah.

Still talking about how good it was going to be, she

142

disappeared behind a screen and showed up again carrying a tray with four tall cups on it. They looked like they were made out of bamboo and, what's more, they were! Then she went through a big ceremony of dumping in whipped cream and sprinkling grated orange peel, for cripes sake, on top of that and stabbing the whole thing with a cinnamon stick.

"Like it, darlings?" she said, passing around some lady fingers.

"Mm-hmmm," Missy said.

" 'Yes, Tante Dorian,' darling," Miss Glen said, in a no-nonsense way.

I saw Missy getting that up-your-bucket look ("intractable" they call it at Miss Farthingale's) so I jumped in to save the day. "This is a very interesting place you've got here," I said—even adding "Tante Dorian," although it made me kind of sick—"is that your trunk?" I pointed to the battered old thing.

"Why, thank you, *chéri*," she said and she was on once again. "No, dear, that's an old Bavarian bridal chest that's been in our family for generations. It was all that was saved after the great fire." I thought that that was going to be interesting, but it wasn't. "Our beautiful place in the country with all of our lovely old family pieces ut-terly reduced to ashes. We were lucky to escape with our lives."

"What country was that?" Missy asked.

Miss Glen charged right on. "And the tragedy was really mine. My father is quite old now and much happier in a small place, but all of our lovely things that were to come to me as the only child . . ." blah, blah, blah. Boy, she really had a stack of L.P.'s for a tongue. "I suppose it's foolish and wicked of me, but I love lovely things. A true perfectionist. One good suit, one perfect ensemble, a marvelous bag, a truly good pair of alligator shoes, one beautifully made blouse, one exquisite jewel that is perfectly simple and simply perfect . . ." blah, blah, blah . . . "That is why I'd a thousand times rather live in an empty room with just one good piece than . . ." blah, blah, blah. Well, she practically did. "Do you *love* the chocolate, darlings?"

"Very nice," I said. Missy didn't say anything. Actually it tasted like plain old Hershey's that some spaz had ruined. Lulu makes much better cocoa with hardly any conversation at all, except telling us to get out from under her feet. I kind of had the feeling that Miss Glen would like us out from under her feet—and her every-. thing else, too. But by this time she was focused on Daddy. ". . . most amusing evening last night, I do wish you could have got out of your other thing and come. After this truly *thrilling* opening at the Parsons Gallery a lot of us all went on to this heavenly little Finnish restaurant run by two friends of Jane's. It only holds ten and you usually have to book months in advance. Not even listed in the phone book! But, by great good luck, it was empty, so we . . ." blah, blah, blah. . . . She was talking about a delicious dish made of smoked reindeer and herring (echhh!) when I said, "Could I wash my hands, please?"

"Certainly, dear, it's right through the bedroom. And then someone suggested that we all go on to Le Club and . . ."

Gadzeeks, for someone who could talk, talk, talk about one empty room with one lovely thing in it, the bedroom was kind of cluttery. There were twin beds (for Miss Glen and who else?), a couple of dressers, a dressing table with about a million bottles and tubes and jars on it and a whole stack of some newspaper I never heard of before called *Women's Wear Daily,* plus piles of Miss Glen's magazine and all the other fashion magazines. The bathroom was okay as bathrooms go, only it was arranged so I could hear somebody taking a shower and somebody brushing his teeth and somebody using an electric razor—all in different apartments—plus me. Kind of a quartet.

But my timing was terrible and when I got back to the living room I could see that I'd missed a far more important quartet—Daddy, Miss Glen, Missy and Lulu, who had just arrived to pick Missy and me up.

"Oh, dear, I had no idea it was so late," Miss Glen was saying. "I must fly if we're ever to get to the Lipsky-Gottschalks' by seven. Really, Kerry, I do wish you could meet their son, Jeremy. He's a true genius."

"I already have," I said. And I had. We were in nursery school together until he got kicked out for being so babyish and ditto for two years at St. Barnaby's. I don't know where he's going now—or care. I mean he's a crud.

"That mean little stinker Ruby used to look after?" Lulu said. "No thanks."

Miss Glen looked kind of miffed, like she thought our "governess" shouldn't be talking like that. And she was right. But Lulu's got a lot of intolerance—especially against people who happen to be white—and she's too old to change.

"Hmm. Then it's all set with Melissa and Kerrington for the thirteenth?"

"Yes, ma'am. I guess so."

"What's all set?" I asked. Poor old Missy looked like she'd just swallowed arsenic.

"The most marvelous thing! These friends of mine are starting up this enchanting marionette theater for children. Of course it's by invitation only—but they said they'd love to have you two. . . ." Miss Glen sure had a lot of friends and they were all busy as beavers setting up businesses that cost somebody (like Daddy) a lot of money. Her pals were always opening places where we (but I guess not just anybody else) could buy our clothes or take riding lessons or get advice on summer camps (echhhhh!) or be treated to special kinds of parties (when we go to about two birthday parties a week and, believe me, they're *all* the same) or do something that Missy and I just plain didn't want to do that's supposed to be some kind of big privilege. This last was a lousy puppet show once every two weeks with programs like an opera by this big musician, Mozart, in German and some play in French and like that.

Now if only *I'd* been in the room when she'd suggested the whole thing, I could have got out of it in one-two-three. I mean it's a sin to tell a *real* lie like "Yes, I've done my homework," when you haven't even cracked a book. But I don't consider it a sin to tell a polite lie like "No, I'm sorry we can't come to your school pageant because we've got to have lunch with our grandmother that day." I mean isn't it more sinful to hurt somebody's feelings by saying "I wouldn't be caught dead at your old shindig," than to make up a fairly decent excuse that doesn't do anybody any harm?

145

And good reasons for not doing something we'd hate to do just come to me naturally. Here I've got Dr. Epston and Dr. Fulton (I'm always getting cavities and like that) and two grandmothers and school and all kinds of easy alibis. But the minute I turn my back the whole system blows up.

"Very nice place you have," Lulu said and I could tell that she hated it.

"Thank you," Miss Glen said. "And you'll ask the children's mother about the spring holidays?"

"Yes, Miss Grim." I could also tell that Lulu hated Miss Glen, too, because she never gets a name wrong except on purpose.

"What about the holidays?" I asked.

"It was to be a surprise, Kerry," Daddy said. "But I thought you and Missy and I might take a trip together. South. You know—fishing, swimming, that kind of thing."

"Hot damn!" I said.

"Just wait," Missy muttered.

"And since *I* have to be down in the Skeleton Keys . . ." the Voice of Doom cut in. "The Skeleton Keys are the most divine islands off Palm Beach; completely unspoiled because only a very few people know about them. We'll be photographing bathing suits for the July issue. So I suggested to your father that it might be fun if he took you down there and we could *all be together*."

Nine

I guess maybe somehow the time passes no matter where you are or what you're doing—like even in solitary confinement. I mean it's hard to realize that the Fourth of July has already come and gone and we've spent almost a month in East Haddock. It seems a lot longer, but like a convict marking off the days on a calendar (which is what I do) it's interesting to see how much time has gone by.

Independence Day probably isn't much *anywhere,* but in East Haddock it's real science fiction. By July first everybody who's fool enough to come here at all has moved into some big, damp house and had the windows washed and the weeds pulled and the wasps killed and what they call the "East Haddock Season" is on. It all starts with this kind of free-for-all at the beach club which is called a Community Clam Bake and which is something the summer children are supposed to give for the local kids.

Even if they do make their livings off them, the couple of hundred people who belong in East Haddock all year round hate the summer people like poison. And that's the way the local kids feel about us, too. As for us summer kids, we don't like the local kids or hate them or anything. We just plain don't know them. And what's more, we're never going to because we're not allowed to. The mothers and grandmothers and nurses all say, "He's a local," like they were saying "He's a leopard," or somebody with some other terrible disease. When the East Haddock kids get big enough to be useful and do things like baby-sit and wait on table and work for the summer people, that's different. But until

147

then there's absolutely no mixing except on one day a year—the Fourth of July. Gran calls it "Democracy at Work."

And do you think we could ever do anything simple at this beach club like go up to some other kid and say "Hi, my name's Kerry and this is my sister. Would you like to take a swim?" Not on your life! Maybe one reason for this is that the East Haddock kids all live on the sea and therefore don't know how to swim or ever even get wet. But the real reason is the summer property owners. Since they haven't one blessed thing to do, they make a big project out of the Community Clam Bake with lots of committees and meetings. I mean there's an Entertainment Committee and a Refreshments Committee and a Fireworks Committee (H. A. was chairman this year) and a Decorations Committee and all the rest of that jazz. Gran is usually called Honorary Chairman because she's the oldest and the richest, I guess, and that means that she doesn't do a thing except moan about what a "ghastly ordeal" it's going to be for her to get into her car with Miss Fitch and have Hughie drive her to the beach club where she has to sit on the porch for a couple of hours watching everybody have a lousy time.

It's supposed to start at six o'clock because by then it's too late to go in swimming and the beach club members don't want the local kids polluting the Atlantic Ocean. The locals show up around six-thirty dressed fit to kill. But all the summer families have been waiting around since five because, like I heard this one dame say, "The rustics are likely to arrive *ages* early —they have so few treats." There's this one family from Boston that didn't turn up until seven, but H. A. says it's because they're very *nouveau* and maybe even Jewish, although I don't see what that's got to do with it. If they were as smart as everybody says Jews are, they wouldn't have come at all.

Well, finally the East Haddock families get to the club and they're expected to act like it's a tour of the White House. I'm sure they all live in nicer places themselves. What the beach club really is is a big kind of living room full of sandy old chairs and sofas and copies of the *National Geographic* and a last year's

Summer Social Register. There's a kitchen and a dining room with some rickety chairs and tables and a big stuffed sailfish some member's wife said she was only too happy to donate. Then there's a big screened porch with a Ping-pong table and a whole lot more chairs for the old ladies to rock in, a men's locker room and a women's locker room and two johns and that's that.

So after our guests all oh-ed and ah-ed over the way we live, the local kids were turned loose and everybody separated. By that I mean the summer grownups all stood talking to each other and the East Haddock grownups shuffled around doing the same thing. I did hear one Boston lady complaining to the guy who owns the general store about the size of her June bill, but that was about as far as the adults went.

We kids were even worse. I swear that the only way you could tell the difference between them and us is that they were all dressed up and we looked like a bunch of slobs. The nurses made kind of a stab at putting us in American flag colors, like blue shorts with red-and-white-striped T shirts and Missy looked kind of cute in one of Hughie's old blue denim shirts with a red bandanna tied around her waist. Ga-ga always said that Missy had a natural sense of style inherited from her, but style or no, Gran made Lulu change Missy into a dress after she picked out her own granddaughter in the mess of kids on the sand. Naturally we didn't talk to the East Haddock kids and vice versa. The one time I tried to say something halfway friendly, H. A. called me away and asked me to get a package in the glove compartment of his station wagon and to bring it to him in the men's locker room without letting anybody see it. As interesting and mysterious as it all sounded, it was nothing but a bottle of booze. I wish I'd dropped it.

Lemonade (pink yet!) was served to everyone while all the kids—both local and summer—would have preferred Coke and all the grownups looked like they'd sell their mothers for a drink. For the past two days the Refreshments Committee—who didn't know anything about a clambake—and Gran's MacKenzie—who did —had been digging a pit and setting fire to stones and messing around with seaweed and lobster and chicken and clams and corn and potatoes and all looking up at the sky and saying it was going to be a beautiful starry night for the big beach bash. All except Mac-Kenzie. He said he felt rain. Sure enough, it had been grayish all day and a kind of drizzle started up just as this big jerk from Hartford, got up in Bermuda shorts and so many kinds of madras that he looked like a patchwork quilt, announced that there'd be fun and games for the small fry. So with a whole lot of confusion and quarreling and arguing and "you are not" and "I am so" we got paired off into teams according to how old you were and whether you were male or female or local or summer.

So there were relay races and sack races and one-legged races in a mist so thick you couldn't see the clubhouse. The summer kids won everything but old Bermuda shorts made us give the prizes "to our guests," which I thought was almost as insulting as the prizes themselves. Later, in the men's can, I heard old Bermuda shorts say to H. A., "It just goes to show that people of our class keep themselves in better condition." And him with a gut the size of a washtub! "Better diet, better schools, better heritage. Better everything." If you ask me, the reason we kept winning was because we were wearing shorts and sneakers and the local kids were all tricked out in their Sunday best.

The rain was oozing down on the tarpaulin that covered the clambake pit. Not hard or fast, but just an occasional plop . . . plop . . . plop-plop . . . plop. There was a big to-do over whether the mess was ready to eat. MacKenzie said it wasn't, but the chairman of the Refreshments Committee said it was. So supper was served. MacKenzie was right. The chicken was kind of bloody at the joints and the lobster sort of rubbery and everything had so much sand in it that it was like when Dr. Fulton cleans my teeth.

Most of the locals claimed that shellfish didn't agree with them (like Gran) and some of the kids came right out and said they'd rather have a TV Dinner any day. But the summer grownups—especially the ones who'd been far-sighted enough to bring bottles, like H. A.—chomped gamely away with butter running down their chins and talked about other clambakes in other places that they'd also enjoyed. Warm water-melon was served, then it was time for speeches. The president of the beach club got up and welcomed all of our dear old friends from East Haddock, and some-body in the crowd muttered, "Welcome to what?" Then the mayor of East Haddock got up and said how the locals always looked forward to the arrival of their "fair weather friends" and some very tony voice said, "At the prices they charge I don't wonder." Then Madame Honorary Chairman was introduced and Gran got up for her big act. All she had to do was read off a list—like "Decorations Committee: Mrs. Sterling Hathaway, Chairman; Mrs. Anthony Baker Bradley, Mrs. Blah blah blah"—but Gran's got these kind of specks on a handle that hang from a long chain around her neck that she needs for reading, only they got all tangled up with her pearls and she nearly hanged her-self trying to see. I thought I'd split. Finally Gran gave the list to Miss Fitch and said, "Would you please read the names out for me?"

Miss Fitch started in with her most social voice, mispronouncing all the oldest names in the summer community, and I hate to think of what she would have done with Mrs. Sebastian Foxhurst Hoare if Moira McGuire hadn't stolen the scene by fainting dead away while she was hefting a trayload of old corncobs, chicken bones, lobster claws and clam shells. What a crash!

"I think we'll dispense with the committees, Miss Fitch," Gran said. "Moira seems unwell." *Seemed un-well?* Poor Moira looked like she'd been mugged in the middle of the city dump. So while Miss Fitch and Lulu were picking Moira out of the garbage and vice versa, the president of the beach club announced that the fireworks were about to begin and then it started raining for real.

All the nurses herded all the summer kids, except for Missy and me, since Lulu was occupied, up onto the porch. There wasn't room for anyone else, so we and the East Haddock kids braved it out in the downpour. Someone gave us some sparklers, but they barely sput-tered in the wet.

From under a slicker, H. A. gave a speech about

how hard he and the men on his committee had worked to make this the most unusual fireworks display ever, but his voice was kind of thick and the rain was really pelting down and nobody was listening anyway.

Well, until they invent some fireworks that go off under water, H. A. and his committee might just as well not knock themselves out. They started with a few Roman candles, but the great balls of fire hardly flickered before they plopped down onto the sand like apples falling from a tree. A couple of aerial bombs were fired out to sea never to be seen or heard from again. The few things that weren't supposed to do anything more than go Bang went Pfffft and one or two of the bigger ones went Pop, but that was all. To say that H. A.'s fireworks were a washout hardly begins to tell it.

The rain was coming down steadily and a kind of wind had sprung up. The East Haddock kids, huddled under the eaves of the porch, looked pretty miserable —the starched, frilly dresses drooping like old dishrags and the dye beginning to run from the boys' neckties.

"Ahem! H. A.," the club president said, "owing to the inclement weather, don't you think we might call a halt to the pyro-somethings."

"We've only got the rockets to go, sir," H. A. said. I almost expected him to do a snappy salute like maybe he was some hot-shot young midshipman talking to his admiral while the ship was sinking.

"Well, if you really think . . ."

Then old Bermuda shorts, who was giving H. A. a hand, said, "We can never get them off the ground against this wind."

"Then fire them *with* the wind!" H. A. shouted. He kind of staggered.

"Toward the club?"

"*Over* the club! Here, watch me!"

"You're drunk!"

"*You're* common." Then H. A. turned this sort of trough around, put a big rocket in it and fiddled around with his gold cigarette lighter. There was a sputtering, a sizzling, a flash of green and then nothing except a long, black thing like a closed umbrella that shot right through the porch screens, over the heads of the crowd and ended up stuck in the side of the stuffed fish like a harpoon. Then all hell broke loose and before you could say "East Haddock Bath and Tennis Club" the East Haddock Bath and Tennis Club was empty.

The parking lot was flooded and cars were stalling and people were godding and damning around to beat anything. H. A. crashed his station wagon square into the side of the spiffy Rolls-Royce that belonged to the Boston people who were so *nouveau* and the man said that H. A. was dangerous to society—hell, H. A. thinks he *is* society—and in no condition to drive.

One of the younger old bags from Philadelphia, who's supposed to be directly descended from the Liberty Bell, just stood out in the rain saying, "No matter how much we try for them they *hate* us. Why? Why? *Why?*"

I am not really certain, but I think I could have told her, told her, *told* her.

And that's what last weekend was like.

I'll bet you think I'm losing track of the story I started out to tell. Well, I'm not. I'm only telling you about Fourth of July weekend at East Haddock to give you an idea of the kind of life Missy and I can look forward to practically forever and also to show you what adults think children like. Or at least we're *supposed* to like that kind of thing and if any kid should be fool enough to come right out and tell the truth and say he hates it, then he's "disturbed" and it's Dr. Epston or even worse.

Two birthdays ago Daddy came to the breakfast table and announced that he was officially too old ever to go away for weekends again. Mom said, "Wonderful, darling. I've *always* been too old." Me, too. And when I get to be eleven—which is only a month off—*I'm* going to be officially too old to go away for weekends.

Like I said before, everybody who had anything to do with Missy and me had some kind of private idea of what we should really be like, whether we could fill the bill or whether we couldn't. Missy is so young (and stubborn as a little mule) that sometimes she'd get her back up, put her foot down and all the rest of it. But before she said or did anything to get her ass in a sling—*and* mine—I could usually reason with her. I used to say, "Come on, Missy. You've always wanted to be an actress. Look at this like a part in a show. It's only for a little while, then we can go back to being ourselves." And you know, that kid could put on some great performances—real Academy Award stuff. It was kind of like this dame called Trilby that gets hypnotized by this old guy—I forget his name—and goes out and sings like a bird when she couldn't carry a tune in a bucket. Sometimes I think I maybe ought to be a diplomat.

Where was I? Oh. Weekends.

I guess I told you that Mr. Reynolds was around the apartment pretty much of the time talking business to Mom. In fact he was around so much that even Gran called off her series of dinner parties and put away her "list of young people" for Mom's "suitable social life." I just happened to pick up the phone once in time to hear Gran say, "Well, dear, I've met your Mr. Reynolds and he seems to be very nice. H. A. says that he hasn't had our advantages but . . . ." Then Mom said, "Kerry! Stop eavesdropping!" And I *wasn't!* So I had to hang up. Anyhow, whenever I got home from school or from a big dream session with Dr. Epston, Mr. Reynolds wasn't far behind—always dressed in his neat, dark suits with hard collars (for business days) and carrying his little suitcase full of legal papers. If he didn't take Mom out to dinner, he'd have it with us, sitting in Daddy's place at the table. And when Mom gave a party, he was always on hand acting as host and mixing the drinks (he was more reliable with the liquor than H. A.) just like Daddy.

Dr. Epston kept asking me if I "resented" Sam's "replacing the father." I told him No. And I didn't. In the first place Mr. Reynolds couldn't ever replace Daddy. Just too different. In the second place, why should *I* care what chair he sat in? The chairs are real old and named after this big hotel on Park Avenue where Elizabeth Taylor stayed—Regency, that's it—and they're always getting shifted around the table anyway. I mean a chair's a chair, for cripes sake. And in the third place, Missy and I never minded about Sambo. There's nothing about him *to* mind—maybe that's his

154

trouble. Square as a city block, but pleasant and polite and always trying to do nice things for us kids—even if they almost never work out that way. I mean I don't mean to be mean about him—no matter how I sound.

But to get back to weekends, one night when Mr. Reynolds was having dinner with us he smiled and said, "How would my two favorite little folks like to spend next weekend out at a farm that's almost two centuries old?"

Missy looked like she'd been slugged. I've never known anybody who hated fresh air and nature as much as she does—unless it's me. So I jumped in with some spur-of-the-moment social lies. "Gee, that sounds swell. It's just too bad that I've got Dr. Epston till four o'clock on Friday . . ."

"We could pick you up at his office at four," Sam said.

". . . and the dentist on Saturday morning . . ."

"I meant to tell you, Kerry," Mom said, "Dr. Fulton telephoned and changed your appointment until the following week."

". . . and then I've got a lot of studying to do for this big history test on Monday . . ."

"History's my favorite subject, Kerry. We can work on it together. In fact, my place in New Jersey *is* history."

". . . and I kind of promised Timmy Brooks that . . ."

"The children would love it, Sam," Mom said.

I could see Missy's lips silently saying one of her really terrible words.

We were pretty impressed by Sam's car, let me tell you. It was this big four-door Continental convertible —really great. Cold as it was, I was about to suggest that we put the top down so Maxl could get a little air, but by the time we got through the tunnel and out into those ugly New Jersey swamps, it had started snowing. And by the time we hit Sam's farm, it was dark and the snow was higher than Maxl's back and coming down faster. It all looked like some Christmas card, for cripes sake—this long, low, old house and all the lighted windows sending reflections out onto the snow. The funny thing was that even with all those

155

flakes falling, the driveway was bone dry and clean as could be. When I asked about it, Sam said, "Electric coils under the pavement."

"Isn't that frightfully expensive?" Mom asked. (And her always telling us not to talk about money!)

"It would have been," Sam said proudly, "but my mother designed the whole system herself and did all the contracting, too. That way it cost about a quarter of what it ordinarily would have." He pulled up to a triple garage and pressed a button somewhere near the steering wheel. Another miracle! The big door slid open and lights came on in the garage. There was a tiny little foreign car, not much bigger than a toy one, and some kind of a tractor parked inside, plus a lot of power tools—don't ask me what they were supposed to do—all neatly arranged. "Here we are," Sam said and we all piled out.

Just then a door burst open and a voice shrieked "Sam?" and a little woman hardly bigger than Missy shot out and leapt up into Sam's arms. "Thought you'd never get here!" she screeched.

"How's my sweetheart?" Sam asked. She seemed pretty darned spry, however else she was.

Then there was a terrible lot of barking and two of the biggest dogs I ever saw came charging out. Maxl jumped right back into the car. The dogs—I found out they were a kind called mastiffs—were followed by a big, gloomy gussie wearing a sweater set and kind of hugging her elbows.

"Put me down, Sam," little Miss Dynamite said. "Rosemary, call those dogs!"

"Here, Ajax! Here, Achilles," the younger woman said without much pizazz.

"That's no way to do it, Rosemary. You know that." Then the little woman put her fingers in her mouth and gave out a whistle that made my hair stand on end. The dogs stopped barking right away. They knew what was good for them. "Now you two get right back in that house. Go on now. *Get!*" "How do you do," she said to Mom. "I'm Sam's mother. And this is my daughter, Rosemary. And these must be Missy and Kerry. I thought you were never coming. Wait. I'll get your bags." Before anybody could say a word she was around the car and then went scooting back toward the house with all of our suitcases—some of them carried kind of up under her armpits the way bellboys do it.

"I can do that, Mother," Sam said.

"Kerry," Mom said. "Help Mrs. Reynolds. Where are your manners?"

"Now don't you worry any about that. You must be tired after that long drive. Just follow me. Son, put the door down. I think we're in for a blizzard." Then she was gone, bumping past Rosemary, who was still sort of clutching herself and looking miserable. We followed her into a big long room that was tricked up with a lot of worktables and a great big loom with half of a rug— I *guess* it was a rug—on it and a drafting table like Daddy's and a whole lot of other mysterious equipment. "Don't mind my workroom," she yipped. "It's a mess. Always is. Hurry up, Sam. Don't dawdle. Rosemary, shut the door." We followed her, on the double, into another room which was full of all kinds of washers and driers and electric ironing machines and like that. "Bring your laundry, Sam?"

"Mother, I told you, the laundry in town can . . ."

"It can ruin your nice shirts and rob you blind and lose every blessed thing you own. That's what it can do. Oh, I let the colored girl go."

"Mother! I just hired her."

"And I just fired her. Sick half the time—or says she is—just moves the dirt around and so everlastingly slow it just plain gives me the jimjams to watch her. I can do the work myself—and far better—in the time it takes me to pick her up and drive her back to Princeton. Isn't that right, Rosemary?"

"Yes, Mother."

"Hurry along, I'm sure our guests are tired and hungry." She zipped into a kitchen every bit as big as the one in Gran's place at East Haddock but much more up-to-date with all kinds of streamlined stoves and freezers and sinks and a desk and about a million electrical gadgets. "Sam," she said, "I've got half a steer waiting for me in Trenton. You'll have to pick it up tomorrow. Didn't have a chance to do it this afternoon. The girls were slow as molasses and all out of sorts and

Rosemary can't ever do anything right. Scat!" she hissed and gave one of the mastiffs a root with her knee that sent him clear through a swinging door. "This is the dining room," she said of the next room. It didn't seem necessary to explain. It had a kind of early-American table and chairs and a great big fireplace (lit) and old plank floor boards so shiny that I skidded halfway out to the hall.

The hall was also very colonial with a narrow, twisting old staircase that led to the floor above. Mrs. Reynolds, suitcases and all, was halfway up it by the time we all made the hall. Maxl looked very nervous. "Rosemary, take their coats. Sam, make drinks for everybody. I'll stow these things in the bedrooms and be right down to start dinner. Unless you want to wash up first?"

"Wh-whatever you say, Mrs. Reynolds," Mom said.

"Then go into the living room and relax. Mind that floor. It's fresh waxed. Didn't have a chance to get at the dining room today. I'll wax it tomorrow before the rest of you are up." Then she shot up out of sight.

The living room was a huge low place also with a roaring fire and floors you could skate on. There was another loom in one corner with most of a rug on it and a lot more woven rugs on the floor—very slidy. Like the dining room, it was filled with a whole lot of early-American furniture.

"Lovely old pieces," Mom said.

"Mother refinished every one of them." Sam said. "In fact, she restored the whole house herself. What can I get you to drink?"

"J-just *anything*," Mom said and kind of sank onto a sofa.

A wheezy old clock on the mantel clanked out six o'clock and Mrs. Reynolds flew into the living room with the mastiffs trying to keep up with her. Maxl got under the sofa. "Lordy-lord! Six o'clock! Where does the time all *go?* We'll eat at seven. I hope you don't mind, but Sunday's the first of March and I've got to get my bills out."

"Mother! Mr. Badian . . ."

"Now, Sam, don't Mr. Badian me! I told that good-for-nothing accountant to pack up his pencils and go.

Mooning around here one whole blessed day every month. Wasting my time with his stupid questions—and Rosemary's, too. Then I've got to get lunch for him and by the time he's out of here there's another day shot. I swear! Hire people to work for you and you end up working for *them*. Sam, get a move on! Rosemary, there's some tiger's milk for the children in the icebox. At least I *told* you to mix up a fresh batch. Excuse me. I'll just get things going." Then she was gone.

"Amazing woman, my mother," Sam said.

"Astonishing," Mom said in a very quiet voice.

"I've asked Mother to put you and Missy in one bedroom and Kerry can come in with me."

"What about Maxl?" Missy asked.

"Oh, Sam! I do hope we're not crowding your mother and . . . and Rosemary."

"Crowding us? Not at all. We have ten bedrooms in the house and Mother has done over every one of them herself. But with the . . . uh . . . situation as it is with . . . well, you know what I mean. Anyhow, I thought it would be better not to take any chances. So if you have Missy in with you and Kerry is in *my* room, then there could never be any suspicion on the part of . . ."

Mom started to laugh. "Darling Sam! I can't believe that anyone would think you'd brought me to a house where your mother and sister live for an assignment [?]," or something like that. Well, they were starting in on one of those boring adult conversations you can't make head or tail of when Rosemary came in carrying a tray with three big glasses full of something the color of Gran's brownstone house. Mrs. Reynolds darted past her. "Rosemary, don't dillydally so. The *rest* of you can ruin your systems with spirits, but we *young* ones are going to have a good glass of tiger's milk. I've improved on the Adelle Davis formula." She flicked a glass off the tray, sat down at the loom and started tearing away at the rug. "Don't mind if I keep busy while we talk. This is a special order for the House of Good Taste but the girls were so poky today I sent them home and decided to finish it off myself. Here's to your very good health."

"What *is* it?" Missy asked.

159

"Tiger's milk? Well, the way *I* make it it is primarily dried flaked high-heat-process brewer's yeast, bone meal, sunflower kernels, raw wheat germ, blackstrap molasses, yoghurt, a capsule of royal jelly, fresh goats' milk—I keep two nannies on the place here; if you're up in time you can help me milk them—papaya juice and . . ."

"May I be excused?" I said.

The dinner was darned good. Mrs. Reynolds cooked well. She did everything well. She'd be the first to tell you that. I could list every herb that was in every dish if I thought you'd really care. Mrs. Reynolds *knew* that we would, so she told us. She raised several kinds of herbs and sold them in jars to fancy grocery stores all over the country. That was only one of the things she did so well. It wasn't late, but at eight o'clock I was so doggone bushed just from watching Mrs. Reynolds race around that I said good night, went up to Sam's room and fell into bed. The first day of our visit had been short but very tiring.

It was only 6:00 A.M. in the morning when I woke up. Maybe it was because I'd gone to bed so early or maybe it was because of the kind of whining drone I could hear from somewhere lower down in the house. I looked over at the next bed and there was old Sambo stretched out sound asleep. If I was supposed to have kept an eye on him for some reason, I sure hadn't. But now that I was wide awake, I had plenty of chance to. He slept just like a corpse with his hands crossed on his chest and the only way you knew he was alive was the steady sort of hiss to his breathing. All the windows were wide open and it was so damned cold in that room that I noticed a little film of ice had formed over the glass where Sam kept his teeth. (Not two whole rows of teeth like Lulu wears, but just a couple of back teeth on a little gold arch—kind of like a croquet wicket.) I slid out from under the covers and raced into the bathroom. If Sam's house was very historical, his own private bathroom was right out of the Futurama—heat in the floors, heat in the mirrors so they wouldn't fog up, sun lamps in the ceiling and all kinds of kookie gadgets. I brushed my teeth, put on my robe and then tiptoed out of the room and down the twisting stairs so as not to disturb my roommate.

The noise was coming from the dining room and the first thing I saw was Mrs. Reynolds, dressed in a skirt I was certain she'd woven herself, riding a big electric waxer around the floor.

"Well! Good morning! This *is* a surprise. I thought you'd be lying abed until at least seven like the rest of them." *Seven?* "You're like me. I can see that. Up with the birds. I can get more done before sunup than most people can in a whole day. A little tiger's milk? Eggs? Buckwheat cakes? I get my buckwheat from this place in Minnesota and grind . . ."

"Just toast and coffee, please, Mrs. Reynolds."

"Toast and coffee? No wonder you're so skinny." (She couldn't have weighed a hundred pounds herself.) "Well, you'll like the toast. I bake every bit of bread that's eaten in this house. No store-boughten bread for me. As for the butter . . ."

I followed her out to the kitchen as fast as I could, slipping and sliding over the slick floor. The kitchen smelled wonderful. It had two stoves, four ovens, four broilers and another big fireplace with some more ovens built into that. Almost every burner was going. They came to ten, all told.

"If you'd been up just a little earlier you could have helped me with the goats. Sam used to keep a man on the place to do it but I had to let him go. Lazy, shiftless, never did it right. Goats' milk is wonderful for you —much better than cows'. And my nannies don't smell, either. They never do unless there's a billy around. What are you looking at?"

"The stove—*stoves*. Is all that for breakfast?"

"Good heavens no. I'm making a *cassoulet* for the P.-T.A. Arts and Crafts Fair. I'm president."

"Do you still have kids in school?"

"Oh, my Lord no! I didn't move out here until Sam and Rosemary were full grown. But nobody else seems able to get the school organized right, so I just stepped in and took over myself. I used to teach, you know."

"In school?"

"Night school. The Rowena Platt Satterfield Elementary School. That's P.S. 202 down on the lower East

Side. Mostly foreigners and immigrants just moping around in their dirty tenements. Well, you can bet that I gave them a good shaking up." Safe bet for sure. "I'd give them exactly fifteen minutes and if they hadn't come to class I'd go right to their miserable hovels and *make* them come. Why, in no time at all they were speaking English and hooking rugs and painting and building furniture and all sorts of useful things. And on Sundays I'd go right through their filthy old railroad flats with Dutch Cleanser and disinfectant and a mop and a broom. A lot of them went back to Europe, but you may be certain that they went home changed people." No argument there.

"Wasn't that pretty dangerous, Mrs. Reynolds? I mean isn't that kind of a tough neighborhood for a woman?"

"*Tough?* Well, I should hope to tell you it was! But I took lessons in the art of self-defense."

"Judo? Karate?" I was getting interested.

"We called it jiujitsu in those days. I'm no bigger than a minute, but I'm wiry. Why, one great giant of a Pole came at me one night with a gun and asked for my purse. Well, I didn't have more than a few cents change in it but I certainly wasn't going to be pushed around by some no-good too lazy to go out and do honest labor. Let me tell you, Kerry, I grabbed hold of that big, brawny arm, and threw him over my shoulder and wiped up the streets with him until he begged for mercy."

"What happened?"

"He was in Bellevue Hospital for six months. Broken back. Well, I got to feeling kind of sorry for him, so I'd go to visit him twice a week. He couldn't do anything with his hands because he was paralyzed, but I made him learn the whole Constitution of the United States by heart."

"Where is he now?"

"He died. Right there in Bellevue. But he went out a better citizen than he went in. Excuse me, dear." She opened a huge freezer, dived in and came out with a whole baby pig. It was frozen stiff and sewn crisscross up the stomach in a way that made me think of one of

162

Ga-ga's most businesslike corsets. "Would you like a liver malted milk, dear?"

"I beg pardon?"

"It's for people who don't care for raw liver. You put it in the Waring Blendor with malt, dextrose, goats' milk and orange juice, and give it a spin and there you are. You need filling out."

"No, thank you. I'm not much of a one for sweets."

"Pity."

All the time she was talking she shot around the kitchen like a billiard ball, taking rolls and loaves of bread out of the ovens, stirring messes on top of the stoves, icing a cake and pouring a big pot of slop into something she said was an electric ice-cream freezer. At one time I counted six different electrical appliances going all at once. She really had living down to a science. Over all the whirring and moaning and clicking and buzzing of the cooking machinery I heard sounds upstairs and said, "Thank you for my breakfast, Mrs. Reynolds. I think I'll go up and get dressed now."

When I got to the bedroom the windows were still wide open and Sam, covered with goose flesh, was standing in front of one of them doing a set of exercises that would have killed Steve Reeves. "Good morning, Kerry," he said, "don't mind me. I'll be through in a minute. I work out half an hour every morning." From the roll hanging over the waistband of his pajamas, it didn't seem to me that the exercises did much good. Daddy doesn't do any more than shower and shave and he's got the figure of a greyhound.

After Sam finished, he closed the window, thank God. Then he lit a big blaze in *his* fireplace. There were enough fires burning in that house to heat hell. It was soon so hot that I was almost melting, but Sam didn't notice as he'd gone to sit in the steam room that was built into his shower stall.

By nine o'clock everybody was up and dressed and fighting off Mrs. Reynolds' suggestions of wild rice pancakes with blackstrap molasses. Missy giggled and said, "Jock strap molasses?" and was sent from the table.

Mom and Sam were dressed in riding clothes. Mom looked a little weary, but very snappy in her jodhpurs, Sam was a bit broad in the beam of his breeches, but he kept whacking his boot with a riding crop and talking about how bracing it was to ride across a field of pure white snow.

When Mrs. Reynolds wasn't busy squirting gold paint on a mess of pine cones and milkweed pods ("Rosemary and the girls and I turned out more than five hundred dried arrangements last Christmas and we couldn't *begin* to fill all the orders. With a little competent *help* I could. The buyer at Bonwit Teller's said . . .") or slapping goo on the dining-room table ("This furniture polish is my own formula. I make it up ten gallons at a time on the stove and the dealers are *all* after it. Mr. Montlor in the antique department at Sloane's says . . ."), she was busy goading Mom and Sam onto horseback. "I make Sam ride every day he's out here. He needs the exercise and so do the horses. As for Rosemary, it's all I can do to get her to groom them."

"I have a cold," Rosemary whimpered, wadding her hankie up into a limp ball.

"A *cold?*" Mrs. Reynolds said, as though Rosemary was having a litter of kittens. "Well *this* will fix you up in *no* time." She threw some terrible-looking things (liver?) into the mixer and splashed it around. "Here! Drink this. Then get on with your sachet bags. The buyer at Bamberger's called yesterday."

"Oh, Mother."

"That's the trouble with that Rosemary," Mrs. Reynolds said. She always talked about people as though they weren't right there in the room. "She has no get-up-and-go. I'd hate to think where I'd be today—and you and Sam, too—if I'd just gone lollygagging around when that no-good Reynolds walked out on me. There I was in 1930—the depression—with two children to feed and clothe. And what did I do? With no experience at all I walked right into the billing department at Harcourt, Brace and convinced them that I could handle the job. Fifteen dollars a week. That's all they paid in those days and there were millions out of work who would have taken less. But I started green as grass and inside of two months I'd reorganized the whole billing system, the collections, the textbook discounts—

everything. You won't believe me, my dear, when I tell you . . ."

"Oh, but I *do* believe you," Mom said. She seemed sort of desperate.

"George Vay *begged* me to stay on at least until I reached retirement age, but Sam, here, wouldn't have it."

"Mother, there was no need of you to go out to a job every day."

"A job every day *and* every night. I was telling Kerry, here, how I taught arts and crafts in the adult education movement. *Wasn't* I?"

"Yes, Mrs. Reynolds. You sure were."

"But Mother, why should you go on working now that I'm a partner at . . ."

"Because I *like* to work. I'll work till the day I drop." I wondered when that might be. "I come from working people and I'm proud of it. Now Sam, here, likes these la-di-da things—society, parties, balls, clubs. Oh, he's a worker, too, I'll give him that. Put himself through college and law school. Not Rosemary. Not on your tintype. But now that Sam's such a success he expects me to sit around out here in the country with a lot of shiftless servants robbing us blind . . ."

"Mother, I just thought a nice couple to look after you . . ."

"I'll look after myself, thank you. Rosemary, did the new labels come for the potpourri jars? That's the trouble with people nowadays. No spunk. There wouldn't be all this crime in the world if people would just do one good honest day's . . ."

"Shall we go out and saddle the horses, dear?" Sam said.

"Y-yes. I think so," Mom said.

Mom hadn't ridden since before she got married but she sure did it a lot better than Sam, whose rear end sort of bounced up and down in the saddle. The two mastiffs chased after them and Maxl came out from under the sofa for the first time since he'd been there.

Some kind of spooky-looking women in old house dresses were sitting at the tables in Mrs. Reynolds' workroom doing funny things—pasting labels on jars and mixing up dead flower petals and cloves and like that. Rosemary was going from one to the other sniffling and saying "No, Zelda, not so much lavender," and "That's very pretty, Ethel [sniff], *very.*"

"Don't mind my girls," Mrs. Reynolds said. "They're all from the mental institution down the road. Oh, they're harmless. This is therapy for them. They get a good lunch and a good day's pay—most of it goes to the asylum, of course—but it keeps them in pocket money. Elsie! Don't dawdle so. No wonder they won't let you go back to your baby." Another one of the "girls" let out a giggle and started saying "Backtoyourbabybacktoyourbabybacktoyourbaby" over and over again. The one named Elsie started to cry. "Now you stop that, Pauline! I won't *have* you teasing Elsie."

"There [sniff], there, Elsie," Rosemary said.

I got out of there fast. Scary!

"Well, now that I've got the girls all working happily," Mrs. Reynolds said, charging into the living room with two bowls of dead weeds (copper colored this time), "maybe you little folks would like to take a spin with me. I've got to leave these pamphlets at the League of Women Voters and try to get a man from Princeton to talk to our Planned Parenthood group and . . ."

Well, that's the kind of weekend it was. Mrs. Reynolds covered about a million miles of New Jersey in her little car. She dragged us through the Arts and Crafts Fair at the schoolhouse and showed everybody there how to do whatever it was he was doing better. She gave a cocktail party for about fifty people after that and then dinner for twelve on Saturday night.

On Sunday Mrs. Reynolds read out the letters to the editor in the New York *Times* and the *Herald Tribune* (she had written the longest ones in each newspaper) and then dragged us all off to church. It wasn't a fancy church like the kind Gran believes in but one where people stand up and say whatever happens to be on their minds. There was plenty on Mrs. Reynolds' mind, believe me, and she had some real cool ideas about how God could run the world twice as well in half the time. Two people from CORE came for lunch and Mrs. Reynolds told them exactly what it was like to be a Negro. At the same time she finished off the rug

166

she was weaving, cooked a delicious lunch of venison (which she had shot right on the property) and a soufflé made of her own white raspberries and explained about Rosemary's marriage that Mrs. Reynolds had had to step in and break up, while Rosemary sat huddled in sweaters and sniffled over her knitting.

Mom was looking a little tense and about three o'clock she said that she thought we'd better start back to town before it snowed. Mrs. Reynolds said, "Nonsense, my dear. Snow? Impossible." Then she got out something called *The Old Farmer's Almanac* and took Mom to look at an antique barometer and proved how it wasn't going to snow. By then it was snowing so hard that Sam said we'd *have* to leave or maybe even be marooned. Nobody wanted that to happen.

Missy and I said thank you, the way we were taught to, and Mom said, "I can't tell you what the weekend has been like, Mrs. Reynolds. I do hope that whenever you're in New York . . ."

"*New York?* Never! I leave that to Sam and Rosemary. Too much hustle and bustle for a homebody like me." Then she loaded us down with a bushel basket of relish and chowchow and white raspberry jam—one each of everything she put up to sell to classy delicatessens—and kissed us all good-by. As we were rolling down the warm dry driveway, I saw her hotfooting it out to the spring to see to her watercress beds. Then both Missy and I fell sound asleep.

Later that night Mom called us to her room and we all got into her big bed. She looked as tired as I felt—and we really hadn't done *anything*. "Did you have a nice weekend?" she asked.

Missy got that tight-lipped stubborn look, so I lied for both of us. "Yes, Mom." We'd had a lousy time and so had Mom. But, like all grownups, she would have been sore if I'd told the truth.

"Sam and I are going to be married," Mom said.

"Why?" Missy asked.

"Why, because we love each other, darling."

"Did he ask you?" Really, that Missy!

"Well, of course he asked me. You need a father."

"We've already got a father," Missy said.

"I mean a real father."

"Isn't Daddy our real father?" (Missy's at the age when kids all think they're adopted. There's nothing you can do about that except wait.)

"Darling, I mean a full-time father who's always here."

"Daddy was always here—except when he was working—until you told him to . . ."

"Children," Mom sighed, "you're tired and . . ."

"I am *not* tired!" Missy said, right on schedule.

"Well, *I'm* tired," Mom said. "Exhausted. We'll talk about it some other time when we all feel a little fresher."

But of course we never did.

Ten

Was our line ever busy during the next week! I can just touch a telephone and almost know whether to pick it up or not, and the extension in the kitchen was usually too hot to handle. The few times I did manage to listen in, very quietly and practically by accident, I could hear Mom and Daddy being very calm and collected and businesslike. I never was able to tune in on a whole conversation but I did get a few odd bits. Like one time Daddy was saying, "You know that you haven't got a leg to stand on, but I won't fight it. What's the use? I didn't marry you to hold you prisoner. As for financial arrangements, you can have whatever you think is fair—that I can afford."

Then Mom said, "That's very good of you, but I don't want alimony and I don't want a settlement. I don't admire these women who take one husband for everything they can get when Number Two is just around the corner."

"Then you really are getting married again?"

"As soon as I can. I don't even expect you to pay for the divorce."

"Well," Daddy sighed, "since I don't want it and you do, I guess that's only fair. I do expect to support my own children—*entirely*—and I'd like to see them as often as . . ."

I burped. Too much Coke.

"Kerry!" Mom shouted. "Kerrington? Are you listening in again?"

Well, since I was, I spun the dial and made a lot of whistling sounds.

"Damned telephone company!" Daddy growled.

"They're so busy fixing it so you can dial Yokohama by mistake that they can't even look after the local service." Then he started clicking the phone and while he was doing that I signed off. Roger and over!

Another time Mom was saying, "Sam thinks that Nevada is the best place. It's only six weeks and we can get it on mental cruelty or some bogus thing like that."

"Why bother with all that?" Daddy said. "You could get it in six minutes in New York. I'll be happy to crawl in with some 'mysterious blonde' while you and the detectives batter down the door. It's no phonier than mental cruelty in Reno." He couldn't have been talking about Miss Glen because during March she was a redhead.

"Yes, I know all that," Mom said. "But that kind of thing is so sordid it's sure to get into some tabloid. It wouldn't help your career and I don't want the children thinking that their father is an adult [?]."

"Just a beast?"

"Oh, come on now! Don't take that tone. There's no point in either one of us being cross and sullen. I'd like us to remain friends if only for the sake of the children. And I want you and Sam to be friends, too."

"That'll be the day."

"You'll like him."

"I adore him already."

"Now, dar . . . I mean, you and Sam are going to have to make arrangements about support and visiting and all the rest of those details. It's going to be a lot easier if we can all be civilized—especially for the children."

"I suppose you're right."

"So why don't you come for dinner on Friday night and we can all have a nice, down-to-earth discussion?"

"I can hardly wait," Daddy said. Then I heard Lulu coming and had to hang up.

On Friday Lulu got us all slicked up and we were waiting in the living room with Mom five minutes ahead of time. Mom was looking real sharp but awfully fidgety. The living room was full of flowers and Mom switched all the vases around and then around again and then ended up with them exactly the way they had been. Then she decided the lamps were too bright and went around turning them down until it was finally so dark she said, "It looks like a funeral parlor." So the lamps all went brighter, then dimmer, and in the middle of it all the doorbell rang and Mom jumped a foot.

Sam and Daddy had arrived at exactly the same time in the same elevator load and there was a lot of "After you," and "Oh, no, after you," at the front door. Finally they came in together and almost got wedged in the doorway. I had to laugh. So did they, but not like they thought it was all that funny.

There was kind of an uncomfortable thing about which man was going to mix the drinks. I mean it was Daddy's apartment, but it was soon going to be Sam's and they'd both been used to taking care of the bar. They probably never would have solved it if I hadn't said, "Allow me." Let me tell you, I didn't stint. I thought it would help to relax them.

Finally dinner was announced and what do you know if Daddy and Sam didn't both head for the same chair and all but knock their heads together. Mom settled everything by putting me in that chair and seating the men opposite one another so they could glare good and proper when each thought the other wasn't looking.

Dinner was very good. Too good, really. And since everybody started out saying nothing, Mom took over the talking department and gabbed away like she was going to go deaf and dumb any moment.

She kept saying things like "Just imagine, tomorrow at this time I'll be in Reno . . ." and "When Sam and I are married . . ." like they were naughty and she was being real daring to mention such things at all. It kind of reminded me of Missy when she tries to see how many times she can say "damn" without getting slapped down.

But when tactful old Missy said, "Daddy, are you going to marry Miss Glen?" Mom dropped her fork and said, *"What?"*

Daddy only said, "I don't know, Missy. I haven't made any plans," and the dinner went on.

After the coffee, Mom said, "Now your father and

Sam and I want to talk, so I suggest that you children say good night now."

Missy had a big to-do about tomorrow's not being a school day and Mom said it was almost nine o'clock and we were going to have a big day of it because of Daddy's taking us to the circus, exetera, exetera, exetera, so the grownups went back to The Room and I wound up in bed with my listening glass.

Well, let me tell you, they were all three being as civilized as Billy-be-damned. But while they were saying things like "Whatever is most convenient for you . . ." and "There's no need for any of us to be selfish . . ." and "We can all be counted on to do the decent thing . . ." and "The children are what really matter . . ." I got the feeling that everybody was thinking most about good old Number One and underneath their nice manners they were all ready to slug it out.

Have you ever heard yourself being passed around like a box of candy? It's some experience! And since the conversation was all about Missy and I—I mean Missy and *me*—I was very interested in finding out exactly what the plans were.

It would be best if we lived with Mom—and Sam, of course. Oh, Daddy agreed with that. He sounded like he was trying to sound nice about it. Mom was a good mother. Daddy was to have us weekends, spring vacation (Mom got us for Christmas), six weeks each summer and at other times by appointment.

Sam said, "Wait a minute, please. Not so fast. I want to get all this down in writing."

Mom said, "Really, Sam! The legal mind at work! Can't we just do this like decent, civilized human beings?"

"Oh, I know. Everybody laughs at us lawyers. But when people are in trouble where do they turn for help? To us. Sentiment aside, divorce and marriage are strictly legal matters—just like any other business agreement."

I'd always figured that love had something to do with it.

"I suppose you're right," Daddy said, "but it seems kind of cold-blooded to carve the kids up like a side of beef." Brrrrrrrr!

172

"I'm trying to do what's best for the little folks," Sam said, "I . . ."

"Sam, dear," Mom said, "would you mind not calling them 'little folks'? It makes me think that they're elves or midgets."

"Sorry, dear. But I feel as though they were my own two children."

"Well, they're not," Daddy said.

"I realize that. Of course. But we must all think of the lit- . . . of the children." So that led to Daddy's will, two trust funds, two insurance policies, our living expenses and school fees, not to exceed, blah, blah, blah. It's all so complicated that I'm beginning to think a lot of married couples stay together just because it's easier than getting divorced. But man oh man, were they ever being civilized. And Mom was pushing that the hardest. "Sam, I realize that in case something should happen to me, it's best to have this all down in black and white. But I think we can all trust each other—at least I hope we can."

"I'm sure we can, dearest," Sam said. "These are just the preliminary formalities. I've already been in touch with your lawyer and he . . ."

"Yes, he told me," Daddy said.

"And I think you'll agree that you're getting off very lightly."

"Getting off *what* very lightly? I got married for better or worse and I wasn't shopping around for bargains."

"Yes, I understand that, but you also married a *lady*. A lot of wives would try to put the bite on you for everything they could get. You're not exactly a poor man, you know."

"I'm not a rich one, either."

"You're only being asked to give up this apartment and . . ."

"And my wife and my children and a few other things. It's a real deal! And now it's all set up for you to move in and take over."

"Ex-excuse me," Mom said. I could hear her running down the hall and then her bedroom door slammed.

So Mom took off for Reno, Nevada, for the next

six weeks and we were left with Lulu and Maxl and school and Dr. Epston and a whole gang of people who decided to heap love on us whenever they thought of it.

It was quite the social whirl and sometimes we were booked up for so far in advance we couldn't handle any more reservations. Gran had us to dinner once a week. Ga-ga took us to lunch almost every Sunday and once to a fashion show, for cripes sake. Miss Glen asked us to tea three times with Daddy, only once it was Mexican cocoa and once it was Viennese coffee and the time it really *was* tea it was some minty mess from Morocco called *atây* (echhhh!) that was so sweet I nearly threw up. And even Aunt Liz got off her duff long enough to charge dinner and a swim at the River Club to her mother's account.

Daddy was very busy being a father—telephoning us every morning, having dinner with us two or three nights a week and spoiling us all he could. Sam was also practicing real hard to be our father. *He* called every day and dragged us around to the most babyish movies you can imagine. Once he took us out to this real swanky place called Le Pavillon (that means the pavilion in French) with his sister, Rosemary. The evening was more expensive than fun. Rosemary looked kind of dowdy under her fruit hat and she still had her cold. She had three Martinis and when Sam said, "Rosemary, do you think you really should?" she whimpered, "Oh, yes, Sam. I can't tell you what a long winter it's been out there with Mother and the girls."

She drank quite a lot of wine with her dinner and when I was being extra polite and said, "May I please have the salt, Miss Reynolds?" Rosemary whined, "Don't call me Miss Reynolds! My name is Mrs. Jackson!"

"Now, Rosemary," Sam said, looking kind of worried, "what Mother did was all for the best."

"Best for *who?*" Rosemary said. Then she broke into tears and went tottering off to the ladies' john and stayed and stayed and stayed until old Sambo had to send the hat-check girl in to get her. Well, I never said it was much of an evening, did I?

But that night was a ball compared to the big stag

party I went to with Sam and old H. A. It took place at their club on the night when Daddy and Missy were at Father and Daughter Evening at Miss Farthingale's, so Sam took extra pity on me and said, "Well, Kerry, we'll have a real he-man's outing together." Honestly, I'd much rather have stayed home with Lulu and Maxl, who are at least entertaining.

People have told me what beautiful manners H. A. has for so long that it's easier to believe it than to hear it again. But if somebody asked me to eat with him (even if it was my club, too) I wouldn't order the waiters around and run up a bar bill like the national debt and practically tell my host what fork to use. I mean I haven't got any gripe against Sam, but H. A. is a real crud.

The club is a real tomb and for a place that's supposed to be the best men's club in New York, they serve food that the St. Barnaby's lunchroom would be ashamed of. I know now why Daddy's been able to resist joining. And that H. A.! At the end of dinner he looked across this empty dining room at a couple of youngish men who were laughing and carrying on like they might possibly be having a halfway good time and then he said, "Really, it's getting so that they'll take *anyone* into the club nowadays." Poor old Sam turned bright red. It occurred to me that he was a brand-new member, too. I know now where Missy inherited her tact as well as her perfect teeth.

Then the two of them got onto putting *me* up for membership, for cripes sake. Sam said, "As soon as I'm Kerry's stepfather I'm going to send his name in so that when he's twenty-one . . ." Then charming H. A. said, "But Sam, since he's the great-great-grandson of one of the founders, a new member's word isn't going to mean nearly as much as . . ." blah, blah, blah. Well, they can put my name up for Sing Sing for all I care, but when I'm twenty-one, *I'll* do the deciding.

Poor old Sam. He must be a real glutton for punishment. After we dropped H. A. off at Gran's and he staggered out of the cab without even saying so much as "Thanks," Sam sighed almost like he was in love

175

with the slob and said, "There are mighty few gentlemen like your uncle left in New York nowadays."

"Isn't that great!" I said, but Sam was off on one of his fine-traditions-of-the-past kicks again and he wasn't even listening.

Then all of a sudden it was Maundy Thursday (that name kills me) and school was out and we were heading for Florida with Daddy and Miss Glen. With Daddy and Miss Glen and practically half the population of New York.

First of all there was Jane, that big roughneck who used to slam out of Miss Glen's apartment every time we were invited there. She was a photographer, I found out, and she showed up at the airport in the old canvas trench coat with about a million cameras and light meters and like that hanging around her neck. Jane didn't seem any gladder to see us than usual and she and Miss Glen were kind of snapping and snarling at each other. "For Christ's sake, Dorie, where are those dumb broads?" "Please, Jane, I'm having trouble enough trying to get the clothes weighed and put aboard. You're the photographer. The least you could do is to see that the models . . ." "That's right. I'm only the photographer. You're the big lady editor . . ." exetera, exetera, exetera.

Finally, two models showed up. They were called Clover and Burma. They didn't seem to have any last names. They also didn't seem to have any brains and I didn't happen to think they were even very pretty, but they smiled a lot and kind of posed every time they stood up or sat down. Clover was very blond—almost white-haired—and skinny as a toothpick. The one called Burma was dark and looked like what Lulu calls a "yalla gal." It turned out that she was a real U.N. —part Chinese and Irish and Cherokee Indian and Hungarian and I forget what all else. Crazy!

Miss Glen was going nuts checking lists and weighing in tons of big canvas suitcases all marked "Fragile" and "Handle With Care" and "Do Not Crush" and haggling with the ticket clerk about the charges for overweight luggage. "Now if Bud would only come," she kept saying.

176

"Serves you right," Jane growled. "*I* never wanted him. More trouble than any of the dames, always late and he's lousy from the left."

"Now, Jane."

They were announcing our plane and Missy and I were sure we were going to miss it when something that looked like the captain of the Yale team came charging in. Gee, but he was big, with broad shoulders and a square jaw and eyes that were so blue they were almost purple. Every woman in the place stopped and just stared at him. Then he opened his mouth. "Dorian, ducky, I'm simply *covered* with shame. I overslept."

"Who with this time?" Jane said.

"Now, Janie," he said. He was introduced to everybody as just plain Bud. He also had forty bucks' worth of overweight luggage and Miss Glen nearly hit the ceiling. "But, Dorian, you said beach things—so I brought twelve pairs of trunks and some odd shirts . . ."

"I'll bet they're odd," Jane said.

". . . and evening clothes—three different dinner jackets; so I'll look different in the backgrounds . . ."

"You'll look different all right."

"Jane! And then you said sports things. So I brought . . ." He didn't have time to finish the list because they started hustling us out toward the plane. But just as we got to the place where they check the tickets, Bud happened to bang the case he was carrying against a post. It flew open and I've never seen such stuff as fell out of it—there were curlers and hair spray and all kinds of bottles and jars of make-up rolling every which way. "Can I help you, madam?" a man said.

"Oh, be still, Mary!" Bud said.

The flight down to Palm Beach wasn't much. Bud and Jane sat together and bickered all the way. Clover and Burma mostly kept dragging mirrors out of their purses to look at their faces. They had kind of an argument about how many calories were in the lunch the hostess served, but it didn't come to anything.

Getting to Palm Beach was only half the battle. After we'd landed and all of the dresses and bathing suits and like that were checked off, the eight of us and the luggage were loaded into three taxicabs and driven from West Palm Beach to just plain Palm Beach and then down to a dock where kind of a big speedboat was waiting to take us to Brigand's Bay out in the Skeleton Keys—some sandy little islands just sitting in the ocean south of Palm Beach.

By then Miss Glen had relaxed a little and since she and her friend Jane weren't speaking (and since the models didn't seem to be able to talk at all), she turned on the charm hot and heavy for Daddy and us. "You'll simply adore Brigand's Bay—absolutely unspoiled. These dear friends of mine, Jennifer and Wade Moultrie, took over the old Cunningham estate and they've had a perfectly wild success . . ." blah, blah, blah.

We skimmed past some desert islands and pretty soon we pulled up to a rickety dock with a big sign that said "Reserved for Guests of Brigand's Bay." I figured that there weren't many other guests because the only thing tied up to the dock was an old rowboat half full of water.

Standing on the dock were a very sun-tanned man in white shorts and a bright orange shirt and two people all dressed to go some place with a whole lot of suitcases.

"Dorian, honey!" the man in the shorts said with kind of a sleepy Southern accent. "Welcome to Brigand's Bay!"

"Wade, darling!"

Then the woman in the dress and the hat piped up, "And if you've got any sense, you'll turn right around and go back to Palm Beach."

"Please, Mrs. Warrington."

"Don't you Mrs. Warrington *me,* Mis-ter Moultrie. And when I get back to Detroit I'm going to tell the man at Cook's just what kind of a place you're running —or *not* running. In all the years we've been coming to Florida I've never . . ."

"Now, Ella," the dressed-up man said.

"Don't you Ella me, Chester. Of all the dumps I've ever seen . . ."

"Come, Ella. The boat's waiting."

"Well, I'm glad of that. It can't get me away from here fast enough. And as for that outrageous bill, I'm going to have Cook's . . ."

There was a whole lot of confusion and loading and unloading of luggage while everybody talked at once and got introduced to Mr. Wade Moultrie, the owner, and pretty soon the other guests were on their way back to Palm Beach and we were left standing on the dock.

"Terrible common scold," Wade Moultrie said. "Not the class of people Jennifer and I like to have here at all."

"She seemed frightfully *outré*," Miss Glen said. "Well darling, here we all are. I'm perishing to see Jennifer. Now about the bags . . ."

"Dorian, honey," Mr. Moultrie drawled, "I can't tell you how sick we are about it, but just yesterday we lost both of our bellboys. It's so hard to get decent help down here."

"Oh, that's all right, Wade. With all these able-bodied men . . ."

"Dorian," Bud said, "I simply can't. You see I've got this trick back and if I so much as try to lift a . . ." The big ox!

"Don't worry," Daddy said. "I'll manage." So Daddy and I walloped all the bags up the hill to the house.

Well, Brigand's Bay was too big to call a house but also too small to call a hotel. If you filled every nook and cranny—and there were a lot of them—the place would hold about forty. But from some of the things Mr. Moultrie's wife had to say while we were there, I figured that the eight of us were about the biggest crowd they'd ever had. The place was put up way, way back in the twenties for some rich millionaire by this famous kook who built a whole lot of terrible Spanish houses around Palm Beach. Daddy winced the first time he saw it and it wasn't from the weight of the suitcases. It had tile floors and a tile roof and walls like a home-iced cake and all kinds of nutty staircases—both indoors and out—and like that.

Miss Glen kept saying, "Charming, charming, charming," while Mr. Moultrie kept saying yes, it did have a lot of charm. Jane said it reminded her of Loew's Barcelona back in her home town and Miss Glen gave Jane a glance like she'd caught her whistling "Twist and Shout" at the Philharmonic. Pretty soon Mr. Moultrie's wife appeared from the gloom and there was a lot of Dorian darling and Jennifer darling.

Jennifer Moultrie was blond except at the part and looked kind of hard-boiled. But I'd learned by then that the look was what Miss Glen called "utterly, utterly smart." This Jennifer smiled a lot, almost like you'd pressed a button to make her do it, but when she turned off the grin, there were always two little lines between her eyebrows. The models (male and female) all went off to their rooms to change their clothes (even when they weren't supposed to be doing it for a living, those three were *always* changing their clothes) and we all sat down in the living room (*"Sala grande,* honey," Mr. Moultrie told me) to make social noises. And boy, could Wade Moultrie ever make them! You couldn't name anybody who was rich or famous any place in the world who wasn't real buddy-buddy with him. "Oh, yes, we were in school at Ashville togethah. . . . He was a class behind me at V.M.I. . . . Ah knew him very well in London. . . . They had the villa next to mine on Capri. . . . She was one of mah sistah's dearest friends, honey." He even claimed to know H. A., but when Missy said he was our uncle Mr. Moultrie didn't mention him again—thank God.

Wade Moultrie said that besides the great, great pleasure of having Dorian-honey with them for a nice, long visit, Brigand's Bay could certainly use the publicity. Then Jennifer Moultrie said that wasn't all Brigand's Bay could use. Then Wade said that it hadn't been too easy getting the Skeleton Keys started as a "truly exclusive resort area." But everybody understood that these things took time. Everybody understood. And everybody understood that you couldn't take just *anyone* as a guest. Everybody understood that, too.

Mrs. Moultrie was up and down a lot, answering the telephone and rustling up what little help there was, but Mr. Moultrie was being a full-time host, all charm and smiles and conversation, mixing drinks for people and telling about the great plans he had for the Skeleton Keys and Brigand's Bay.

From what the two of them had to say to the grownups (they hardly spoke to Missy and me at all,

180

but we're used to that) the Moultries had been in quite a lot of businesses over the years and somehow none of them had ever quite panned out but it was always somebody else's fault.

After a while Daddy said why didn't he and Missy and I all go swimming. So we did. It was great. I mean we were on our vacation and we were there with Daddy and even if the food was lousy (very pretty to look at, but awful to eat) and the place kind of spooky, it was fun. At least it was interesting.

The next morning I was woken up by a kind of droning sound in the bathroom that reminded me of Mrs. Reynolds and her floor waxer. When I looked in, there was Bud (he had the room next to mine), all muscles and brawn and like toilet paper rolls in his hair, shaving his chest with a lady's electric razor. That big hulk had so much junk stowed away in the bathroom that I could hardly find my toothbrush in the mess. He gave me one of his big, beautiful smiles and said it was a godsend having me next door and please rub Bain de Soleil on his back while he "did" his teeth. Then he coated them with some kind of white paint, for cripes sake, and started going to work on his eyes. He put on three coats of some stuff called Out of Line that took away the little wrinkles he had from flashing his famous smile. He pressed his lashes into some kind of curler and then put dark stuff on them and on his eyebrows. Next came his hair—first taking out the curlers, then fussing away at it with a special brush and comb and squirting it with a spray can. By that time the sun was getting warm and he was out on the roof with a timer tanning himself on all four sides. I guess he's a very famous model. Around Father's Day I counted six different pictures of Bud in a magazine with child models giving him pajamas and cartons of cigarettes and cigars and underwear (but not the kind he actually wears that flattens your stomach) and stuff like that. But if kids could see what this father is *really* like (Bud isn't even married) they'd all save their allowances to buy dear old dad a home-permanent-wave kit.

As far as Miss Glen was concerned the real

reason for the trip was to take pictures of Clover and Burma in bathing suits and summer dresses and like that. So the photographing started in real earnest down on the beach that very morning, with Mr. Moultrie lolling around in a bikini being charming. I don't know how good of a photographer Jane is considered, but she sure was a temperamental one, trudging around in old khaki pants and snapping and snarling at everyone in sight—especially Miss Glen. There were about fifty different bathing suits to shoot and it always took Clover and Burma quite a time to get every hair in place ("in place" was usually hanging down in their eyes like mine) and every eyelash going the right way. But it always took Bud even longer and he was just kind of out of focus in the background for atmosphere. My job was to hold a big tin reflector and from the way Jane cussed and swore at me you'd think *I* was working for their crummy magazine. Once Daddy even said, "Jane, remember that Kerry is only ten and this *is* his vacation." Boy, the look she gave him! And then Daddy gave it right back.

Half the time the reflector wasn't doing any good anyhow because Bud was standing in front of it flexing his muscles and admiring his reflection. "Wade, do my eyes look bloodshot? Is my nose getting red? Jane, can you hold it until I get my hair right?" For cripes sake, Clover and Burma were about the vainest two dames I've ever seen in my life, but they were nothing compared to Bud.

Finally Jane wanted a shot of the girls in the water —not far enough in so that the bathing suits would get wet, naturally—with Bud a bit farther out looking like a fairly fuzzy Greek god. Well, you'd think Jane was asking Bud to get into boiling oil. He asked about sharks and undertow and I don't know what all. When everybody promised him that it was perfectly safe (for cripes sake, even Missy had been in and out of the ocean about a million times), he went tiptoeing out waist deep shivering and shaking like it was the Arctic Sea.

"Is this far enough, Jane?"

"Little farther, Bud."

"Careful, Bud, honey," Mr. Moultrie called. "It drops off right sharply about . . ."

And just then Bud went down like an anchor. "Help!" he called as his head bobbed up, and then he disappeared again. And do you suppose any of those slobs could do anything about it? The women all stood on the shore and screamed while Mr. Moultrie said, "We had to let the lifeguard go, honey. It's just impossible to get good help nowadays."

Daddy plunged in fully dressed, fished up Bud, who was thrashing around so bad that Daddy had to knock him out before he dragged him back to the shore. Bud just lay there, all muscles, looking like the dead All-American Boy—only with his eye make-up a little smudged. His first words were, "M-my hair . . ." Some athlete!

Mr. Moultrie, who hadn't even bothered to get his feet wet when the poor spaz was out there drowning, was suddenly all attention and loving care. "Bud, honey, let me help you back to the house. Man, you gave me such a fright."

"Thanks, Wade," Bud whimpered and stood up like some kind of wounded gladiator, carefully sucking in his stomach.

"Here, honey, just lean on me," Mr. Moultrie said. Then there was a terrible scream of pain. Bud had stepped on a Portuguese man-of-war. And that was the end of the shooting for that day.

There wasn't much to do around Brigand's Bay, fashionable as it was supposed to be. There was kind of a weedy, overgrown tennis court, but there was no net, no tennis balls and the two warped old rackets that Wade Moultrie had needed restringing. The same went for the badminton. Mr. Moultrie messed up my hair and said, "Honey, next season you're going to see four championship tennis courts out here. The pro I hired this year was just no good. I had to let him go." So Missy and I ended up with most of a croquet set —like out here at Gran's.

Mrs. Moultrie managed to keep busy as a bird dog, always smiling except when she thought no one was looking. She was on the go all day long, helping the maids set tables and tidy up the rooms; dealing with the cook (who quit while we were there); arranging flowers; writing out the menus in her fancy penmanship; and saying mysterious things on the phone like "Mr. Moultrie is away, but I know that he mailed the check to you last week." As for Mr. Moultrie, he hardly ever turned a hand at anything more than mixing a drink, although after Bud got stung by the man-of-war, Mr. Moultrie did take sort of an interest and insisted on carrying Bud's trays to his room and keeping him company most of the time. I thought it was kind of nice of him—Bud being such a boring dope —but Mrs. Moultrie didn't act like she was any too pleased about it.

Meantime the picture-taking went right on, with me holding the reflector and getting yelled at by that big, tough Jane. To me a dress is a dress, but to all of them it was a matter of life or death. The only thing that was at all interesting was to see how absolutely one hundred and one per cent phony the whole thing was. I mean you see these fancy pictures in magazines with everybody looking like royalty and I guess nobody realizes that the dresses are only pressed where they show and all pinned up the back to make them fit like the models' skins. I mean like without my telling you right here and now, who could open up the July issue of that magazine and see those three mental re-tards dining on the terrace by moonlight (it happened to be 11:00 A.M. in the morning) and know that that big muscle man Bud had one bare foot soaking in a tub of Epsom salts while he whined about running out of nail polish and see Burma lifting her wine glass (full of cold tea) to Clover—both of them grinning like apes—and realize that they'd just had a terrible row about which one got to wear the most fake diamonds and that they'd only stopped chomping on their gum long enough for Jane to snap the pictures? In the year-end report from St. Barnaby's the Head wrote, "Kerry is alert, intelligent and precocious"—I guess that's supposed to be good—"but distressingly blasé and totally lacking in the beautiful illusions of youth." That's bad. But I mean any slob ought to be able to know what's real and what's fake when it's put there right in front of his nose, for cripes sake. And it didn't take me long to get the idea that everybody at Brigand's Bay, except for Daddy, was just as phony as a nine-dollar bill.

The photographing was supposed to last for just three days—one day for bathing suits, one for regular dresses and the last for evening dresses. Except for Bud's practically drowning and carrying on about his sting like it was a shark bite, everything went off just the way Miss Glen had arranged it. She was a pretty sharp planner, I'll say that for her. But at lunchtime on the third day, a real breeze started up. *Breeze?* It was so strong it sent the tablecloths to flapping and even knocked over one of Mrs. Moultrie's artistic centerpieces, spilling water all over Clover's scrawny lap.

"Jennifer, darling," Miss Glen said, looking up at the sky like maybe God hadn't been paying attention when she laid out the shooting schedule, "you *don't* think it's going to rain?"

Mrs. Moultrie didn't bother to smile, for a change. In fact she frowned even harder. "I—I don't know, Dorian darling. The equinoctial storms . . ."

"I'm real scared of storms, doll," Burma said.

"Nonsense, honey," Mr. Moultrie said. "There *are* no storms in the Skeleton Keys. Oh, maybe a little rain in September, but in the spring . . ." A gust of wind came along that sent all the doors in Brigand's Bay to slamming and whatever our weather expert was going to say got drowned out in the banging and crashing.

"Well, by Christ, I know one thing we can do," Jane said. "And that's to get some good wind shots of those long summer dresses down on the beach."

"My hair!" all three models said at once.

"Oh, that's a marvelous idea, Jane!" Miss Glen said. "Better than any old studio electric fan." It sure was. The clouds went scooting by about a hundred miles an hour so that sometimes the beach was bright as could be and other times almost pitch black. While the sand flew and the models complained, Jane bawled out orders like Captain Bligh and one gust was so strong that it knocked me and the reflector flat. "Thrilling!

185

Thrilling! Thrilling!" Miss Glen kept crying and it did look kind of exciting with the waves crashing in and the palm trees bent almost double and the girls' big, filmy skirts flying all over the place.

"I've simply got to call New York and tell Monica to give us an extra six pages for these shots," Miss Glen said. But she was out of luck. The telephone wires had already been knocked out. "I've *got* to call Monica. The Managing Editorship will be open next month and there won't be any question about my not getting it when she sees what I've done."

"What *you've* done?" Jane said.

"I've got to go into Palm Beach and call—or at least wire. When's the next boat?"

"You can't go out in any boat in weather like this, Dorian," Daddy said.

"There's the grocery boat at four—if they can make it at all," Mrs. Moultrie said. "But, darling, I doubt that they'll . . ."

"And isn't that divine! Here it comes now!" Miss Glen said.

"Dorian, you can't," Daddy said.

"Honey, this is no storm. It's just a breeze from . . ."

"Dorie, you're outta your mind," Jane said.

"I'm going! I've got to. My whole career . . ."

"Then I'm coming with you," Daddy said, "if Jennifer will keep an eye on the kids."

"Come along, then. Darlings, we'll be back in time for dinner!"

"Hey! Wait a . . ." But Jane might just as well have been yelling at the wind.

"My hair's all full of sand," Bud said. "I've got to get indoors and shampoo it."

"Let me give you a hand, Bud, honey," Mr. Moultrie said.

Then it started to rain.

I don't know if you've ever been stuck in a place where it's not supposed to rain but it does—like Florida or East Haddock. Well, let me tell you, there's nothing gloomier or colder or damper. And this wasn't just any April shower, like Mr. Moultrie was saying. The wind was howling, trees were snapping in two like

186

matchsticks, the waves were coming all the way up to the terrace and the rain was pounding against the windows so hard that I thought sure the glass would break. It was kind of exciting but I didn't like to think of Daddy out in any open boat in a storm like that.

Indoors, with the lamps lighted and a big fire going it was cozy enough, but still kind of weird—especially when one big blow swept all the furniture off the terrace.

Bud wasn't the only one who'd washed the sand out of his scalp. So had Clover and Burma and pretty soon they were all down in the living room—excuse me, *Sala grande*—having tea with rum in it and bickering over Bud's hair drier. That is, until the hair drier went off and so did all the lights.

"Cantcha do something about the lights, doll?" Burma whined.

"Honey, it's just a little windy spell. They'll be back on directly."

"But, Wade, I get so scared in a storm."

To make Burma feel better, Clover told a long story about another model who was a friend of a friend of hers and had got struck by lightning and killed while she was posing in raincoats. It didn't comfort Burma much. From then on she huddled up blubbering on the sofa and every time there was a clap of thunder she'd scream until Missy finally said, "Oh, stop being so babyish. We've got a dog that's smarter than you are." That sent Burma off to her room in hysterics while the rest of us sat around in the candlelight waiting for Daddy and Miss Glen to come back.

Miss Glen had said by dinnertime, which gave her a lot of leeway as there wasn't any dinner. The stove had gone out with the lights and so had the refrigerator and the freezer and the water heater and just about everything else. Jane had given up tea and was just drinking plain rum and every couple of minutes she'd march to the telephone and click it like crazy and then cuss a lot into it—not that there was anybody at the other end to hear her—and pretty soon she got over being sore at Miss Glen and, for some reason I could never quite figure out, the whole crazy boat trip got to be Daddy's fault.

The junky old place was so drafty that the candles kept going out almost as fast as Mrs. Moultrie could light them. The fire finally burned out and it never could be relighted because all the wood was kept outside and it was soaked clear through.

By then it was good and dark and everybody was drunk and kind of quarrelsome except for Mrs. Moultrie. About nine o'clock she took us out to the kitchen and gave us some milk and sandwiches and cookies. Then she said, "You children aren't to worry about your father. I'm sure he's all right. So I want you to go upstairs and go to bed and keep away from that riffraff in the living room."

"You mean the *Sala grande?*" Missy said.

"I mean that hog wallow full of swine," she said. Gosh but grownups can be odd! Here they were talking with "honey" and "darling" and "dearest" every other word and all hating each other's guts. I mean if you don't like somebody, why bother?

We said good night, which I thought Daddy would want us to do whether he was here or not, but nobody paid much attention. Mr. Moultrie was reading Bud's palm off in one corner and Jane was telling Clover exactly what was wrong with her face. "Whadaya mean I oughta have my nose done, Jane? I've already had it done twice," Clover sobbed.

I tried to find my toothbrush in the dark, but with all of Bud's cosmetics it was hopeless. It took me a long time to get to sleep with all that wind and rain and the ocean pounding away and it seemed like the minute I did doze off I was awake again. This time there was a terrible uproar going on in Bud's room. Both Mr. and Mrs. Moultrie were in there. Bud's wounded foot, I thought at first, but I guess not—at least not from all the yelling and carrying on. Even over the noise of the storm I could hear Mrs. Moultrie screaming—not everything, but enough to figure that she was plenty sore about *something*. "Give up a good job in New York . . . follow you around from one bankrupt business to the next . . . work like a slob from dawn to dusk . . . minute I turn my back . . . sneaking off to some cheap little hustler . . . insulted under my very nose . . . sick and tired of it, Wade Moultrie . . . phony Southern aristocrat . . . I understand plenty . . . two eyes in my head . . . far as I'm concerned the bank can have this rotten island and you with it . . . no more 'Now Jenny, honey' for me . . . getting out of this pigsty on the first boat . . ." Well, I don't know what she was so miffed about, but I guessed that Mr. Moultrie had done something that didn't please her.

When that commotion was finally over—and it lasted better than half an hour—Missy was at my door. She was crying. "Can I sleep with you, Kerry?"

"Oh, I suppose so. Why?"

"I'm scared."

"Of what? You've seen it rain before. Remember what you told that kookie Burma about Maxl in a storm?"

"It's not the storm."

"Then what is it?"

"S-suppose D-daddy should drown and . . . and Mom would get killed coming home from Reno and . . . and . . . and we'd be orphans."

"For cripes sake, Missy. Is that all you can think about? You're always saying you're an orphan anyway."

"Y-yes. But then we'd *really* be orphans and . . . and they'd send us to this big home with a fence all around it and we'd . . . we'd have to wear you-oo-oo-oo-ni-forms and . . ."

"Missy! We have to wear uniforms anyway. At least the Miss Farthingale ones are . . ."

"But not over weekends we don't. Kerry, I . . ." Then she was asleep, leaving me to toss and turn and worry about Daddy. Isn't that just like Missy?

The next morning it was so bright and sunny and still that you'd never guess there'd been what was practically a hurricane except for all the trees that had been knocked down and all the stuff thrown up onto the beach. It was also very still in the house as nobody was speaking to anyone else, except for Missy and I—I mean Missy and *me*.

A little after nine we heard the sound of a motor and everybody ran out onto the terrace. Sure enough, there was a launch with Daddy and Miss Glen aboard looking like they'd never heard of the word "storm." Missy and I were so glad to see our father again that we went racing down to the dock to hug him and make sure he was really alive. But Jane got there first and she was really spitting tacks. "God damn it, Dorie, where the hell have you two been? Leaving me stranded out here with no food or light and a pack of . . ." Some welcome home!

But Miss Glen was full of charm. "Darlings! The most exciting time! We got to Palm Beach and I called the office and then there wasn't a hope of finding any boat that would bring us back . . ."

"You could have called."

"Jane, darling, *how?* You know the lines were down. They still are. I tried and tried and tried. Didn't I, dear?"

"Huh?" Daddy said. "Oh, sure."

"So we went to the Petite Marmite for dinner and guess who I ran into?"

"The Duke and Duchess of Windsor!" Jane snapped.

"Well, no, but we did see them at the Everglades Club afterward. And then it was storming so hard that there wasn't a prayer of getting back. But as luck would have it, there was room for us at the Colony Hotel. Otherwise I don't know *what* we'd have done."

"I've got a pretty good idea," Jane said.

"And Jane, I want you to be the first to know. We're engaged!"

Jane didn't seem to be any happier about the news than Missy and I were. But at least Missy and I had the manners to say "Congratulations, Daddy." Jane just turned on her heel and stomped back to the house.

Then Daddy took us for a walk around the island to see how much damage the storm had done—and it was plenty—and tell us how he and Miss Glen had suddenly discovered that they were in love. Well, maybe it was sudden for Daddy, but Missy heard Lulu telling Mary Courtney Rogers' nurse that Miss Glen had Daddy earmarked as Mr. Dorian Glen from the word go. That's crazy. Everybody knows that when two people get married it's the woman that changes her name. According to Daddy, everything was going to be just the greatest when he got married to Miss Glen and Mom got married to Mr. Reynolds and we were going to be twice as happy as ever before with twice as many parents to worry about. Maybe he was convinced, but I wasn't so sure and from the fish eye Missy kept giving him, I don't think she was buying it either.

When we got back to the house, Miss Glen was pacing up and down on the terrace, stumbling over a lot of luggage (ours), while Jane and the models were all down at the dock sitting in the launch.

"Darling," she said, briskly, "where have you been? I've looked high and low for you."

"Not very high or very low," Daddy said. "We just strolled around the shore. Where's everybody going?"

"Well, darling, I can't explain right now. *Pas avant les enfants*. But there was some trouble here while we were gone and Jennifer and Wade are closing up for the season—possibly forever."

"Well, that's dandy, but the kids and I happen to be booked into this dump for two weeks and paid up until . . ."

"Darling, I know that Wade will send you a check for the difference. And you do understand?"

"No, I don't, but I can't say that it breaks my heart. We shouldn't have much trouble finding another place now that April's here and then the four of us . . ."

"Oh, but darling, *I've* got to get back to New York!"

"What for?"

"Why, I've got to get the models home and . . ."

"Aren't they bright enough to find the way themselves? Well, I suppose not. But who cares? We're getting married. You can call long distance and turn in your resignation and . . ."

"My *resignation?* Are you out of your *mind,* when the Number Two job is mine for the asking? Really, dear, I've got to dash. If we miss the noon plane . . ."

"Listen, I don't expect my wife to go on working when . . ."

"But, darling, how stimulating would you find me if I just sat . . ."

"I'd find almost anything more stimulating than that hairy-chested Jane or those two dumb cadavers or a silly fag like . . ."

"Precious, I simply must run. Call me at the apartment tonight. Kiss Tante Dorian, darlings." Again the cheekbone.

"*À bientôt!*" And she was off.

The rest of the vacation was great. Daddy and Missy and I moved into a little apartment right on the ocean at Riviera Beach, which doesn't even pretend to be fashionable. We rented bikes and went fishing and swimming and shopped in our bare feet at the Publix Market or the Greater Gator and did our own cooking or went out to keen places like Pancake Palace or Hamburg Heaven and Missy learned to dive without landing on her gut and we bought all kinds of junk at the International Bazaar and sent a souvenir coconut to Mom in Reno and a live baby alligator to Lulu up in Harlem. (A funny thing; Lulu swears she never received it and yet her signature was right there on the shipping slip.) I mean we really had a ball—just with Daddy and nobody else.

We got home the same day Mom came back from Reno. Then real life started in all over again.

Eleven

If this was a real book I'd give the chapters titles instead of just plain old numbers and I'd probably call this one "Brides and Brothers" or something like that. I don't know how those authors think up all that stuff.

But what got me started on that was just this morning Missy came up to me before we were taken off to the East Haddock Bath and Tennis Club and said, "Kerry, if you tell me something, I'll tell you something."

"What?" I said.

"Well, you have to tell me first or else I won't."

"You won't what?"

"Tell you."

"Tell me what?"

"That's what I mean, Kerry, you've got to tell me first."

"Tell you *what*, for cripes sake?"

"Do you know how babies get born?"

"Well, sure. Yeah. Kind of." Well, to level with you, I do and I don't. Oh, I've had my chances. In fact I've been told three times. The funny part is I could never work up much interest in the whole thing. When I was only like four and Missy was on the way Mom and Daddy tried to drag me into it and explain how a new little life was inside Mom, exetera, exetera, exetera. Well I am here to tell you that I couldn't have cared less. The kindergarten I was going to at the time was very big on this "sibling rivalry" (it's one of Dr. Epston's best words and it means you're supposed to hate your brother or your sister). Well, like I said,

I took to Missy right away. And I still do except when she gets me mad. As a matter of fact, when they brought Missy home I was the only one who *did* like her. Ooba-dooba, but she was ugly! And a real, thoroughgoing bitch—always screaming or spitting up or messing herself or like that. Well, that was the first time it was explained to me.

The second time was around a year ago when Daddy came home with this book that had some damned baby sitting on a cloud on the cover and read it aloud to me. It was full of all these nine-dollar words like womb and ovary and spermatoga [?] and gesticulation period [?] and all that jazz. Dull as all get-out and it happened to be at the time when "Car 54, Where Are You?" was on TV. What a drag!

The last—and I hope the final—time was at the school this year during study hall when the Head came marching into our class all hot under the collar, pulled down the shades and turned on this projector. We were afraid it was going to be movies of his trip to the Holy Land, but it was worse. Just some slides—and most of them upside down—of eggs and a lot of wiggly things squirming around and some real obnoxious kind of unborn baby all curled up into a ball. Well, the Head went on and on and on and on and on about God's glorious plan and the beauty of it all, like it wasn't something any alley cat could do. I mean if he'd only had the sense to *ask,* any one of us could have told him that you lay a dame and nine months later you get a baby—if you want one that bad. But at St. Barnaby's they practically won't promote you into the sixth grade unless you're a father. I mean they act like it was as important as long division or irregular French verbs.

What really bugs me about grownups is that they're all sitting around worrying about how much we kids are worrying about the facts of life instead of realizing that we don't hardly ever think about it at all.

Well, like I told you, I could care a whole lot more, but I guess you could say that I *know.* So I gave Missy a quick rundown on as much as I could remember about "life's most beautiful experience" (that's

194

what the Head calls it) and she just said, "Oh. *That,*" like I knew she would.

"So now what's your big scoop?" I asked Missy. "Don't tell me you finally dragged Hughie up to the hayloft."

"No, Kerry. This is for real."

"Well, *what?*"

"It's about Moira. I heard Lulu talking to Nellie up on the top floor just now and Nellie says that Moira's got this big baby in her stomach."

"That's impossible," I said. "Moira's not even married."

But now I'm getting ahead of the story again.

Anyhow we were back in New York and Mom was back, all divorced but otherwise the same, and the World's Fair opened (in a real downpour of rain) and it was spring.

Miss Glen saw to it that she got lots of practice at being a mother and I tried to go along with it and make the best of things. Not Missy, though. She's so stubborn that she wouldn't budge an inch.

Like I said before, Miss Glen was a big planner and she was really swarming with plans for Daddy and us and especially for herself. Whether Daddy liked it or not—and he didn't—Miss Glen was going to go right on working at her magazine. She pointed out how Monica, the big boss, had had three very successful marriages while she was being an editor and how all the really top women in her office were wives, too. However, she was willing to take the whole summer off and let Daddy take her to Europe for a honeymoon.

Since Daddy was such a hotsy-totsy architect, Miss Glen was also full of plans about how he could buy a town house and do it over into "something really striking, so that we can do our important entertaining there—and also make a gracious home for the children, darling." Until then Miss Glen thought it would be nice just to live out of suitcases at the Plaza.

"I hope you don't think it's trite of me, darling, but I'd like to be a June bride. Now I'll be putting the

195

fall furs issue to bed at the end of May, but there's Decoration Day weekend, so let's say the first week in June just to be on the safe side. The *United States* is sailing on Friday the fifth. (The French Line's smarter but their schedule doesn't fit in with mine.) We'll be married Thursday, June fourth, then I can really unwind on the ship. That'll get us there in plenty of time for Ascot. (I'm so glad they've relaxed that silly rule about divorced people in the Royal Enclosure.) And I've promised Monica to give the London office a good shaking up. Now I do have to be in Paris for the openings so . . ." blah, blah, blah.

What really surprised me about Daddy was that he just let her go on and on leading him around by the nose. When Daddy puts his foot down he does it hard enough to go all the way through the floor, but somehow he seemed to have lost all his old pizazz.

And at home old Sambo was pretty big in the planning department, too. I kept hearing Mom say, "But, Sam, dear, I've already had one of those white satin, St. James's and Colony Club weddings. It didn't work the first time and I'm not going to go through it all again. Let's get married right here in the living room with Judge Spencer doing the honors, if he's still alive by then. Just our families. Then we can go off by ourselves somewhere." Somewhere turned out to be Newport. Sam said that even if it was a miserable place quite a lot of fine old families still spent the summer there. *Their* wedding was set for four o'clock on Thursday, the fourth of June.

I'd kind of expected Miss Glen's plans to be on the fancy side, but they turned out to be even simpler than Mom's.

"Darling," she said to Daddy one afternoon while she was treating us to something she called Chocolate Coffee à la Russe, "about our wedding?"

"Anything you say, Dorian," Daddy said.

"Well it seems to me that a big, elaborate, ostentatious wedding coming so soon after your divorce would be in very questionable taste."

"And also expensive," Jane growled from the corner.

"So I thought we might have it right out on the terrace. It's a lovely terrace." Actually it was okay, and

196

about twice as big as Miss Glen's apartment. "And not a lot of people around either. I suppose you'll want your mother and the children."

"I certainly will. I plan to have Kerry as best man."

"Gee, Dad!" I'd never been to a wedding before, let alone *in* one.

"How nice," Miss Glen said. "Of course I'll have to ask a few of the girls from the magazine. No sense in hurting any feelings."

"And your own family, too."

"Darling, I have no family."

"Really, Dorian? I thought you said . . ."

"You're mistaken, darling. I'm all alone in the world."

Jane got up with a snort and slammed off to the bedroom.

"We can be married at noon in case Monica and the girls have to get back to the office. A buffet luncheon, I think. But everything kept just as small and smart and simple as possible."

"Are you going to come to Mom's wedding afterward?" Missy asked.

"Darling, I hardly think . . ."

"We haven't been invited," Daddy said.

"Mom said we could each bring one friend. I asked Mary Courtney Rogers but I can un-invite her. She may be in Nantucket by then and . . ."

"That's sweet of you, dear," Miss Glen said, "but I think not. Now about the wedding breakfast. How do you feel about lobster mousse?"

In all the movies I've ever seen people who are getting married are all starry-eyed and sappy like they didn't have much sense. Not Mom and not Daddy. From the way they acted you'd think that their weddings were something they had to go through with like a checkup with the doctor. But Ga-ga was thrilled enough for everybody. She even called up Mom and asked if she could come to that wedding, too, and Mom was so surprised that she said yes. "Oh, what fun! Two weddings in one day! Now I've got to dash out and find something decent to wear. You're a darling to ask me and I accept with pleasure. There's *nothing* I love like a wedding!"

Daddy had met old Sam and said, like he didn't mean it, that Sam was very nice. But Mom had never before clapped eyes on Miss Glen. However, her chance to be civilized was just around the corner. The Lipizzaner Horses from Vienna, Austria, came to Madison Square Garden for a week in May and Daddy booked Missy and I—and *me,* sorry—for the opening night. Well, right after Mom said yes to that, old Sambo turned up with a couple of million-dollar tickets from some charity for the same night. Ever since Mom and Sam got engaged, it seemed like he got more and more social every day, with his name in the newspapers for being on this committee and that committee for all kinds of good causes. One week he took Mom to a different charity ball every night for five nights in a row, although when it comes to charity balls Mom has always said she'd rather give twice the amount of money and stay home. But Sam kept getting bigger and bigger and bigger on the good work done by the Sheltering Arms and the Spence-Chapin Adoption Service and the Yorkville Association and some of those really spiffy old New York charities, while he didn't have much to say for like the Red Cross. Well, what do you know if Daddy and Miss Glen and Missy and I didn't end up in the box right next to Mom and Sambo!

The horses were just great, but I'll bet if you'd ask Mom or Miss Glen even what color they were neither one of them could tell you, Mom was so busy taking in Miss Glen and vice versa. Miss Glen was giving Mom plenty to look at, too, being got up in a rig that was so far out I'd have sworn she was kidding if I hadn't known her better. So of course at the intermission Mom leaned over the rail and said, "Do join us for a drink," and everybody was so civilized I could have puked.

When we got back home Mom was already there and full of how beautiful and charming and stylish Miss Glen was and how lucky Daddy was to be marrying her. She did such a good job of it I halfway believed

198

she believed it herself. But not Missy. Old Missy got that mulish look and when Mom said, "Don't *you* think Miss Glen's lovely, Missy, dear?" Missy just glowered and said, "I think she's a bitch!" So Missy got sent to bed and got her television time cut by five hours and had her allowance docked for that week. (It's fifty cents per dirty word in our family, even if you only say "damn" and the fines all go to cancer research so if we cuss a blue streak we know it's doing some good for somebody.) Missy said she didn't care —and what's more she didn't.

In New York the more you pay to go to school the less you have to do it. I mean the public schools keep open all through June and the parochial ones nearly as long but the private ones give up the ghost around the first week in June and Miss Farthingale's (where nobody learns anything anyway) calls it quits with Memorial Day. So we were both at ease in time for the big wedding day.

I will say that they couldn't have picked better weather even though Missy had been praying for a cloudburst to louse up Miss Glen's terrace. It came a day too soon. Missy is very shaky on dates. I was looking as much like a best man as I knew how in my best blue suit when Daddy showed up in *his* best blue suit to take me off to the barber—not just the kids' barbershop on Madison Avenue, but the one where Daddy goes. Missy's hair had grown long enough since Christmas at least to curl and Lulu was nattering at her to hurry up and get dressed so that Lulu could take her to Best & Company for a quick frizz job. Mom who was also going out to get *her* hair done, was being supercivilized. "Since we're all together for what is going to be absolutely the last time, come in and sit for a while. Coffee? Drink?"

"No thanks," Daddy said. "But I will take one last look at the old place."

"Well, don't look in the living room. The florist is turning it into a veritable fairy bower. Sam is so corny about things like weddings. I try to convince him that my debutante days are done and . . ."

"You look younger today than you did when we were married."

199

"Why, thank you," Mom said. "Are you sure I can't drink to your health. I know it's early in the morning but there's lots of champagne on ice."

"All right," Daddy said, "but just one." He opened the bottle with a mighty pop and poured out champagne into the two glasses.

"Here's to health, wealth and happiness all the rest of your life," Mom said.

"Same to you."

"Missy!" Lulu called, "if you don't come along with me this very minute you're going to look like a scarecrow at both those lovely weddings."

"So what?" Missy said.

"Aren't you excited about going to two weddings and then spending the whole summer in East Haddock?" Mom asked Missy. She looked a little worried.

"Not especially," Missy said.

"Well, bottoms up," Daddy said.

"Good luck again. And if you and . . . you and Dorian would like to stop by at *my wedding* . . ."

"Thanks, but no thanks. I have other plans for four o'clock."

"Yes. I suppose you have. I do hope you'll be happy, darling, honestly I do. Dorian's perfectly beautiful. Really she is."

"And I hope you will, too. Sam's a brick."

"He's a what?" I said.

"A *brick*."

"Oh."

Daddy and I got to Miss Glen's apartment about eleven o'clock. Jane was pounding around the place in her stocking feet, but at least she looked kind of decent for a change in the only real genuine dress I ever saw her wear. It was made kind of like a man's bathrobe but at least it was a dress.

"Well, the bridegroom cometh!" Jane said. It sounded kind of nasty to me, but at least she was smiling. I never got the feeling that Jane was very fond of any of us. "Dorie's out at the hair-burner's but come in and make yourself comfortable. Or else try the terrace. It's a beautiful day."

"Did the flowers come?" Daddy asked.

200

"What the hell do you think all this is, stinkweed?" There were big vases of white tulips, white lilacs and white carnations around Miss Glen's frosty little living room. Very classy and expensive, but they looked more like they were on display in some kind of flower shop than like trimmings for a simple home wedding. Out on the terrace there were even more flowers, except there everything was white and yellow to match the furniture.

"I didn't mean *those* flowers," Daddy said. "I meant the ones I ordered for Dorian to carry and for you to wear."

"Oh, Christ, do you expect me to wear a lot of flowers at this thing?"

"I don't care if you eat them. Have they arrived?"

"No."

"In that case I'd better go out and pick them up myself. You wait here, Kerry. I'll be right back."

As Daddy was going out of the apartment a colored couple was coming in loaded down with crates of plates and glasses and like that.

"Oh, Jesus," Jane said, "the caterers! Here, I'll show you the kitchen and where to put all that stuff." Then she slammed off behind the screen.

The doorbell rang.

"Get that, will you, kid?" Jane barked.

I opened the door and there stood this great big beefy guy, *also* in a blue suit. But when I say blue I mean blue like the neon sign on top of the Americana Hotel. "Is this Miss Krausmeyer's place?" he said.

"Miss who?"

"Miss Krausmeyer, sonny. Miss Glendora Krausmeyer."

"I'm afraid you've got the wrong apartment. It's a big building."

"Or maybe a Miss Jane . . . Jane . . ." He reached into a pocket with at least half a dozen pens clipped into it and pulled out a letter. "Miss Jane Waldo. Does Miss Waldo live here?"

"Oh, sure," I said.

"Well, then everything's ginger-peachy." He turned and yelled down the hallway. "This here's the place, Delma."

I went to the kitchen and said, "Somebody to see you, Jane."

"Who?"

"I didn't get his name. He was asking for a Miss Krausmeyer."

"Oh, baby!" Jane said. I never noticed before but she sure had a mean pair of eyes—just like a lizard's. "Tell him I'll be right out."

When I got back to the living room old blue suit had been joined by a real dowdy-looking woman wearing a flowered dress and a hat all rose petals with her glasses caught in the veil. There was also a kind of snively girl about my age. With the World's Fair on you see a lot of people like that around New York. They're usually going the wrong direction on a one-way street in a car with baby shoes hanging from the mirror and a hula-hula doll in the back window and fox tails and pennants and a whole lot of streamers and stickers advertising all the places they've been to. But in Miss Glen's living room with all her "lovely things" this bunch looked real out of place.

When old Jane got a load of them her eyes really popped. "You're Mr. Krausmeyer? Mr. *Henry* Krausmeyer?"

"The same. But folks just call me Heinie. Is Glendora here? I sure hope we ain't too late for the wedding. We left the mo-tel at six this morning and I been driving ever . . ."

"You haven't missed a thing," Jane said with a mean smirk. "Do come in."

"Nice place Dorie's got here," the woman said. "Kinda plain, but cute. Blow your nose, Darlene."

"Oh, do forgive me," Jane said real sarcastic. "Kerry, this is Mr. and Mrs. Krausmeyer—Dorian's brother and sister-in-law."

"Her *what?*"

"Isn't this going to be a wonderful surprise for Dorian *and* for your father?"

"You know, Miss Waldo . . ."

"Just call me Jane, Heinie."

"Surest thing, Jane. You know we haven't heard from Dorie—not even at Crissmuss—for more'n ten years. Isn that right, Delma?"

"Not since she left Talcum and took that trip to Paruss, France. Why, she don't even know little Darlene here is even born. Blow your nose, Darlene, I said."

"Well, Jane, when I got yer letter asking Delma and I to come to Dorie's wedding and just surprise her you could of knocked me over with a . . ."

Jane said, "You're really more than I'd even dared to hope for—*all three of you.*" The words were just fine, but she said it in such a doggone funny way— like she was making fun of them right to their faces.

"Well, we was planning to drive on for the Fair anyway, but when I got yer letter I just said to Delma, here, I said . . ."

"You know that we dint even realize Dorie was living in New York City. Darlene . . ."

"Heinie and Delma and Darlene Krausmeyer," Jane kept saying over and over, like she couldn't believe it. "It's too perfect. And I gather from your letter that you are in the meat business?"

"Krausmeyer's Quality Meat Market," Heinie said proudly. "It's the best butcher shop in Talcum, Illinoise.

"Here, sonny, maybe you'd like a souvenir pen. Writes in four colors."

He unclipped one of the ball-point pens from his pocket and handed it to me. There it was in big gold letters: "Krausmeyer's Quality Meat Market. Henry ('Heinie') Krausmeyer, Prop. Prime Cuts Our Specialty. Talcum, Illinois." It's a great pen!

"Th-thank you," I said, "Mr. Krau . . ."

"Just you call me Heinie, sonny. *Uncle* Heinie. And this here's your new little cousin, Darlene." Missy and I never had a cousin before and if we had to settle for this one I decided to get off on the right foot. "Would you like to borrow my hankie, Darlene?" I said.

"No."

"No *thank you,* Darlene."

"Now where's my little sisturr, Glendora?" Heinie bawled. The room was real small but everything Heinie said it was like he was calling trains.

"Dorian's at the hairdresser but she'll be back at

any minute. I can't wait to see her face—especially when she sees *yours*." I just don't dig that Jane. I mean if you're not going to be *really* nice and polite to people, why invite them in the first place?

"Gee, I'd like to go to a real New York beauty parlerr—like Ullizabuth Ar-dunn," Delma Krausmeyer said.

"You ought to," Jane said. There it was again: All the right words said all the wrong way. And Jane was sure no oil painting herself.

The doorbell rang again and I hoped it was Daddy. When Jane was being bitchy—like now—or just plain ornery, he could always shut her up fast. But it wasn't. Instead it was Ga-ga and Missy. As Jane was busy insulting the people she'd invited a little more, I answered. "Kerry! Kiss Ga-ga! Careful dear, my *maquillage*. I ran into Missy and Lulu downstairs and as our dresses looked so sweet together . . ." Ga-ga was in baby blue with a great big hat and gloves up to her armpits. "Do I look all right, darling? Dorian is *so* chic. *Elle a beaucoup de chien!*" Ga-ga had taken Daddy and Miss Glen to Passy for dinner and both ladies had been pretty bowled over—Miss Glen especially because about a million years ago Ga-ga had known a Mrs. Chase and a Mrs. Snow and a Mr. Nasty [?] and some other magazine people like that who were all dead but very fashionable.

"You look very nice, Ga-ga. You, too, Missy."

"I bought a different outfit for each wedding, but when it came to deciding wh . . ." Ga-ga caught sight of the Krausmeyers and for just one second she was silent, her red mouth ajar. Then she put on her social face and said, "Oh, how do you *do*? I'm the groom's mother, Mrs. . . ." Then Jane took over.

When Ga-ga finally got the connection between Miss Glen and the Krausmeyers she looked like she'd just heard that bridge had been outlawed. But once a social star always a social star. "How *lovely* that you could be here for the wedding! And you must promise to dine while you're in town. We'll go to . . . well, we'll go to *some* nice restaurant, or perhaps just have something sent in." She stretched her glove out to Heinie, expecting it to be kissed, and he darned near yanked her arm out of the socket. When Heinie shook hands with you, you knew it.

"That'd sure be a pleasure, ma'am," Heinie shouted. "An' maybe while Dorie and the new hubby are off in Yurrup you an' the kiddies here will have supper with Darlene an' Delma and I. There's this place in Flatbush, Brooklun that only us butchers know about that's got these turrifuc steaks." Maybe Heinie looked kind of out of place in this crowd, but he sure was nice.

"B-Brooklyn?" Ga-ga said. "Why, I'd *adore* it!"

"I'm *sure* you would," Jane said. Boy, talk about nasty! You can say a lot of things about Ga-ga and they'd probably all be true, but one thing *I'll* say for the old clown is that even if she is kind of an idiot, she's got nice manners and a good heart and no matter how silly she looks or acts, when Ga-ga shows up people know that *somebody* has just come into the room. I've never noticed any twenty-one-gun salutes for a tough cookie like Jane.

The doorbell rang again.

"Here comes the bride!" Ga-ga cried, clapping her gloves together.

"Allow me," Jane said, stamping to the door. But it wasn't Miss Glen, it was Daddy. "Well, it's the next best thing. Come right in. I've got a little surprise for you and Dorian. It's the Krausmeyers. This is Heinie and Delma and little Darlene, chum. Heinie is Dorian's brother."

Daddy looked kind of stunned, too. Well, who wouldn't to see a big friendly ox like Heinie and then find out that he was blood brother to a scrawny clotheshorse like Miss Glen?

"Her brother?" Daddy said. "But I thought Dorian said . . ."

"A long-lost brother," Jane said.

"Put 'er there, brothernlaw," Heinie said, pumping Daddy's hand. "Welcome to the Krausmeyer fammly. An' let Delma and I tell yuh, yer getting one smart little gurl fer a missus. Isn that right, Delma?"

"Oh my yes. Doruss—Glendora always liked to be called Doruss back home—was the prettiust and the

205

smartust girl in Talcum, Illinoise. We haven't seen nor heard of her since . . ."

"And that's why I planned this big surprise to-day," Jane said. "Shhhh! I hear the elevator door. Now why don't we all run out on the terrace and just leave Heinie and Delma and Darlene here to surprise Dorian?"

"Hey, Janie, that's a swell idea. Outcha go, sonny." Heinie gave me a gentle shove that sent me through the door and almost over the railing.

"Isn't this fun!" Ga-ga giggled.

"Fun doesn't *begin* to describe it," Jane said.

"Jane," Daddy said. "What is this?"

"It's just a little wedding gift from . . . Shhh. Here she comes."

We could hear a key being jabbed into the door, then Miss Glen's fluty voice. "Really, that tiresome hairdresser! He kept me waiting for . . ." There was a silence for just about a second and then Miss Glen screamed. No other word for it. She screamed.

"Surprise!" Heinie boomed.

"Doruss! I'd hardly of reckanized you," Delma cried.

"What in hell are you two doing here?" Miss Glen asked. She sure didn't seem very happy to see her brother after all these years. "How did you know where I was?"

"We never would of, Doruss," Delma shouted, "but . . ."

"Except that Miss Waldo wrote this letter to General Delivery back home in Talcum and it come straight to the store."

"*Everybody* knows Heinie's Markutt," Delma said proudly.

"Poor Papa, he wanted to come, too, Dorie, but he's awful bad off. They say at the Home poor Papa can't last much longer. I know yer busy, Dorie, but if yud just write to Papa once in a while he'd be so . . ."

"Jane!" Miss Glen said, like she was spitting poison out of her mouth. "That bitch!"

"Doruss!"

"Now listen to me, Heinie—and you, too, Delma

206

—I don't know what kind of a joke this is, but whatever you and Jane have cooked up between you, I'm not having any."

"Doruss!"

"Why, Dorie, I would of thought you'd want yer own family at yer . . ."

"Well, I don't!"

"Why, Glendora Krausmeyer!"

"Shut up! There isn't any Glendora Krausmeyer. I had it changed years ago. And there isn't going to be any butcher from Talcum, Illinois, and his frumpy wife at my wedding."

"Doruss!"

"Now listen to me and listen fast, because when I finish you're getting out of here—all three of you. This is the chance I've been waiting for. This is my chance to marry a gentleman. . . ."

"He seemed like a swell . . ."

"Shut up! This is what I've always wanted—money, position, a place in New York society and I'm not going to have it loused up at the last minute by you."

"Is that my Ant Dorie?" Darlene asked. Nobody answered.

I felt so awful I thought I'd be sick right there on the terrace. Poor old Heinie! And poor Daddy! What a dame to be getting married to! I looked at Jane's face and it was enough to stop a clock. All of a sudden Ga-ga let out something between a sneeze and a sob and said, "Oh, my poor little boy!"

"Who's there?" Miss Glen snapped.

Then Daddy stood in the doorway. "*Everybody's* here, Dorian," he said.

"D-darling, I . . ."

"Come on kids, Mother. Let's get the hell out."

Miss Glen closed her mouth. Her eyes looked kind of wild, but she managed to keep calm and cool. "Darling, these people . . ."

"These people are the only decent people you'll ever know, Dorian. You'd better hang onto them now. Good-by, Dorian. Let's go, kids. Coming, Mother?"

"*Au revoir,* Mr. Krausmeyer," Ga-ga said, working up some sort of a smile. "Do call me about dinner. I'm—I'm in the book." But all of a sudden Ga-ga kind of drooped and she walked like her feet were hurting something awful. As we were getting into one of the Mondrian elevators a lot of ladies who looked just like Miss Glen were getting out of another one.

I love a lot of people, but I've never been *in* love with anybody so I can't quite tell you what Daddy must have felt like. Ga-ga said that she was just too *hors de combat* to go on before the next wedding and so Daddy said, "Okay, kids, let's go to Oscar's—a good, honest fish restaurant with nothing fishy about it." Poor Missy hates fish and it wasn't even Friday, but even she got the message. So we went to Oscar's.

It was just about three o'clock when Daddy dropped us off at the apartment. He'd had a lot to drink, but it had cheered him up. "When I think what a narrow escape I've had it gives me the shakes," he kept saying. When the cab pulled up to the door he kissed us good-by. "Now that I have the whole summer ahead of me without Dorian—or Glendora, whichever you prefer—you kids won't have to go to East Haddock unless you want to."

"Yea!" Missy yelled.

"We can go to the Fair and Coney Island and maybe take a trip out West."

"You know what, Daddy," Missy said, "I'm glad you didn't marry Miss Glen."

"So am I. I hate to cheat you out of an extra wedding but maybe your mother's will be good enough for two."

"Why don't you come to it, Daddy?" Missy said. "Mom asked you and Mary Courtney Rogers can't come and Kerry didn't ask anybody and there's chicken salad and since you didn't have a wedding of your own . . ."

"Sure, Dad," I said. "Come on up. Mom really did ask you and as long as everyone's so civilized and you haven't got anything better to do . . ."

"Well, maybe I'll come up for just a minute and kiss the bride."

"Do you and Mom kiss each other?" Missy asked. The dope!

"We used to."

Even when Missy and I are in it our apartment is a calm place. I mean it kind of takes care of itself and it's usually pretty quiet. But not on the day of Mom's wedding. The cateress Mom usually hires was standing out in the front hall jamming a hat down on her head and giving Lulu what-for.

"In all the years I've been doing parties in this house nobody has ever had one word of anything but praise and now that old busybody is telling *me* how to stuff eggs!"

"Now just you calm down, honey. How do you think *I* like it—having my whole kitchen changed around to suit *her?* And all the time telling me my civil rights. I said, 'White gal . . .' "

There was a loud sniffle and Sam's sister, Rosemary, appeared. She was wearing a dress I'd seen her knitting out of pink ribbon and a hat made out of the same stuff. But there was a bobby pin hanging from her back hair and a lot of underwear straps kept slipping down over her shoulders. "I'm awfully sorry, but you mustn't mind Mother. . . ."

"*Who* mustn't mind her?" Lulu growled. "Would I go into her house, move all the furniture around; change everything in the kitchen; go poking around for dust where I had no business to be?"

"Mother's only trying to help," Rosemary said with a long sniff.

"She help a whole lot more if she just keep her nose out of my kitchen. Wedding isn't until four o'clock and she's been . . ."

Mom came out of her bedroom wearing the dress she'd bought for the wedding and kind of a grim expression. Aunt Liz, all gussied up as Mom's matron of honor, was hot on her heels. "Liz, this is the third time I've tried to finish packing. I may just as well forget it."

"Well, if that human steam roller would just get out of the . . ."

"Rosemary," Mom said, "it's sweet of your mother to try to help but . . ." Then she saw us and Daddy. "Good heavens, what are *you* doing here?"

"You asked me to dance at your wedding. Remember?" Daddy said.

"Well of course. You're more than welcome. Where's . . . where's Dorian?"

"I don't know," Daddy said, "and what's more I don't care."

"Daddy didn't marry Miss Glen after all. And her name isn't even Miss Glen, it's . . ."

"Shut up, Missy," I said.

"My God!" Aunt Liz said.

"You're joking," Mom said.

"I was never more serious in my life," Daddy said. "In case you and Sam would like two tickets on the *United States* for tomorrow . . ."

"Really, the waste that goes on in this miserable little apartment is a scandal!" I looked out toward the living room and saw what I thought was a walking mushroom, but it turned out to be Mrs. Reynolds. She was wearing a dark blue-and-white dress printed like a road map and a blue straw hat so big that you couldn't see her face. But you sure could hear her. "This room would look much bigger if the sofa was back against this wall and these two chairs . . ."

"I . . . like . . . the . . . sofa . . . where . . . it . . . is," Mom said. I could see that she'd been pushed pretty far.

"Well, it'll be a happy day when the lease runs out here and you and Sam and the little folks can move out to New Jersey. The rent you must pay for all this waste space."

"If you don't mind, madam," Daddy said, *"I'm* still paying the rent and I happen to like it this way."

"Who are you?"

"Oh, excuse me," Mom said. "Mrs. Reynolds, this is my husband."

"Your *what?*"

"My former husband."

"How do you do?" Daddy said.

"I don't know how you have the nerve to show your face here today."

"I guess because I was invited," Daddy said.

"After the way you've acted!"

"After the way who's acted?"

"Mother, please," Rosemary said with a long sniffle.

"If Sam were any kind of man he'd horsewhip you."

"I'd like to see him try!"

"Mrs. Reynolds," Mom said, kind of desperately, "my husband—that is, my *former* husband—and I are still very friendly. We always were. We've had our little differences, but that's all water over the bridge or under the dam or whatever you call it. Now, Lulu, if you'll please take the cateress back to the kitchen the rest of us can all sit down and have a drink or something until everyone gets here."

The doorbell rang and in marched Gran, all purple lace, with Miss Fitch bringing up the rear. "Good afternoon, my dear. H. A. has gone to the club to collect your bridegroom and . . . What are *you* doing here?" Gran said to Daddy.

"I've come to the wedding."

"Oh, now really, my dear," Gran said to Mom. "This is too much. It's quite bad enough to indulge that fool Evelyn by inviting her. But to have your last husband . . ."

"That's just what *I* tell her," Mrs. Reynolds said from under her hat. Beside Gran she was a little like a sparrow with an eagle.

"I beg your pardon?"

"Mother," Mom said, "I don't believe you've ever met Sam's mother, Mrs. Reynolds, and this is his sister . . ."

"No," Gran said. "We have not met. It's customary for the man's people to call on the bride's family."

"I'm a busy woman. I haven't time for all that fancy la-di-da."

"I see," Gran said in that tone that meant that she didn't see at all. "But my dear child, inviting your recent husband here this afternoon . . ."

"Well, Mummy, he happened to find himself rather at loose ends. It is *my* wedding and *my* ex-husband and unless you blab it all over town I don't see who's to know—or care."

"It's just a matter of ordinary, decent taste," Mrs. Reynolds said. It was the wrong thing to say.

"Are you suggesting that my daughter lacks taste?"

"Darling," Mom said to Daddy, "would you mix drinks or do *something?* Now let's all go into the living room and . . ."

"Darling?" Mrs. Reynolds said. "Well, I must say . . ."

"Force of habit, Mrs. Reynolds. Now let's all sit down and relax."

"Please, Mother," Rosemary sniffled.

"Lovely flor-eal pieces," Miss Fitch said. The living room was bristling with all kinds of flowers. They had been Gran's contribution. "I love fresh flowers, don't you?"

"You call those fresh?" Mrs. Reynolds said.

"I do," Gran said. "My family has been trading with the same florist since before I was born and . . ."

"Highway robbers, all of them. Why, on our place we have acres of peonies and glads just to pick for the asking."

"Is there anything about the apartment or the wedding or me that happens to please you, Mrs. Reynolds?" Mom said. I recognized that dangerous tone.

"Yes, Mother," Rosemary said, "after all, this is . . ."

"Be still, Rosemary. Well, dear, I only meant that if you want to throw your money away on . . ."

"And it is my money, isn't it, Mrs. Reynolds?"

The doorbell rang—and just in the nick of time, if you want my opinion. It was Sam and H. A. They were both wearing cutaways and striped pants—only Sam's clothes were so new they were shining and H. A.'s so old they were green.

"Oh, Sam, thank God you've come!" Mom said.

"Honey! I'm not supposed to see you before the ceremony."

"Sam, stop being silly. I've been so busy acting as referee . . ."

"But it's a tradition."

"Well, it's a tradition we'll have to do without. Now as soon as Judge Spencer gets here . . ."

"Don't forget Ga-ga," Missy said.

"And Ga-ga, we can get on with the ceremony. If anybody's speaking by then."

Daddy came in with a trayload of drinks.

"My God, what are *you* doing here?" H. A. said.

"Tending bar, sir," Daddy said. "Good afternoon, Sam."

"Now see here, dear," Sam said. "You can be as unconventional as you want, but I think having your ex-husband around at a time like this . . ."

"You know, I think I'd better put on my hat and cut out of here," Daddy said. "If I'd known that I was going to louse up your wedding . . ."

"And it *is* my wedding," Mom said.

"But, dear," Sam said, "what will people say?"

"They're saying plenty already," Daddy said.

"And the press?"

"What press?" Mom asked.

"Well, I had my secretary call the *Times* and the *Trib* to send their photographers around. Thursdays are slow, socially speaking, and after all, dear, your family is . . ."

"Sam, if I thought that you were just using me—and my family—to further your own ambitions, whatever they may be . . ."

"Oh Lord," Daddy said. "Not again today! Now, if you don't mind, I really will go. I've done enough to wreck your life already."

"Really?" Mom said. "You know, try as I will, I can't honestly name one single thing you've ever done to make me unhappy."

"Well, there was Christmas and the Applegate Arcade . . ." Daddy said.

"And striking your poor brother," Gran said.

"And running around with another woman," Sam said.

"Well, haven't I been running around with another man? You?"

"That's different, dear."

"I don't see how."

"I'm respectable."

"That's the trouble with you, Sam. Sometimes I think you're not in love with me. You're in love with respectability. You're in love with this apartment and the children's schools and your club and H. A. and Mummy's house—all of those unimportant things."

"Maybe they're unimportant to you. You were born with them. Other people have to struggle to get them."

"And I've told you before, Sam, they're not worth the struggle."

"Struggle?" Mrs. Reynolds said. "Don't talk to *me* about struggle. . . ."

"I am not aware that anyone was talking to you about anything," Gran said.

I guess she's not used to being interrupted, or maybe she just doesn't listen, because Mrs. Reynolds charged right ahead. "When that shiftless Reynolds left me . . ."

"Now why would any man do a thing like that?" Daddy said. "Champagne anyone?"

"Just bring the bottle—several bottles," Mom said.

"Amen," Aunt Liz said.

"I went right out and found the first job I . . ."

"I know, Mrs. Reynolds. In the billing department of Harper's for twenty dollars a week," Mom said.

"It wasn't Harper's. It was Harcourt, Brace and they only paid . . ."

"Now calm down, Mother," Sam said.

"Maybe *you* can be calm, Sam Reynolds, and be pushed around by these high mucky-mucks. But while there's a breath left in my body . . ."

"I'm afraid there's quite a lot of breath left in it," Mom sighed.

"Do you realize that you're insulting my mother?" Sam said.

"Does your mother realize that she's insulting me and has been ever since she came charging in here to take over my apartment and my food and my servants and me?"

"Why Sam wants to marry some spoiled society girl who never did a lick of work in her life! Just like Rosemary. That Jackson! Called himself an artist . . ."

"Mother!" Sam said.

Rosemary burst into tears.

"Now I've heard just about enough, Mrs. Reynolds," Gran said. "My family . . ."

"I know all about your high and mighty family," Mrs. Reynolds said. "Sam's always telling me how grand they are. Sit around living on money you didn't earn. Now in *my* family . . ."

"A little more champagne, anyone?" Daddy said, coming in with four open bottles.

"You know, darling," Mom shouted across all the

214

noise of everybody talking at once, "that's the key word in this whole mess."

"What is? Champagne?" Daddy said.

"No. *Family*. If two people could ever be allowed to get together and just go off by themselves instead of having to kowtow to the whims and crotchets of a lot of other people who are only thinking of themselves, why then . . ."

"I can't quite hear you," Daddy said, "but I'm with you."

"Why is it," Gran said, "that every time you come near my daughter she . . ."

". . . and teaching in night school down on the lower East Side . . ."

"Could I have just a drop more?" Liz asked.

". . . loved him and he loved me until Mother . . ." Rosemary sobbed.

Well, there was so much racket that you couldn't hear yourself think until Ga-ga shot through the kitchen door. She was wearing a dress exactly like Mom's. "Am I *hours* late?"

The shock of seeing a sort of Number Two Bride shut everybody up if only for just a minute.

"I had to come up in the service elevator, my dears," Ga-ga said. "It stopped on *every* floor. But the most frightful thing—poor old Judge Spencer is stretched out cold down in the lobby and all the building staff is swarming around him like . . ."

"Judge *Spencer?*" Sam said. "He's the head of my firm! Why, if anything happened to him, I'd be in line for . . ."

"You'd be what?" Mom said.

"Well, I mean he's nearly ninety and he's put my name in for . . ."

"Nipped in the bud," Daddy said.

"It's the finger of God," Aunt Liz said.

"I've got to get down there," Sam said. "This is very important."

"Isn't marrying me important?" Mom asked.

"Well I don't exactly know who'd do the job at this late date," Aunt Liz said. "I've always used . . ."

"You're upset, dear," Sam said.

"You bet your boots I am," Mom said.

"But what you don't understand, dear, is that Hewlett, French and Spencer is one of the oldest law firms in the country. The chief reason I asked Judge Spencer to marry us was . . ."

"Was what?" Mom said.

"Can't you realize that my whole future could change if . . ."

"I realize that it's changing pretty radically right now, Sam. I'm sorry the poor old man is dead, but . . ."

"He's not dead, darling," Ga-ga said. "He's drunk."

"Impossible!" Gran said.

"It happens in the best of families," Daddy said. "Eh what, H. A.?"

"Now you listen to me . . ." H. A. growled.

"Sam, you must rush to Judge Spencer's side," Mom said. "Don't let anyone or anything stand in your way."

"What's the quickest way downstairs?"

"The window," Mom said. But old Sambo wasn't even listening. He was out the front door and ringing for the elevator.

"Sam!" H. A. yelled. "Wait!" But it was too late. "Now see what you've done," H. A. said to Daddy.

"What *I've* done?"

"The photographers from the society pages are down there. What are they going to do now?"

"Well, I think they'll get one hell of a picture of Sam and Judge Spencer."

"That's the trouble with you—with *both* of you," H. A. shouted, turning on Mom and Daddy. "You have no reverence, no respect for anything or anybody."

"It becomes increasingly hard to have," Mom said. "And now I hate to let everyone down, but there isn't going to be any wedding."

"I, for one, think that's a blessing," Mrs. Reynolds said.

"And for the first time, I agree with you," Mom said.

"Oh, dear," Ga-ga pouted, "two heavenly new outfits and not one single wedding so far."

"Well, what about me?" Mom said. "All dressed up and no place to go."

"It's a little early for dinner," Daddy said, "but if you've got nothing better to do this evening . . ."

"The scandal!" Gran moaned.

"You know, that sounds like the best idea I've heard since Christmas," Mom said. "And if you don't mind a simple suggestion, we might get into a cab this very minute and go down to the license bureau before it closes. Of course I was there only yesterday with Sam . . ."

"Me, too," Daddy said. "They must get sick of the same old faces."

"Have you gone insane?" H. A. asked.

"Yes," Mom said. "But it was only temporary. I'm much better now. And the *next* time around . . ."

"You little fool," H. A. roared. "You can't make a laughingstock of our family, I won't . . ."

"There goes that word again," Mom said. *"Family.* Did you hear it?"

"I wasn't listening," Daddy said.

"And I never will again," Mom said. "If it weren't for families—mine, yours, the whole lot of them interfering . . ."

"Aren't Kerry and I your family?" Missy said.

"Yes, Missy. But that's different. And *we're* going to be different from now on. That is, if I get another chance . . ."

"If you don't shut up and get down to that license bureau, you may not," Daddy said.

"Have you ever *seen* anything so romantic?" Ga-ga said.

"Help yourselves to all the food and liquor you want, everyone," Mom said. "I hate to run out on you this way but . . ."

"Stop them, H. A.!" Gran cried.

"Come back here, damn you!" H. A. bellowed. He made a lunge toward Mom. But Daddy was there first and H. A. got the same fist in the same eye as he had on Christmas Day. And then Daddy and Mom were gone.

Well, we weren't cheated out of a wedding after all. Mom married Daddy all over again in their stateroom on the *United States* just before it sailed the next day. I was best man, just like I was supposed to have been for Daddy and Miss Glen. Missy was maid of honor and Lulu and the cabin steward were witnesses. It was all over in about two minutes.

"I guess I know what this means," Missy sighed.

"What, darling?" Mom asked.

"A summer in East Haddock."

When we got back from the beach club this afternoon there was still another bride's brother on hand. It was Moira McGuire's brother and he was waiting for H. A.

Twelve

Well, yesterday was quite a day in East Haddock and today is going to be quite a day, too. Mostly because it's our last.

If the fireworks were a fizzle on the Fourth of July, they sure were a sensation yesterday. Things started popping in the afternoon just as soon as H. A. pulled up in his snazzy new station wagon. He didn't even have a chance to get into the house before both McGuire sisters and their great big burly brother, Eamon, were all on top of him shouting and screaming and crying and all talking at once.

Poor old Eustace came to the front door and tried to order Moira and Bridget in and Eamon out, but it didn't work. Eamon McGuire even had a gun with him, although I could have told him that there's no hunting allowed in East Haddock—ever.

All of them were still out in the driveway hollering at each other when Gran's old Packard came creaking in with Hughie at the wheel. Gran got out and shook her parasol at everybody and said a lot of things like "What is the meaning of this?" and "Get off my property at once or I'll have the law on you." But she wasn't able to cut any more ice than Eustace was. For some reason the whole McGuire family got it into their heads that H. A. was going to marry Moira and he was going to do it P.D.Q.

Missy and I were terribly interested and we were creeping closer to all the excitement, but behind this hedge from where we could hear and not be seen. Then all of a sudden we both got a good whack across the backside. It was Lulu. "Doggone your time!" Lulu said.

"If you two aren't the worst. Now you come away from here. It's not fit for your ears."

So Lulu dragged us off on a long, boring walk—and her always complaining about her feet! It was almost dinnertime when we got back to Gran's house and the whole place was still as death.

The meal (fish) was late and when it was finally served there was nobody in the big old dining room but Missy and me. There was only Eustace to serve, although every time the pantry door opened I could hear Lulu and Nellie laughing like they were going to split their corsets.

"Where's Gran?" Missy asked.

"Your grandmother is unwell," Eustace said. "Miss Fitch has had to put her to bed."

"Where's H. A.?"

"Your uncle is getting married," Eustace said. And then he broke up. He started to laugh so hard the tears came and finally he just put the platter down and staggered out of the room holding his sides. Nellie took over serving dinner—or trying to serve it—but she kept going off into giggles, too.

"Where are Bridget and Moira?" Missy asked. Talk about curiosity!

"They . . . they've gone," Nellie said.

"Gone where?"

"Gone to a . . ." Then Nellie started in even worse than Eustace. "Gone to a wedding!" That gave her such a charge that she could hardly get through the swinging door and there was a whoop from the three of them out in the kitchen that nearly brought the house down.

Miss Fitch came downstairs looking like she'd heard the world was coming to an end. "You children will have to be very, very quiet. Your dear grandmother has had a complete emotional collapse. There's to be no more laughing and screaming in this house."

"We haven't made a sound," Missy said. Then, almost like to prove she was right, another big whoop came from the kitchen.

"Really! The lower classes!" Miss Fitch said and went out to settle everybody's hash.

Lulu was still wiping tears away when she came to shoo us off to bed. "What's so funny?" I said. "If there are good jokes going around there I'd like to hear them."

"Don't let on to your grandma that I told you, but your uncle's getting married."

"No kidding? Who to?"

Lulu started to break up again, but not so bad that I couldn't understand her saying "To Moira McGuire."

"Are we going to have *another* wedding?" Missy said.

"Not here. Him and the McGuires will all be back in New York State by now."

"Why in New York?" I asked.

"Because you don't have to wait so long there."

"But if H. A.'s waited for almost fifty years why does . . ."

"Now brush your teeth and get to bed, hear?"

This morning the house was even quieter, although I heard some long, low moans as I passed Gran's door. When I asked Miss Fitch how Gran was feeling, she just shook her head and sighed.

"Poor, poor woman," Miss Fitch murmured. Her voice was so low and gentle I thought *she* must be sick. Maybe she meant Gran had lost her money and really was poor. But in a minute Miss Fitch was her usual cruddy self. "Kerrington, throw this trash out!" She pushed a wad of crumpled paper into my hand and grumped off toward Gran's room. Miss Fitch sure doesn't know the magic word—I've never once heard her say please.

But if Gran wasn't up to talking to us kids, she sure was able to use the telephone. I just happened to lift the receiver off the hook in time to hear the tail end of a conversation with New York. "Tell Judge Spencer that I want him out here immediately with a copy of my will," she said.

Then the East Haddock operator broke in and said, "I have your call to Southampton, Long Island, ma'am."

"Thank you, operator," Gran moaned.

I was about to hang up until I heard Ga-ga's voice so far away that it sounded like she was in South America.

"Evelyn," Gran said, "I've got to ask you the most enormous favor."

"What, darling? Louder. I can barely hear you."

"I say, I must ask you an enormous favor."

"Well, this *is* unusual. What is it?"

"Could you take the children?"

"Take the what? This is the most ghastly connection."

"I said, could you possibly take Kerrington and Melissa for the rest of the summer?"

"Why, yes, of course I could, darling. You know how Ga-ga loves having her babies and how the babies love being with Ga-ga. But *why?*"

"I can't tell you over the telephone, Evelyn. Not with all of East Haddock listening in."

"What? Speak up, darling. I can barely hear."

I hung up to make the connection a little better and went to find Missy and tell her to start packing. She was sitting about halfway up the stairs with her head in her hands and looking bored.

"What you got?" Missy asked, looking at the wad of paper I still had in my hand.

"I don't know. Let's see." I sat down next to her and unwadded the paper and flattened it out. It was an envelope addressed to Gran and a Christmas card and the handwriting was Mom's.

"Hey, Missy, look at this. Daddy finally mailed the Christmas cards." Now maybe Mom wasn't mad at Daddy about anything. I looked at the envelope again. "Know where he mailed this from? Paris."

"Paris, France?" Missy asked.

"Yup."

Missy giggled and said, *"Joyeux Noël, Kerry!"* And then she kissed me, for cripes sake.

"That was a dopey . . ." I started to say and then stopped. "Merry Christmas, Missy. Come on, let's go!"